MURDER
at PRIMROSE
COTTAGE

BOOKS BY MERRYN ALLINGHAM

MURDER
_at_ PRIMROSE
COTTAGE

Merryn Allingham

bookouture

Published by Bookouture in 2022

An imprint of Storyfire Ltd.
Carmelite House
50 Victoria Embankment
London EC4Y 0DZ

www.bookouture.com

ISBN: 978-180314-072-8
eBook ISBN: 978-180314-071-1

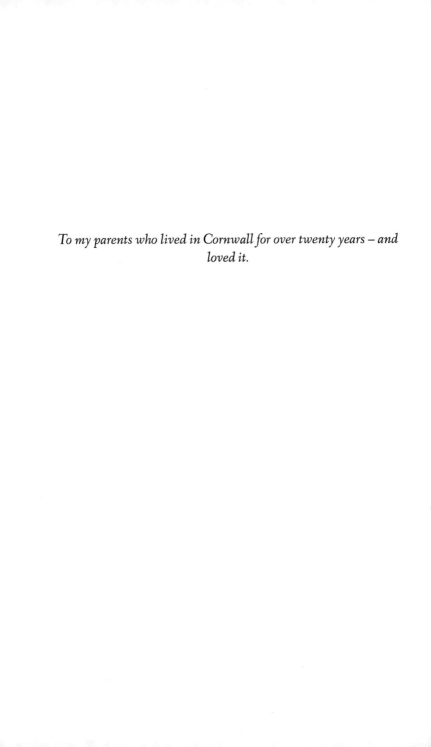

To my parents who lived in Cornwall for over twenty years – and loved it.

1

ABBEYMEAD, SUSSEX, MAY 1956

Flora Steele pedalled slowly along the high street, past the bakery, already busy despite the early hour, past Mr Houseman arranging a tray of cauliflowers and past the butcher, his burly figure at the window of his shop. This morning everyone wore a smile – for once this spring, the sun was shining. Even her bicycle was happy. Betty had not enjoyed the weeks of trundling through cold rain and deep puddles.

Coming to a halt outside the All's Well, Flora wheeled the bicycle round to the cobbled yard at the rear of her bookshop. It would be a while before she packed books into Betty's tray for the weekly delivery round. She was going away! Leaving the village of Abbeymead for the first time in years, not to travel far, it was true, but Cornwall sounded magical and she would enjoy every minute of her stay there.

Opening the shop's wide, white-painted door, she stood for a moment, breathing in the earthy smell of paper and leather and wood. This was home and, for a moment, she was gripped by a mild sense of panic. Sally Jenner, who was to manage the All's Well in her absence, was due at any minute but, tossing her jacket to one side, Flora felt compelled to wander. She zigzagged her way around the angled bookshelves, inspecting each cabinet very carefully, nudging a book back into line, displaying another more prominently, allowing her fingers to linger on her favourite volumes. A small sigh of satisfaction – the All's Well was in good shape and she could leave with a quiet heart.

Towards the rear of the shop, where the interior narrowed to little more than a passageway, the shelves were crammed against one wall, allowing customers just enough space to view the rare second-hand books that Aunt Violet had loved so much. Flora had added few herself – unlike Violet, she was not an enthusiast for auctions – but she made sure she kept the section as shining and pristine as her late aunt would have wished.

It was here, she remembered with a start, as she turned the last corner, that she'd found the body all those months ago, last autumn. Strictly speaking, it had been Jack Carrington who'd found the young man – rather too close to home for a crime writer – and it was Jack she was to travel with tomorrow. For the next few weeks they would be close companions but, with luck, they'd find a Cornwall devoid of dead bodies and could leave their sleuthing behind.

The shop bell rang as Flora was making her way back to her desk and a head of tight blonde curls appeared round the open door.

'Am I too early?' Sally asked. 'Auntie's here, too.'

Alice Jenner's plump figure appeared at her niece's side. 'I won't be gettin' in the way, though,' she said cheerfully. 'I'm here to make the tea. I've brought fresh milk.'

'Perfect!' Flora's smile was warm. 'Come and sit down, Sally, and we can make a start.'

Delving beneath the desk, she heaved an impressive-looking ledger into view and opened it at April's figures. 'I make sure I do the accounts every month. I like to check I'm solvent!'

Her companion nodded, running her finger expertly up and

down the columns of figures. Admittedly, Flora's bookkeeping system was simple, but Sally's understanding was immediate, and it was plain she had a good grasp of what running a successful bookshop would entail.

Sally Jenner was a gift, Flora decided, looping strands of copper hair behind her ears. Almost a saviour. She'd been on the point of giving up her trip to Cornwall, having found no one she trusted to manage the All's Well in her absence. Several women had answered her advertisement in the local paper, but either they'd had little experience in running a shop or so much that they'd wanted to rearrange the All's Well according to their taste. That was certainly not what Flora wanted, determined the bookshop would stay exactly as she'd inherited from Aunt Violet, no more than twelve months ago. Then, out of the blue, Alice, a long-standing friend, had suggested her niece.

Sally had been in Abbeymead for several months, staying with her aunt and picking up casual work here and there. *Mostly there*, had been Alice's tart comment. Disappointed by the applicants she'd interviewed, Flora was more than willing to consider Sally for the job and, from their first conversation about the business, it was clear that she would run the All's Well efficiently and Flora could relax.

'Sally knows all about accounts.' Alice bustled towards them, a tray of tea in her hands. 'She was in the finance office at the embassy, you know – had a good job there. I still don't think she's done the right thing leaving Germany, but I know she'll look after the bookshop well.'

'Auntie, stop the lamentations!' Sally shook her head, spiky blonde hair dancing. 'I'd had enough of the Foreign Office, and enough of Germany. I was ready to leave.'

Flora sighed inwardly. Sally was in her early twenties, only a few years younger than Flora herself, and she could understand the girl's frustration with her aunt, but she'd been witness to the same wrangle for several weeks and was keen to finish the handover. She needed to be home. There were still things she had to do at her cottage before tomorrow morning.

'I'm sure you'll be brilliant with the figures,' she said quickly, turning to the girl at her side, 'but just in case, I'll leave you the name of the accountant who does my books.'

She was scribbling the name and telephone number on a sheet of paper when the shop doorbell rang and Jack's lanky figure appeared in the doorway, fedora under his arm and his hands thrust into his overcoat pockets.

Flora looked up at him. 'What's the matter?' she asked, knowing immediately that something was wrong. Jack had the slightly haunted look he wore when he didn't want to impart bad news.

'I'm not sure you should come with me,' he blurted out.

'Not come? To Cornwall?' Flora's expression was bewildered. Jack had a contract to fulfil. He was to write a crime novel set in the county, and their journey had been planned as a research trip. A research trip with a friend, nothing more, Flora had told herself severely.

'Yes, of course to Cornwall,' he said a trifle testily. 'Where else?'

Alice put the tray heavily down on the desk, pushing aside Flora's paperwork. 'I warned you,' she said triumphantly. 'I warned you there'd be a problem.'

'And what is the problem?' Flora's hazel eyes registered confusion.

Jack hesitated, then withdrew a sheet of paper from his pocket. 'You'd better look at this. It may change your mind.'

Flora took the page he handed her, and smoothed out the creases. It didn't take long to read. One simple sentence:

STAY AWAY FROM CORNWALL, OR ELSE. YOU HAVE BEEN WARNED!

'What on earth?'

Each letter had been individually cut from a newspaper. Different newspapers, by the look of the print.

Alice Jenner took her spectacles from her apron pocket and peered over Flora's shoulder. 'It's a warnin',' she said cryptically, 'and you should heed it. Jack might have to go – he's got this contract, hasn't he? He'll need to write that crime book. Though I'd say this' – she poked a worn finger at the sheet of paper – 'is reason enough to refuse. But that doesn't mean you have to, Flora. You've had enough trouble this year and there's nothin' to stop you stayin' in Abbeymead. Sally won't mind backin' out of the job, even at this late stage.'

Sally had joined her aunt and was glancing down at the message. 'It will be a crank, for sure. You get them everywhere,' she said confidently.

'But who? Who would send it?' Flora couldn't feel the same degree of certainty.

'Someone who knew where I lived.' Jack retrieved the letter and thrust it back into his pocket.

'Has to be someone who knew you were travellin' to Cornwall,' Alice said sagely. 'That's creepy and I don't like it. Crank or no, there's people in this world who just want to hurt others.'

'Jack?' Flora looked at him enquiringly.

'I don't know what to make of it,' he said at last, taking the teacup Alice offered him. 'I could contact Arthur, I suppose. He's my agent,' he explained to Sally. 'The Cornish novel was his idea and he's rented a cottage for us in a village on the Helford river. Nanleggan, Treleggan, something like that. He knows the chap who owns the cottage and says it should be a good base for exploring the county. There's been no mention in his letters of any trouble, but this...'

'Like I say, it's some crank,' Sally repeated. 'The news that a crime writer is renting a cottage has probably spread round this village, and someone there doesn't like the idea.'

'Why not?' Alice put the teapot down with a thump. 'We've had a crime writer livin' in Abbeymead for years and no one here's been bothered.'

'This is Cornwall, Auntie. They're a bit cut off down there. More insular. They probably think Jack will ruin their village. Bring murder and mayhem all the way from Sussex!'

'Perhaps it's simply that I'm a foreigner.' Jack furrowed back the flop of hair that always refused to lie straight, as though trying to clear his mind. 'As a child, I remember being called an "emmet" when I was on holiday. It's what the Cornish call tourists – it means ants. Not exactly welcoming.'

'Did you notice the postmark?' Flora asked practically. 'It might not even have come from Cornwall.'

'The envelope came from there, all right, and I think Sally's correct. Someone in that village doesn't want me there.' He hesitated an instant, then turned to Flora. 'There may be some ugliness ahead and I don't want you involved. Not after all that's happened recently – that wretched business last autumn and then the Polly Dakers case. You should stay.'

'He's right,' Alice put in before Flora could speak. 'When you said you were off to Cornwall, I wasn't happy. I didn't say anythin' at the time, mind. It was after that dreadful stuff at the Priory and you were still feelin' a bit shaky. I could see that Jack's suggestion you make the trip with him cheered you up. But I wasn't happy.' Her motherly form quivered slightly, as though in warning. 'Cornwall is a dangerous place, in my opinion.'

'Dangerous?' Flora couldn't stop herself smiling. 'Why would it be dangerous? Because Jack has received some stupid, anonymous letter? Like Sally said, there'll be some poor misfit behind it, probably harmless.'

'He or she isn't that harmless. They've made sure to cut the letters from different newspapers to hide their tracks,' Alice retorted. 'And sent a threat all the way to Sussex.' She pushed a strand of wiry grey hair back from her forehead and fiddled with the spectacles she'd begun to wear. 'It's not just that, though. We've known trouble in Abbeymead before. Trouble that came from Cornwall.'

Sally looked intrigued. 'What do you mean, Auntie?'

'During the war, it was. Young Tommy Martin – you know the Martins, Flora? At Birds Acre Farm? He was their son, their only child.' Alice shifted on her feet and Flora made haste to offer her the stool she kept behind the desk. 'Volunteered early and went into the Signals,' Alice continued. 'He was always a bright boy. A few years on, he was stationed in Cornwall. That dreary-lookin' bit, you know, right near the tip.'

'Land's End?'

'No, the other bit.'

Sally laughed out loud. 'Your geography, Auntie. Do you mean the Lizard?'

'That was it. It was a big postin' for him. A centre where they did very important work... hush-hush, you know. Lord Edward Templeton was in charge of the place. Anyways, Tommy was gettin' on fine, or so it seemed, then suddenly he disappeared. No one saw him go. No one knew anythin'. Just disappeared in a puff of smoke. Lord Edward did his best to find out what had happened, the Martins bein' friends as well as tenants, but he drew a blank. To this day the Martins have never heard a word from Thomas nor anythin' about him.'

'He couldn't just disappear,' Flora protested. 'When was this?'

'Well, he did,' Alice said, a truculent note entering her voice. 'It was around D-Day, if I remember. We were all so excited that the Allies had made it to France and were pushin' those beastly Jerries back, all of us but the Martins. They weren't. They were grievin' for their boy.'

In the silence that followed, Jack absent-mindedly picked up Flora's cup and drank from it. She could feel his unease and saw he'd schooled his face into blankness. Whatever he was thinking, he wasn't about to share. Not at the moment.

'At the time, there was some talk of a scandal,' Alice went on. 'But no one knew exactly what and, if the Martins knew, they never said. It was all very sad.'

'That may be so, but what happened twelve years ago doesn't make Cornwall dangerous today.' Flora sounded firm. Violet's illness had meant she'd lost her chance to travel and, though Cornwall wasn't the Paris or Rome trip she'd planned, it was a special place and she was determined to go.

'Maybe not, but it would be good to know what did happen,' Jack put in. 'I wonder if my father knows anything? He was in Cornwall during the war and, at some point, worked alongside Edward Templeton. We'll probably never find the answer, but Alice is right. You should reconsider, Flora.'

'If you'd rather not leave the village, I'll forget the bookshop and look out for something more permanent,' Sally put in. 'I know Aunt Alice is happy for me to stay as long as I want.'

Flora straightened her shoulders, her slim figure erect. 'Thank you all for your concern – that's my tea, by the way, Jack – but I'm not going to be put off by an old story and some idiot's idea of fun.'

There was a tense silence, Sally lowering her cup into its saucer with exaggerated care. They were waiting for her to change her mind, Flora thought, to back out of the Cornish trip.

'Are *you* still going?' she demanded, looking hard at Jack.

'I must. I don't have a choice.'

'Then I'm going, too. Sally, if you come to my cottage early tomorrow, I'll hand over the keys you need.'

2

Flora had only just finished explaining to Sally how to coax the outside water tap into more than a dribble, essential now that spring flowers were in full bloom, when a red Austin saloon rolled to a stop outside the cottage.

Jack extricated his long limbs from the front seat of a vehicle that had seen better days. 'What do you think of it now?' He waved his hat proudly in its direction. 'A car transformed! Spring cleaned inside and out – washed and polished by Glittins' best mechanic.'

The garage had done a good job, Flora had to agree – the car's headlights gleamed, its tyres sparkled in the morning sun, its bonnet flashed bright – but it was unmistakably the same old Austin. Happy to be embarking on a new adventure, though, she kept her thoughts to herself.

'If you need any help with the garden, ask Charlie,' she said, turning to Sally. 'The Teagues live along Swallow Lane, first cottage on the right. I know Jack has asked the boy to water while we're away, and he'll be glad to do the same here. Mind you, you'll have to pay him!'

'Charlie has a birthday while we're in Cornwall,' Jack added cheerfully, walking up the path towards them, 'and once he gets to thirteen, he'll probably charge double.'

'I'll be sure to remember that.' Sally straightened up from stowing a watering can against the cottage wall. 'But you best get going. It's a long journey to the Cornish border, let alone all the way down to its tip.'

'Not quite the tip, I hope,' Flora put in.

'Pretty much,' he said. 'I'm not sure why Arthur thought Helford would be a good base.'

'*I'm* not sure why he couldn't have provided you with a different car.' In the end, she hadn't been able to resist voicing her doubts.

'What's wrong with the Austin? It looks splendid and it works.'

'At the moment, but for how long? It's not proved exactly reliable, has it? And we've a long distance to travel.'

His mouth settled into a mutinous line. The car had been well and truly used – if you were being generous – but Jack had become its champion. Probably, she thought, because it had gobbled up most of the advance he'd earned for his next book.

'I'll fetch my case,' she was quick to say.

'Stay there, I'll go,' Sally called over her shoulder, dashing back into the house and scooping up Flora's case from the hall.

'You can't wait to get rid of me,' Flora teased, when the girl reappeared.

'That's right! I'm looking forward to being sole mistress of your lovely cottage.' Sally looked back at the old brick and flint building, dozing in the early morning sun.

'You will let me know if anything goes wrong,' Flora said anxiously. 'You've got my telephone number in Cornwall?'

'You've asked me that twice already. Stop worrying. I'll look after everything. Now go. Shoo, both of you, or you'll make me late for work. I have a bookshop to run!'

Flora settled herself into the car's worn leather seat and

waved a final goodbye, feeling almost tearful. It was ridiculous – she was travelling a mere three hundred miles west, hardly the journey of a lifetime. But she hadn't left Abbeymead since she'd arrived back from library college to discover how ill her aunt had become during her absence. She'd hoped desperately for Violet's recovery until they'd received the dreadful diagnosis of inoperable cancer. For nearly three years, Flora had cared for the person who was dearest to her, years passed in a daze, with little time to think, some days not even time to change her clothes or brush her hair. Through all the months caring for Violet and the weeks since her death, Flora had barely travelled out of the village. This morning marked a break from the past. A new start, she told herself bracingly. A new project: helping Jack to write his Cornish novel.

Just now he wasn't thinking of work, she could see, but concentrating on the road ahead, intent on the journey. Despite the large map spread across the back seat, he'd evidently memorised the route, ticking off the place names as they passed. She wondered if it was his way of pushing to the back of his mind things he'd rather not think about. He'd said no more about the anonymous note, but Flora was certain it troubled him.

She'd known Jack for only a matter of months – had been aware of Jack Carrington, crime writer, for considerably longer, of course – but the man himself for a relatively short time, yet she was already attuned to his moods. Right now, she could feel his disquiet.

'Is that letter still bothering you?' she ventured, as they passed the county sign for Hampshire.

He took some time to answer. 'It's not exactly what you need, is it? I'm travelling to Cornwall to get a sense of the place, talk to Cornish people, learn about life there, and if there's already hostility...' He left the sentence hanging.

'You could have refused to go.'

Jack half turned towards her, for a split second taking his

eyes off the road. 'How could I?' His face was grave and, for a moment, he seemed to have aged beyond his thirty-five years. 'Telegram Arthur to say that some crackpot had sent me an anonymous letter and I'd taken fright and was breaking the contract? Not exactly professional.' He paused. 'Alice was right, though. *You* didn't have to come. *You* don't have a contract.'

'Maybe I have one with myself,' Flora said spiritedly. 'You know how much I've been longing to travel, and this is my first chance.'

'I do know, but your plans were for Europe, not a few hundred miles west of Sussex.'

'Small steps, Jack, small steps.'

They had travelled a good many more miles before she broke the silence again. 'Have you kept writing the Cornish book? You made a strong start.'

'Then abandoned what I'd done,' he said gloomily.

She glanced quickly across at him. 'You didn't tell me. But why? The chapters I read were good. Very good.'

'I suppose I might go back to them eventually – I'm not sure. Truthfully, I'm beginning to flounder, even before I get to Cornwall. I had a clear idea of how the story would develop, but when Arthur wrote last week, brimming with enthusiasm, to say he liked what I'd sent, he suggested the book went in quite a different direction from what I had in mind. At the moment, I can't visualise what he wants.'

'Isn't it always like that – at the start of a new book?'

'A bit, I guess, but this feels awkward. The story has to be particularly Cornish, and Cornwall itself painted in glowing colours. At the same time, I need to concoct a hideous crime that will attract readers wanting blood and thunder.'

Flora lapsed into silence for a while, before saying, 'Helford will provide inspiration, you'll see.'

Jack's expression was gloomy. 'I'm fairly sure I shouldn't have agreed the contract. I signed in a moment of weakness and didn't think it through. The book I was writing at the time was going nowhere and this was something different. It offered an escape, I suppose. A new series, a new place. I thought I'd be visited by a host of sparkling ideas and the words would flow – and they did for a while.'

'And they will again.'

Jack pulled down the sides of his mouth. 'I have to accept that I'm more or less writing to order. Arthur assures me it's not so, but his letter laid out in detail what's expected of me. I guess reality has begun to bite.'

Reality was biting Flora, too, as the miles trundled by. The further west they travelled, the narrower the roads became. Narrower and slower, though the Austin was never going to be a speedy vehicle. At one point, Flora wondered if it might have been quicker to get Betty out of her shed and cycle to the county.

They stopped several times along the way to stretch aching limbs or grab a cup of tea and a sandwich at some dingy roadside café, but within minutes they were back in the car. Jack seemed desperate to reach their destination before dark, and Flora suspected that more than likely the headlights, though gleaming, didn't work that well. She had never travelled in the Austin at night.

It was a wearying ten-hour drive before at last they passed the sign for the village they'd been looking for.

Flora perked up. 'Treleggan,' she read, shielding her eyes against the setting sun. 'The name is Treleggan.'

'And now for Primrose Cottage.'

'It sounds charming. I hope there'll be primroses.'

But when they pulled off the main road and into a narrow lane, stopping outside a slate-roofed cottage, Flora looked likely to be disappointed. The front garden was a mass of long grass and overgrown bushes, without a flower in sight. A short, stocky man was waiting for them at the garden gate.

'Here you are at last,' he said, bouncing up to them, moustache quivering, and a flustered look on his face. 'I was beginning to worry.' Two slightly florid cheeks attempted a welcoming smile. 'I'm Gifford, Roger Gifford.'

Jack untangled his long legs and slid from the car. 'Jack Carrington,' he said, taking the man's hand. 'And this is Flora Steele.'

The name had Roger looking slightly bemused, and when Flora's trim figure walked around the car to shake his hand, the man's eyebrows rose alarmingly.

'Miss Steele is my assistant,' Jack said quickly.

Flora hoped that made their relationship clear. It was plain that Mr Gifford had been ready to assume the worst. Jack was an attractive man, she conceded, but he was ten years older than her, and had set his face firmly against any romantic entanglement. And so had she, knowing the pain it could inflict. She enjoyed Jack's company too much, valued his friendship too greatly, to jeopardise it.

'There are two bedrooms?' she asked their landlord, in case Mr Gifford was still in any doubt.

'Certainly,' he said hurriedly. 'I remember, Arthur asked that in particular.'

'How do you know Arthur Bellaby?' Jack heaved their suitcases from the car boot and lined them up at the garden gate.

'He and I go back a long way,' Roger said after a pause, sounding a little calmer now. 'As a young man, he worked for a London publishing house and his firm banked with us. I was in the city training as a bank clerk,' he explained. 'Over the years, I made it up the ladder to manager. Not in London, naturally, but here in Cornwall. In Falmouth – it's very close. You'll have heard of the town, I'm sure. Here, let me take those.'

A suitcase in each hand, Roger made his way up the garden path to the open cottage door, with Flora following. After locking the car, Jack was close behind, carrying his beloved Remington.

'I thought of getting one of those myself,' Roger said, pointing at the typewriter Jack was nursing, 'but I'm an old-fashioned pen-and-paper man at heart. Now... the cottage layout's pretty simple.' Roger's rounded form almost filled the hallway. 'Two rooms up and two down. The kitchen's to your left and the sitting room on the right. The bedrooms follow the same pattern, though with a small bathroom between them. Very small, I'm afraid.'

'I'm sure it will be adequate,' Jack said smoothly. 'Do you usually rent out the cottage?'

'Not that often. Occasionally to holidaymakers. The Helford river is quite beautiful – do you know it?' When Jack shook his head, he said, 'You'll see for yourself very soon. Treleggan is at the head of the river but there are plenty of other villages to explore. If you walk back along the lane and turn left at the main road, you'll reach the village. There's a pub, a baker's, a general store which functions as a post office and, of course, the river. There are boats to hire – it makes a delightful day out.'

He smoothed a toothbrush of a moustache with his little finger. Flora noticed that on one side it had been trimmed too short, giving Roger's face a slightly lopsided appearance, as though permanently surprised.

'Most of the people I have staying here are friends or friends of friends – Arthur has stayed several times,' he went on. 'Otherwise, Primrose is all mine.'

'You normally live here?' Flora was uncomfortable. They must be dislodging this man from his home.

'Gracious me, no.' Roger patted his substantial stomach. 'I've a big place on the high street. River House. Georgian and very grand. It was my wife's choice, not mine. But I use the cottage when I'm researching. It's quiet here, tucked away, and I can leave papers wherever I like without Jessie getting in a fuss over them.'

'Jessie is your wife?'

Roger gave a subdued snort. 'Jessie Bolitho cleans for me. Really, she's my unofficial housekeeper, but her passion for tidiness can be a nuisance. Hence the value of a hideaway!'

'What are you researching?' She thought it sounded important.

'Local history, Miss Steele. I've developed a deep interest in the local area since I retired. As a bank manager, you know, your horizons can be quite narrow but, since I received my gold watch, I've been delving more and more into the history of Cornwall and into this part of the county in particular.'

'That must be fascinating,' she said, hoping they could soon put the kettle on.

But Roger Gifford was now started on a topic that evidently consumed him. 'I began with trade along the Helford river,' he said enthusiastically. 'It was a very busy waterway at one time, though you'd never know it now – then passed on to mining. Everyone knows about the demise of tin mining in Cornwall, of course, but there are some wonderful individual stories told from the miners' point of view. I've made a note of a good many of them. I did dip into monks in medieval times for a while, but monasteries weren't quite my thing. It's military history that is rapidly becoming my passion – it was an honour for me to captain the local unit of the Home Guard.' There was a streak of pomposity in Roger Gifford, Flora thought, but it was more comic than unattractive.

'I find the subject enthralling!' he continued. 'But don't worry, my research won't clutter the cottage. I've whisked away my papers for the time you're here – I always do when I have visitors – it means they don't disturb my current line of enquiry. And it means that Jessie doesn't either. I've asked her to call every day, keep the cottage clean for you and do any shopping you need.'

'That's very kind.' Flora was grateful. It seemed she'd be relieved of most of the household chores.

'Nonsense. I'm delighted to welcome you to Treleggan. Once you're settled, you must come to tea at River House. I'll give you a call. Meanwhile, enjoy the cottage – and the garden. It's a bit of a wilderness, but it makes a pleasant place to sit when the weather's good.'

'Let's hope the sun keeps shining then,' Flora said.

The garden could well be another project to tackle, as well as a place in which to relax. If Jack's progress with the new book proved elusive, she would have plenty of time on her hands.

3

Flora hadn't slept well. She had fallen into bed exhausted, yet found it impossible to settle. The bed was comfortable, the intense dark of a country night familiar. So why was she still awake? It was the strangeness of the room, she decided. The shape of the furniture, sensed rather than seen, the window at a different height, a door in the wrong place. Tossing from side to side, she heard the grandmother clock in the hall chime two before she finally succumbed to sleep, only to wake again just after dawn. Giving up the unequal struggle, she swung her legs from the bed, her feet searching for slippers. Then wrapping her dressing gown around her for warmth – there was a chill in the air despite the promising glow of early sunshine – she crept down the narrow stairway to the kitchen.

She'd heard nothing from Jack since he'd bade her good-night at his bedroom door. If he was still asleep, that was all to the good. Over supper last night, his face had looked pinched and white. Until a few months ago, he hadn't driven for years and, since then, had made only short journeys. A long day at the wheel had evidently tested him. Jack never mentioned the wound he'd sustained fighting across France, but she knew that at times it pained him, and last night he'd been surreptitiously holding his arm when he thought she wasn't looking. But he'd done them proud. They had arrived safely – and there was a new world out there to explore. Flora's spirits rose at the thought.

She filled the kettle and lit the gas, thankful for a stove that was relatively modern and that last evening had produced a delicious casserole left for them by Jessie Bolitho, Roger's 'unofficial housekeeper'. She must remember to thank Jessie when she put in an appearance.

Seeing the old cottage for the first time yesterday, Flora's heart had sunk a little, anticipating an outdated kitchen. It seemed, though, that Roger Gifford had equipped it well for the few holidaymakers he entertained. Flora had thought him a nice enough chap, perhaps a little too hearty, but well-meaning. And the cottage, despite its age and simplicity, appeared to have everything necessary for a protracted stay. How protracted, she had no idea. In part, it would depend on how smoothly their research progressed. Jack was intending to visit any number of towns and villages, she knew, and there was a stack of books in the Austin's boot ready for her to study and review. Crucially, though, it was Jack's imagination that would decide how long they were here.

Opening the kitchen curtains, she looked out on a ragged wilderness of garden. Still no primroses. But the jungle of grass and bushes in every shade of green was strangely inviting, and she had an urge to push through the dew-covered grass and discover what lay beyond. If she borrowed a pair of Wellington boots – she could see several lined up by the back door – she could take her tea into the fresh air and enjoy the first few hours of what promised to be a beautiful morning.

Immediately outside the back door, patches of a paved terrace showed through the encroaching moss and grass, its stern granite sparkling beneath a sun that was growing warmer by the minute. South-facing, it would make an ideal place to sit if she cleared the greenery and could find some garden chairs. Perhaps they were stored in the shed she could see at the end of what had once been a lawn.

Finishing her tea, she tramped through the wet grass to investigate. It was clear the shed had stood here for many years, but it appeared solid and the door was unlocked. Flora teetered on the threshold, peering into deep shadow, and eventually made out what she'd hoped for – two or three folding wooden chairs, the paint faded and scratched, but looking as though they would hold firm. And even better, a small wooden table. Brilliant. She would begin work on the terrace immediately after breakfast, unless Jack had other plans. A quick scan of the cupboards had revealed that the estimable Jessie had provided cereal and milk as well as bread, butter and marmalade.

Closing the shed door, she turned to retrace her steps to the kitchen, but then saw an archway to her right. It hadn't been visible from the house and she'd thought the garden must end at the shed, but now she walked through the narrow hoop of entwined rose and clematis and into what, if possible, was an even greater wilderness.

She came to an abrupt halt, her eyes wide with surprise. Not only a wilderness, but an orchard. How wonderful! An apple orchard, billowing with blossom. Cloud after cloud of pale pink flowers unrolled into the distance and she wondered just how large the orchard could be. The grass looked fiendishly high and the edge of her nightdress was already soaked, but her feet remained dry thanks to the rubber boots, so why not see for herself? It would be something with which to surprise Jack when he finally made it downstairs.

Wending a path through the knee-high grass was hard going, but she continued to trudge forward, determined to discover the true extent of this amazing garden. In Abbeymead she did as much as she could with the patch Violet had left her.

Her aunt had been a brilliant gardener, managing to grow nearly every vegetable they needed, but space was limited and Flora was nowhere near as expert. And she loved flowers a little too much – their shape, their smell, their jewelled colours – planting pansies, asters, lupins, a whole host of blooms, wherever she could.

The dew had begun to creep along the edge of her dressing gown and her cotton nightdress was flapping wetly against bare knees. She would have to go back to the house, she decided regretfully, and leave exploration until later. Turning to go, she was momentarily confused – the archway had disappeared from sight and she could no longer see the trail her steps had left behind in the grass. The garden lay due south, she told herself and, if she turned, keeping the sun on her left, she should find her way back.

Fixing her eyes directly ahead, Flora stumbled and, for an instant, was in danger of falling headlong. She had tripped on something solid lying in her path. Looking down, she parted the dew-laden grass with one hand. Then jumped back, horrified.

A body.

A man's body with an angry red slash across his neck. The figure was somehow familiar and, sickened, she made herself look again. It was Roger Gifford. Roger, their poor landlord, lying in his orchard with his throat cut and his blood spattered across the grass.

For several seconds her limbs refused to work, then as though every demon of hell was chasing her, Flora ran. She had lost any idea of direction but, somehow, she was bursting through the archway, haring over the sodden lawn, across the lichen-covered terrace, and in through the kitchen door.

Jack was standing at the sink, bleary-eyed but looking considerably younger than he had last night. He was filling the kettle. 'Thought I'd make some coffee if we've got any. How about you? It might get us going—' He broke off. 'What's the matter? What's happened?'

Flora stood just inside the door, her nightclothes dripping, her boots filmed in dew, and tried to speak. He put down the kettle and walked over to her, taking her by the shoulders. 'Flora, you're worrying me. What is it?'

Wordlessly, she pointed through the window.

'The garden? What about the garden?'

'Not the garden,' she burst out suddenly. 'The orchard. There's an orchard and... and... Mr Gifford.'

'Roger? Our landlord?'

She nodded, her face crumpling. 'He's lying there, Jack.'

'He's had an accident? But what's he doing at Primrose Cottage at this time in the morning?'

'You don't understand. It's not an accident. He's been murdered.'

Jack looked as though he might be about to laugh, but when she began visibly to shake, his expression changed. 'Sit down,' he ordered. 'You're in shock. Hot tea with half a bowl of sugar is what you need. Brandy would be better but tea will have to suffice.'

Flora allowed herself to be pushed into a kitchen chair and, within minutes, was sipping a cup of Jack's very sweet tea. Gradually, her shakes began to subside, but her heart was beating far too fast. She looked across at Jack slumped in the chair opposite. He was shaking his head.

'It's unbelievable,' he said. 'You are sure?'

'I know when a man's throat has been cut,' she replied tartly, the old Flora coming to life for a moment.

For a while they sat in silence, but once Flora put down her cup he said, 'You must show me,' and ditched his slippers for the larger pair of boots by the kitchen door.

'You can't go out like that,' she protested. 'It's too chilly and very wet.' Jack was still in his vest and pyjama bottoms.

'Never mind that. Just show me.'

Reluctantly, Flora led the way out of the house and across the lawn, passing through the arch of rose and clematis once more. She wasn't sure just where she had seen Mr Gifford – the orchard was a vast space – but she need not have worried. Jack had strode ahead of her, following the pattern of flattened grass, and come to a halt.

'My God!' he exclaimed. 'I thought for a moment you'd been at the kitchen sherry, but...'

'What do we do?' She averted her eyes from the sad bundle at their feet.

'We ring the local police, I guess. But what a dreadful thing... The poor chap.'

Flora turned away, desperate to leave the scene. 'The whole thing is crazy. By the look of it, Treleggan is a small village, miles from anywhere. Roger was a jolly little man, a retired bank manager, for goodness' sake. Who would want to kill him?'

Jack had no answer and they walked back to the house in silence. They had regained the terrace when she was struck by an unwelcome thought. 'You don't think it has anything to do with the letter you were sent?'

Since their arrival, Flora had almost forgotten the anonymous threat. Pleasure at being somewhere new, enjoyment of the cottage and its garden, had pushed it to the back of her mind.

'I can't see how there could be any connection.' Jack dragged a hand through his hair. 'But whatever's behind the chap's death, it's left us with a problem. Once I telephone the police, they'll be swarming everywhere – over the cottage as well as the garden. Finding peace and quiet to write will be impossible.' He pushed open the kitchen door. 'Still, I have to phone, but first we'd better find some dry clothes or we could be joining Roger with pneumonia.'

She followed him up the narrow stairway to the landing

above.

'How are you feeling now?' he asked, his hand on the bedroom latch.

'Queasy.'

'I'm not surprised. You really shouldn't keep finding dead bodies. This is the third in six months!'

'I don't. They keep finding me,' she protested.

Jessie Bolitho arrived at ten that morning, shortly after two police cars had pulled up outside the house. The detective inspector was from Falmouth and after he'd interviewed them both briefly and Jack had taken him to view the body, he immediately ordered his men to cordon off the cottage and its infamous orchard.

As soon as Flora heard the key in the front door, she sprang up to greet their visitor – a sprightly sparrow of a woman – meeting her in the tiny hallway. 'Mrs Bolitho? I'm Flora Steele.'

'Jus' call me Jessie, my luv.' The housekeeper's spare figure bent to undo a pair of battered lace-ups. 'What's all this to-do then?' She waved her hand at the police cars parked by the front gate and the white tape that now adorned the garden fence. 'Young Will Hoskins let me through. He weren't goin' to. Got all formal-like. But I said to him, look 'ere, Will, I've known you from a baby. Stood in the church when you were christened. You let me through, my lad. And he did,' she finished triumphantly, her sharp brown eyes alight.

'I'm so sorry for the confusion,' Flora murmured, wondering how best to break the dreadful news. 'You'd better come into the kitchen and sit down.'

'No sittin' for me, Miss Steele. I've a mornin's work to get through. Mr Roger's told me what he wants, but you can let me know, too. I'm happy to do your shoppin' an' all.'

Flora took a deep breath. 'There won't be much you can do.

Not for a while. Not while the police are here.'

'I arsked Will what it were all about but he wouldn't say.' Jessie led the way into the kitchen and plumped herself down on one of the chairs.

'Can I get you some tea?' With lots of sugar, she thought.

'Nothin' for me, my 'ansum.'

Flora lowered herself into the other chair. 'It's Mr Gifford...' she began.

'Mr Roger? Wha's he gone and done?' Jessie rested her elbows on the scrubbed wood table. 'It'll be a storm in a teacup, you'll see. Not filled in some form or t'other. Since he started lettin' the cottage, he's 'ad all these forms to fill. You'd never think it were so difficult—'

Flora reached out for her hand. 'Mrs Bolitho, Jessie, I have to tell you that Mr Gifford is dead.'

The woman's face paled. 'Dead? What d'you mean dead? I saw 'im yesterday and he were as fit as a fiddle – as always.'

'He's been killed,' Flora said quietly. Then when her companion stared at her blankly, she added, 'Murdered.'

Jessie gave a sharp intake of breath. 'Murdered,' she repeated. 'Mr Roger? He can't be.'

'I'm afraid it's true. I found him early this morning.'

'But how?'

'The police are investigating,' she said weakly. She couldn't bring herself to describe Roger Gifford's death, not to a woman who seemed as much a friend as an employee. The image was vivid still: bulging eyes, the thin red line, the splashes of blood on Roger's otherwise pristine white shirt. Flora hadn't been able to dislodge it from her mind and she wouldn't wish it on anyone else.

Jessie was looking bewildered. 'Why?' she asked forlornly.

'I have no idea. We've only just arrived and obviously don't know Mr Gifford, but I'd have thought he was well liked in the village.'

'He were.' Her companion gave a sharp nod of her head. 'A very respected man. Did a lot for Treleggan, even before he retired.' There was a silence while both women grappled with the conundrum, before Jessie burst out, 'It were that Mercy Dearlove. That's who it were.'

Mercy Dearlove was a name that could have stepped out of a long-ago folk tale.

'She were always bad mouthin' Mr Roger,' her companion said fiercely, leaning towards Flora across the table. 'Always rantin' and ravin' about 'im.'

'Who is Mrs Dearlove?'

'Not so much of the missus,' Jessie snorted. 'That one'd never 'ave got 'erself a man. Calls 'erself a wise woman, would you believe? I've another word fer it.' She lowered her voice. 'She's a peller, a witch, that one. Used to live Nanwartha way, but turned up 'ere about a year ago. Ever since she's been in Treleggan, stuff's been 'appenin'.'

'Like what?'

'Chickens goin' missin', a barn catchin' fire, Farmer Truscott's wheat crop jus' witherin' and dyin'. She's a peller all right.'

'Couldn't all those things have happened naturally?' Flora asked mildly.

Jessie gave a vociferous shake of her head. 'She were behind it, that's fer sure. If anyone crosses 'er, that's what they get.'

'And how did Mr Gifford cross her?'

'The village wanted 'er gone, specially when we 'eard 'ow she were run out of Nanwartha. Mr Roger is chairman of the parish council. Were chairman,' Jessie added, a catch in her voice. 'He tried to get 'er to move on – persuadin' like – but she refused point-blank. He tried several times and she got angrier and angrier. There's no doubt in my mind. It were 'er.'

Flora said nothing, too astonished to respond. Treleggan, it seemed, was not the quiet Cornish village she'd been expecting.

4

'He's gone.' Jack loomed large in the kitchen doorway. 'Inspector Mallory and his sergeant. But they've left a small team behind, rummaging through the undergrowth. Did Jessie Bolitho arrive?'

'She did, but left for home a few minutes ago. I had half a mind to insist she take the rest of the week off, she was so badly shaken.'

'But you didn't?'

'No, I didn't. Jessie is our sole link with the village and I think we might need her in the days to come. She's promised to return tomorrow. Did he say anything – the inspector? Does he have a theory?'

'He wouldn't admit it, but I don't think he has a clue, other than distrusting us as strangers to the area. But, since we only met Roger a few hours ago, we'd be a pretty long shot. The inspector knew Gifford quite well from the chap's days in Falmouth and appears bewildered as to why anyone would want to kill a seemingly harmless man.'

Flora filled the kettle once more and set it to boil. 'Coffee? You never got your cup.'

'Please.' Jack sat down on the chair recently vacated by Jessie. 'And toast if there's any bread. I'm ravenous.'

'I've discovered butter and marmalade and here's the coffee.' Flora had found what she was looking for on the top shelf of the larder cupboard. 'It's that instant stuff that's all the rage. Jessie is a treasure – she seems to have thought of everything.'

Once she'd made toast and coffee for them both, Flora sat down opposite and fixed him with a steady gaze. 'I wonder how much of the orchard the police will search,' she said. 'There's a large area beyond where Mr Gifford is lying.'

'He's gone, by the way. The ambulance turned up shortly after the police. But to answer your question, I imagine they'll give the whole place a going- over. Why do you ask?'

Flora sipped her coffee. 'When I first walked through that archway, the grass in front of me was untrampled. I had to push my way through and only stopped because I became so wet and because... because I found Mr Gifford. Which means—'

'That you were the first person to walk that way.'

'At least for some time. I don't know how long it takes for grass to spring back into place, but I'm sure it hadn't been disturbed for several days.'

'And Roger was alive and well at eight o'clock yesterday evening,' Jack finished for her. 'So how did the body get there?'

'Exactly. And how did the murderer get there? There only seems to be one way into the back garden and that's through the cottage, but that can't be. There has to be a gate somewhere. At the bottom of the orchard perhaps?'

'If so, the grass at that point will be well and truly trampled. The police will be sure to note it.'

'Still,' she said thoughtfully, 'I wouldn't mind having a look myself. Do you fancy a walk?'

~

Jack was conflicted. He wasn't at all keen on taking a walk, if it meant pursuing a killer. The police were here and it was their responsibility to find the villain. Flora had discovered the body, but beyond the brief interview she'd given the inspector when he'd first arrived, Jack had hoped her role in this horrible death would be minimal. He was determined that this time she would stay safe. He'd had enough of last-minute rescues.

Unfortunately, Flora was equally determined. And stubborn, too. He knew the more he tried to dissuade her, the harder she would cling to whatever plan she had in mind. It might be better to stay close, rather than leave her to her own devices.

The memory of the letter was never far from his mind either. She'd asked whether he thought there might be a connection between their landlord's death and the anonymous note that had found its way to Abbeymead. He'd dismissed the idea, but in his heart he wasn't certain. Could it be that Roger had been killed by mistake, that it was he, Jack, who had been the real target? It might be wise then to confront the threat by following Flora's lead into what was sure to become another investigation. On the other hand, it could simply be an ugly coincidence that a dead body had appeared yards from where he was sleeping so soon after his arrival in the village.

Flora was looking at him enquiringly, waiting for an answer.

'A walk sounds good,' was all he said, 'but let me finish my toast.'

'We can buy some bread and milk while we're in the village.' Flora locked the front door behind them. 'It will give us a chance to meet some of the locals, and hear what they have to say.'

'You think they'll have heard what's happened to Gifford?'

'Of course they will. This is a village, Jack. You should

know by now how villages work. There will be a network of spies here, just as in Abbeymead, and someone will have reported seeing the police at Primrose Cottage. I bet Jessie is fielding questions at this very moment.'

Jack opened the garden gate and looked up and down the lane. 'We turn right for the main road, then left for the village? I think that's what Roger said.'

'He did, but first I want to find that other way into the orchard. There has to be one.'

He sighed inwardly. She wasn't going to let it drop.

'So... I think we need to turn left instead and then keep walking along the lane.'

Two hundred yards further on, the track appeared to come to a dead end, halting at the edge of a small river with no discernible bridge in sight.

Jack pushed back the brim of his fedora. 'This doesn't look promising.'

To the right of them, an open field stretched into the distance – it must adjoin the main road, he thought – and to the left a high hedge ran parallel to the water.

'This hedge must mark the perimeter of the orchard,' Flora said. 'I'm sure if we walk along the riverbank, we'll find a gate.'

'That's if we don't fall into the water first.' It was the narrowest river path he'd ever seen.

'If you're scared your size twelves will be too big, I'll go alone.'

'I'm not scared and I don't wear size twelves.' She half turned to smile at him.

'Well, OK,' he amended, 'elevens, but I can manage.'

Gingerly, they made their way along a track that was no more than a foot wide and, halfway along the hedgerow, came to a metal gate.

'There's no seeing through that,' Jack said pessimistically.

'Or over it. It's much too high, even if I jumped for it. And I'd probably end up taking a swim.'

'We'd see inside if we open it.' Flora grabbed the gate handle and pushed, but it stuck fast. 'Damn,' she said softly.

'It's as well we can't get in, or we'd be contaminating a crime scene.'

'I wasn't going in. Not right in. I just want to see if my suspicions are correct. Can you put your shoulder to it? I'm sure it would budge then.'

'Hang on a minute. Let's think about this. If Roger and his murderer are supposed to have passed through the gate, it would open easily, wouldn't it? So it's likely they didn't.'

'Just push.'

Jack resigned himself, battering the gate with his shoulder while Flora held down the latch. The metal door creaked open a few yards, sufficient for her to peer into the orchard.

'I can see why the gate isn't opening easily. There's a thick ridge of grass and mud behind it, as though it's been forced and,' she continued excitedly, 'there's a pathway of flattened grass ahead.'

'A single line, as though someone has walked through it?' Jack edged closer and peered around the gate.

'More like a swathe, as though a body has been dragged across it and dumped.'

Jack closed the gate behind them and stood leaning against it. 'What's your theory?'

'Roger arranged to meet his killer outside this gate,' she said firmly. 'Maybe because we were in the cottage and he didn't want to disturb us, since the only way to the orchard from the front is through the cottage and out of the kitchen door... so they meet here and then slip into the orchard – to avoid being seen? Or because this path is too narrow to feel safe for long?'

'OK, they heave the gate open as we did. What then?'

'They stand just inside and talk, but then they quarrel.' Flora sounded more certain than Jack considered likely. 'They quarrel and the killer produces a knife and strikes. To cover his crime, he drags Roger's body further into the orchard.'

'But why? Why not leave the body where it fell? And why meet in such an awkward place in the first instance?'

'If Roger was left lying where he fell, he'd probably be half in and half out of the gate. Someone walking along the river-bank, either on this path or the opposite one, could have spotted him. But if he was left lying in the middle of the grass, he could be there for days. It would give the murderer time to make his or her escape and for the trail to go cold. Who's going to find a body that's so well hidden?'

'Flora Steele?'

'A fluke. I only walked there because it was a lovely morn-ing, we'd just arrived in a new place, and I was keen to explore. The killer must have assumed that if there were any visitors at the cottage, they wouldn't stray that far. From the house, you can't see the archway that leads to the orchard and, even if someone spotted it, the place itself is a jungle. Apart from visi-tors, who else might wander among the apple trees? Jessie? I don't think so. Even if she continued to work at the cottage after Roger's death, she'd stay inside. There's a very good chance that no one would think to look for him in the orchard. Not for a long time.'

'It would probably be the last place you'd think of checking,' he agreed. 'And I guess that if anyone opened that rear gate for whatever reason, all they would see was an ocean of grass.'

'Which, by then, would have sprung upright again, completely concealing what had gone on.'

'I grant you that for someone determined to kill, it's a good place to meet,' he conceded, as they wandered back down the lane towards the main road, 'but why would Roger agree to it?'

'Perhaps the killer knew something that Roger needed. Maybe knew something that Roger wanted to keep secret. He'd be willing then to come to an out-of-the-way place.'

'Gifford doesn't seem the kind of chap who'd have secrets.'

'Everyone has secrets, Jack. Even you. Even me.'

5

'Jessie Bolitho thinks she knows who did it,' Flora said, as they walked into the village along a main street lined by granite stone cottages, their slate roofs shining in the sun. Interspersed with the grey, the occasional splash of whitewash signalled a more recent building.

'Jessie knows? That's more than the police do. She must be clairvoyant.'

'She was quite serious,' Flora said severely.

'And you believe her?'

'I'm not sure I do. She's decided it's someone called Mercy Dearlove who, she says, is a witch. Or rather a peller. That's what Jessie called her – the word must be Cornish. The woman is evidently someone Jessie dislikes intensely and it's satisfying to pin the murder on her, but she did say that Mercy was at odds with Roger and that they'd quarrelled badly.'

'Did she say why?'

'Apparently the village is keen to see Mrs Dearlove – or Miss Dearlove, as Jessie insisted – to move on and move out. The woman came to Treleggan a year ago and she's widely mistrusted. It was Roger's job as chairman of the parish council to persuade her to leave.'

'He couldn't have done a very good job.'

'Perhaps his heart wasn't in it. There's no doubt prejudice against her exists in the village and Roger seemed a good-natured man. Or perhaps Mercy was just too much for him.'

'If that was so, she'd no need to kill him.'

They had reached a small square of green grass, around which clustered the few village shops. Jack came to a halt outside a solid stone building, a rusting sign swinging from the wooden post at its entrance announcing it was the Chain and Anchor.

'Looks a nice pub,' he remarked. 'Pity I'm not a great drinker.'

'Never mind the pub, let's start with the bakery. That must be it, just ahead.' She pointed to a rambling grey stone building on one side of the green, its single window filled with a mountain of different-shaped loaves.

The aroma of freshly baked bread hit them as they walked through the door and Flora breathed it in appreciatively. A small knot of people were waiting to be served and, with one accord, they turned and stared at the incomers.

'Good morning,' Jack said cheerfully.

'Mornin'.' A woman in a thick wool jacket and floral head-scarf nodded an acknowledgement, followed by a murmur of greetings from her companions.

'You've come from Primrose Cottage then?' she said.

'That's right.' Flora was glad to have broken the ice. 'We arrived last night. We're... we're on holiday.' It was definitely not the moment to mention that Jack was here to write a crime novel.

There was a general shaking of heads. 'It's a bad business,' the woman behind the counter offered morosely – the baker's wife? – ringing up the cash register with a loud clang. 'That'll be fourpence, Mrs Hoskins.'

'It's a bad business all right,' Mrs Hoskins said, handing over the coins and addressing the rest of the shop. 'Like I was tellin' you, my boy Will is up there now. A murder! And in Treleggan of all places!'

'And Mr Gifford of all people,' another voice joined in.

'He was well-liked, I understand,' Jack said in his smoothest manner.

'More'n well-liked. He did a lot for Treleggan. Got the village hall repaired, stopped them shuttin' the post office. Made sure we got some money from that thievin' bunch who run the county.'

'It don' make sense, do it? Everyone liked Roger.'

''Cept Mercy Dearlove. She didn't. And we know what pellers are.'

'She ain't that bad,' the baker's wife said. 'Jus' a bit different. Cured my Carol of the warts. One day her poor little 'ands were covered in 'em, then Mercy 'eld 'er tight, and next morning Carol woke up and them warts were gone. Jus' the tiniest white scars where they'd been.'

'That's as mebbe, but what about Dolly's chickens?'

'And the way Kenver took sick. He runs the Anchor,' one of the group explained obligingly. 'Refused to serve the woman, and the next thing he's rollin' round, 'is stomach all aquiver.'

'She's got a temper on 'er, that's for sure,' the headscarf woman said. 'I 'eard the row t'other day. Mr Gifford tryin' to speak and that Mercy shoutin' and screamin' at 'im. Do you know 'ow the poor man died?'

Every head turned to look at the visitors. There had been just the slightest hint of suspicion in the woman's voice, Flora thought. They were strangers here and twelve hours after they'd arrived in the village, a much respected inhabitant had died for no apparent reason.

She felt Jack glancing at her, seeming unsure how he should reply, but Flora had no qualms. It was evident that not everything had yet reached the village grapevine and honesty would bring its own rewards. 'He had his throat cut,' she said baldly.

There was a collective gasp. Then a long silence. 'Mercy Dearlove do 'ave sharp knives,' one of the women said at last.

'Really? Why is that?' Flora asked.

'Whittles wood, don' she. Makes ornaments, toys, that kinda thing, and sells 'em in whatever fair's goin' on.'

'What can I get you, my 'ansum?' It was clear the baker's wife wanted them gone. No doubt the entire group wanted them gone, to talk over their horrendous discovery without foreign ears listening in.

'One of those, please.' Flora pointed to the row of loaves sitting on the top shelf.

'It's a cob you're wantin'?' The woman was smiling now.

'And a couple of pasties,' Jack put in.

The toast had long since disappeared, Flora guessed, and the excitement of their first morning in a supposedly drowsy village must have given him a hunger.

Purchases made, they wandered down the main street and found themselves once more by the river. It was wider here than at the end of the lane and several rowing boats were drawn up at a rudimentary jetty.

'Fancy a gentle drift downstream?' He nodded at the vessels bobbing close by. 'We could hire a boat.'

Flora started to shake her head – their last trip down a river had been anything but gentle – yet, suddenly, the freshness of the water, the freedom it offered, seemed important.

'Maybe,' she extemporised.

Jack stood waiting. 'Well, is it yes or no?'

There was an even longer pause. 'OK, Jolyon,' she said at last, teasing him with the given name he hated, 'but if we drown, it's down to you.'

'We're not going to – I've decreed it. Unless, of course, you call me Jolyon again.' Screwing up his eyes against the sun, he read the faded notice propped against a wooden shed. 'A shilling an hour. I think we can afford it.'

'I think we should, after the morning we've had.'

An elderly man in a tattered sailing cap appeared at the square window that had been cut into one of the shed's walls, taking their shilling and pointing them towards the nearest boat. Its bright blue paint had begun to flake but otherwise it appeared seaworthy. Or so she told herself. When her confidence, never robust, began to ebb, she clambered quickly into the boat before she could change her mind.

'Don' go too fer,' the man advised, coming out of his shed and unlooping the rope that tied them to the jetty. 'The river ain't tidal these days, and 'ere it's not much more'n a creek, but two mile down' – he pointed towards where the river broadened considerably – 'you'll be gettin' into rough water, and a mile on, you'll be gettin' to the sea.'

'Thanks for the warning,' Jack said, as their grizzled companion pushed them out into the river.

Taking the oars, he gently steered them away from the bank. 'The bakery was an interesting experience. Mercy Dearlove seems to be Treleggan's choice of killer.' There was a laugh in his voice.

Flora relaxed her hold on the side of the boat very slightly. 'I assumed it was the village ganging up on her. Well, it is, but it's clear she had a grievance with Roger and also that she quarrelled with him. It's possible, too, that she asked to meet him in a quiet place, but none of it adds up. Except... it's the sharp knives that are making me wonder.'

'Then again, if Mercy is the witch the village says she is, she surely wouldn't need to use a knife. Nothing so crude – a spell or two would do the trick!'

'It's a puzzle, certainly. And I think it's one we should try to solve, Jack. If we leave it to the police, they'll take far too long.'

'Too long for what?'

'For you to write your story.' There was a pause before Flora tumbled into speech again. 'I've just had a brilliant idea! Maybe it wasn't just a dead body I found. Maybe it was something else. Your elusive story – right here on our doorstep.'

'You're seriously suggesting I should include this murder in the new book?'

'Why not? It's Cornish enough even for Arthur Bellaby, and you're a good writer. You could easily weave it into what you've already done.'

When he grimaced, she said with some exasperation, 'You said yourself that you're floundering.' She let a few minutes drift by before adding, 'It would work really well. You could start the weaving, while I do the digging around – try to discover how the story ends.'

'No! Keep out of it, Flora. Speaking to the natives this morning is one thing, but tracking down a cold-blooded murderer is quite another. We already know how dangerous that can be.'

'I'll be discreet,' she said with an impish smile. 'You won't even know I'm at work and no one else will either. I won't get into trouble again, I promise.'

'That's what you said last time.'

'Treleggan must have a ferry,' Jack said, pointing to the small quay they were passing on the outskirts of the village.

'I wonder where it goes to? I must ask Jessie – I could take a trip one day. When you're hunched over the Remington.'

Pulling on the oars, he steered them past the jetty and clear of the village. Once in the countryside, they drifted slowly past one sandy inlet after another, a small boat anchored here and there, ready for the next fishing trip. Inland, daffodils still bloomed and vast carpets of wild garlic covered the woodland floor. The creek they were rowing along was a deep thrust of water, overhung by trees on either bank, their branches trailing in the stream. Occasionally, the tip of a whitewashed cottage was visible through the dense clusters of foliage, but of people there were none. Gradually, the creek transformed into a wider expanse of water, the sun-dappled river bending itself in and out of sheltered coves as it rippled towards the sea.

'It's beautiful,' Flora said, looking around her. 'Quite beautiful.'

Jack said nothing, but there was a smile on his face.

'Very different from Sussex,' she went on. 'Enclosed, almost secret.'

'Magical?' he teased.

'Why not? We all need a little magic in our lives. Tell me when you've had enough of rowing.'

'And you'll take over?'

'I'll try.'

'This boat has a mind of its own, so perhaps not. And the oars weigh a ton.'

'If you're sure...'

She leaned back against the wooden hull, her face raised to the sun, and breathed in the clean smell of fresh water. Through half-closed lids, she watched as muddy banks, trailing leaves, shingle beaches, drifted by. What made her open her eyes fully, she didn't know. But there on a scrap of sand was a woman's figure, tall and wild-haired, standing lone and still. She had appeared from nowhere, it seemed, and was watching. Watching them?

Flora felt her stomach harden to rock, caught by a strange fear. Scolding herself for being foolish, she twisted in her seat to get a better view, but the figure had vanished as suddenly as it had appeared. The beach was deserted, the grass bank beyond bare of human presence, and the trees rustled their leaves in solitude. Could she have dreamed the moment?

Jack hadn't noticed the woman, it seemed, and Flora decided to keep her counsel. The figure might have been an illusion, conjured from the flowing water and skittering sunlight, and was probably best forgotten.

Trying to distract herself, she asked teasingly, 'Is this better than rowing in Central Park?' Jack's time in New York and his ill-fated love affair was never far from her mind.

He didn't respond and some deep-seated twinge of jealousy made her go on. 'Do you think of her at all – Helen?'

Smart New York Helen, who had jilted Jack, not quite at the altar but nearly.

He stopped rowing for a moment, his head to one side.

'Almost never. Her visit to Abbeymead seems to have freed me. I've not heard a word from her since I put her on the train to Bournemouth and I've no idea where she might be. Maybe still with her grandmother or home in Canada. Or even back in New York. I don't know and, truly, I don't want to.'

'Time heals, or so they say.' Flora gave a wry smile.

'Clichés are clichés because they're true. Time does heal. The hurt stops eventually. Do you still think of... what was his name?'

'Richard. Very rarely. I don't think I *was* hurt, not really. It was more disappointment with myself that I could misjudge a person so badly.'

'That comes into it, certainly,' Jack agreed, taking up the oars again and rowing with long, leisurely strokes. 'But betrayal cuts deep.'

'It definitely makes you wary.' She settled back once more against the warm wood of the boat. 'I'll never be quite so gullible again.'

Not gullible, she reflected, but still able to trust. Her trust in

Jack ran deep – she had a faith in him that she'd never had in Richard.

There was a long silence until a flurry of wings broke the quiet as a white-plumed egret came to land on the small beach they were passing, its yellow feet strikingly bright against the green of the steep hillside behind.

'I'd like to meet Mercy Dearlove,' Flora said at last. 'Not to accuse her of murder. Just to meet a real-life witch.'

Had she somehow conflated the figure she thought she'd seen with the mythical Mercy? It was certainly a possibility.

'You don't know that she is a witch. It could be village gossip.'

'But what if it's not? Think of the warts!'

'Do I have to? And warts have a well-documented habit of disappearing suddenly.' He stopped rowing again and rested the oars. 'It's probably time we turned round.'

'This should be an interesting manoeuvre. Shall I hold on tight?'

'I've a feeling that for the next few weeks, we'll both be holding on tight.'

6

'It will have to be bacon and eggs for supper,' Flora announced that evening, scanning the larder unsuccessfully for an alternative.

'Sounds fine.' Jack came into the kitchen, a map in his hand. 'We can do some shopping early tomorrow unless Jessie Bolitho reappears.'

'I'm really hoping she will. Her chicken casserole was delicious, far better than anything I could muster.'

'You're not here to cook. You're supposed to be enjoying a break.'

'So in the absence of Jessie, you'll be chef?' She couldn't help teasing.

'I can try,' he said gallantly, 'though I'm pretty useless. But you know that already.'

'If I fancied surviving on ham sandwiches, you'd be ace.'

He grinned. 'Shall I slice the loaf? I have skill in that department.'

'Good idea. There's butter in the larder.'

'Now the police have gone – for the moment at least – we

can get organised. It's a simple matter of studying the map and deciding where we go first.'

He began to hunt through the cutlery drawer. 'Ah, got it!' he announced, pouncing on the bread knife. 'Not in the drawer, though. Slotted into this odd-looking block.'

'Do you have a list of places in mind?'

He shook his head. 'I've no idea where best to head for. Perhaps we should plan military fashion! Divide the county into sections and make one or two day trips to each area.'

'In a way, we started researching today, by exploring Treleggan and the river.' Flora shook the pan and turned the sizzling rashers of bacon.

'If it's a start, it's a very small one. There's a lot more of the Helford to explore, not to mention the rest of Cornwall. It used to be a lively waterway, like that old chap said, with ports lining each bank, but Helford, Gweek, Constantine – they're just sleepy villages now. I was wondering' – he paused in buttering the bread – 'if possibly the river's faded glory could be the nub of the new story. Some deep-seated grudge perhaps that stemmed from business dealings years ago, or maybe a crime committed in one of those ports and covered up, but now in danger of being revealed. It would mean completely rewriting those early chapters though.'

'That would be a shame. But after the Helford district? I've done two eggs each. Is that OK?'

'Perfect. The pasties have long since disappeared. I've brought several books on the history of the Helford with me. You probably saw them in the boot.' Jack's mind, it seemed, was still focused on the river. 'When you have time, could you give them a read? Make notes on anything you think potentially interesting?'

'I'll do that. And after Helford?' she asked again.

'Land's End maybe, or we could trot across country and

drive along the north coast. The terrain there is more rugged – wilder seas, dramatic rockfalls, a host of abandoned tin mines. There could well be a story there.'

The talk of where in Cornwall they might visit over the coming weeks encouraged Flora to say what was foremost in her mind. 'I've been wondering how long we can stay at Primrose Cottage, now we haven't a landlord,' she said, taking a seat at the table.

'It crossed my mind as well and I phoned Arthur Bellaby this afternoon – sorry, I forgot to tell you – it was when you were outside weeding the terrace. It took a while to run him to ground, but I needed to give him the sad news. He was shocked, of course, and quite upset. I think Roger must have been a nice chap.'

'And the cottage?'

'We seem to be OK here for the moment, but Arthur is looking into the legal position. He believes that until probate is granted, we can continue to be tenants based on the agreement he signed and the rent he paid in advance. His advice is to sit tight, at least until he can find us another place.'

'Does he know who will inherit the cottage?'

Jack shook his head. 'He's never met Roger's family and doesn't have a name for the solicitors. He signed the rental agreement with the local estate agent.'

'I wonder.' Flora reached across for a folded sheet of paper she'd left on the kitchen counter. 'It could be these people. This letter was under a pile of library books I found while I was looking for somewhere to store my writing materials. It mentions an appointment with a firm of solicitors in Falmouth.'

She passed the letter to Jack and he took a quick look. 'Sadler and Sadler. They could be the chaps. Roger was the manager of a bank in Falmouth and it's likely he used local solicitors. I'll pass their name on to Arthur, just in case. They probably hold Roger's will, not that they'd disclose anything if we asked.'

'Whoever inherits his estate will have a fair amount to sort out. Two houses, two enormous gardens, and a mountain of paperwork. Somewhere there'll be boxes of material from all the research Roger undertook, though I've seen nothing of them.'

'He must have taken it back to the grand house in the high street he mentioned. Or, possibly the cottage has a loft and he's hoisted the boxes up there.'

Flora took a mouthful of bread and butter. 'This loaf is wonderful. We must buy another tomorrow. The books I found with the letter came from the library in Helston. They'll need to be returned.'

Jack put down his knife and fork, his eyes suddenly alert. 'That's it! It's decided. That's where we'll start – Helston. We'll combine a research trip with our good deed for the day. And returning those books might prove useful. If Roger was borrowing them for research, it suggests the library has a good local history section.'

He pushed back his chair, taking their empty plates to the sink. 'It's not going to be a desperately interesting day, Flora, so if you'd rather stay and weed your terrace, it's OK with me.'

'Thanks, but I think I'd prefer a trip to Helston. The terrace won't be going anywhere.'

The table cleared and the kitchen tidied, they decamped to the sitting room where Jack switched on the wireless, fiddling for some time with the dial in an attempt to find a programme worth listening to.

'Nothing,' he muttered despondently.

'Never mind the wireless. Come and look at this.' Flora had been leafing through the books they were to return tomorrow, her forehead creased. Pointing at the open page, she held it up for Jack to see. 'I flicked through a couple of the books to see what kind of stuff Roger was reading – and see what he's underlined.'

Jack peered over her shoulder. 'Something about signals, is that right?'

'Not just something, but hidden Signals units here in Cornwall during the war. I wonder where exactly.' She picked up a second book and checked the index, quickly finding what she wanted. 'According to this book there were several of these outposts in this part of Cornwall, though Roger seems most interested in... where does he say?' She went back to the original book and scanned the page, her finger moving from line to line.

'The Lizard?'

'How did you know that?'

'Remember what Alice said? About the Lizard – about Thomas Martin, wasn't that the name, posted to a signals centre there during the war? My father was in the Signals, too, and in Cornwall for a few years.'

'On the Lizard?'

Jack nodded.

'I wonder if he knew Thomas. Did he tell you about his work?' Flora closed the books and set them into a neat pile on the small square table that filled the centre of the room.

'Very little. Only that he was posted to the Lizard and the stuff he was assigned to was very hush-hush. I thought he was just bragging and that it hadn't been half as secret as he made out.'

'What do signals centres actually do?'

'Control intelligence mainly, which is pretty vital. Identify targets for bombing and report back on the results. Follow troop movements, pass on information on enemy tanks and troops, that kind of thing.'

Flora picked up the second volume again and found the page she'd been reading. 'I don't think your father was bragging unnecessarily. Apparently, the chain of radar stations in the county were part of an early warning system against enemy aircraft. Sussex was filled to bursting with troops and tanks and landing crafts, but I hadn't realised that Cornwall was a wartime base, too.'

'I knew the RAF sited their fighter aircraft here, as escort to the heavy bombers on their raids over France, so I'm not too surprised there was more. Cornwall enjoys a huge stretch of coastline after all – numerous coves that would be perfect for landing enemy tanks and troops. Like Sussex, the ports would need to be defended and the beaches mined and blocked by barbed wire and anti-tank structures.'

Flora reached out for the book she'd first looked at. 'D-Day seems to have been of special interest to Roger, if you go by the paragraphs he's asterisked. See how many pages he's marked.'

Jack took the book she handed him and read several pages. 'The signals centres here were clearly very valuable on D-Day. They provided bogus traffic – setting up false movements of non-existent regiments – persuading the enemy that the offensive would take place in an area where it wouldn't. Decoy and deception, that's what it's called.'

'Maybe one of the librarians in Helston can throw some light on why Roger was so interested.' Flora took back the book and returned it to the pile. 'He's got a real thing about the event.'

'He was in the Home Guard, remember?' Jack said mockingly, a laugh in his voice.

'Don't be unkind. Roger must have done his bit.' But she laughed as well.

Flora struggled awake from a deep sleep. Someone was knocking on the front door, knocking hard and persistently. She made a grab for her watch lying on the bedside table and saw that it was nearly eight o'clock. She'd overslept, but who was the impatient caller and why come so early?

Reaching for her dressing gown, she wrapped herself against the morning chill and fished her slippers from under the bed, then padded down the stairs to open the door. The man who stood on the threshold was thin and sinewy, around fifty years old, Flora judged, though his face was deeply lined and his hair sparse.

He looked her up and down. 'Oh, sorry. I got you up.'

'Yes, you did.' She waited for him to state his business, annoyed that he didn't seem in the slightest bit sorry despite his words.

'I'm Lionel Gifford,' he offered.

'Gifford?'

'Roger was my brother.'

She felt immediately contrite. 'I'm so sorry, Mr Gifford. I didn't realise. Would you like to come in?'

'Thanks.' He walked through the door with alacrity, his smile hardly suggesting a grieving heart.

Flora flattened herself against the wall, the hallway was so narrow, and she felt a strong need to keep a distance between them.

'I suppose you've come to see where... where...' It sounded ghoulish but she'd read how often people were impelled to visit the last place their loved ones had drawn breath.

'Gracious no,' Lionel said chirpily. 'But poor old Roger, eh? Done to death in his own orchard.'

Lionel definitely wasn't a grieving brother, so why was he here? Perhaps as Roger's beneficiary, he had inherited the cottage and come to turn them out. It seemed a little previous, but then he was evidently a man in a hurry. Flora withdrew any sympathy she had felt and decided she didn't much like Lionel.

'In that case, what can I do for you, Mr Gifford?'

'I've come to collect my brother's stuff, that's all. Get it out of your way.'

'I don't believe your brother had any stuff, as you call it, unless you mean the furniture. Surely that belongs with the cottage?'

Lionel gave a tinny laugh. 'I've not come to take your bed away, Miss, Miss—'

'Steele,' she said impatiently.

'It's the papers, I've come for. Roger's papers. He was quite clear he wanted me to have them.'

Whether or not that was true, Flora had no chance of checking, but she was pretty sure that until probate was granted, everything should be left just as it was.

'There are no papers here, as far as I'm aware.' Even if she'd known where Roger had stored his private documents, she wouldn't have told this man. 'Your brother lived elsewhere, I believe – in the high street.'

'I know where he lived,' Lionel said truculently. 'I'm staying there right now. But he worked in this cottage. You might not know it but he was doing vital work and I want to protect it.'

'You're talking of your brother's research? Naturally, you would want to protect it, but I'm afraid I can't help you.'

'Help you with what?' Jack had come downstairs, similarly attired in a dressing gown. There were three of them now, squashed together in the small space.

'Morning, squire,' Lionel greeted him. His gaze travelled between them, a salacious smirk touching his lips. '*Miss* Steele was saying as how she didn't know of any papers, but I can assure you that my brother had plenty stored somewhere.'

'Then I suggest you visit his home and ask there. This is a rented cottage and at the moment we are tenants. I'm extremely sorry about your brother, but as Miss Steele has told you, we know nothing of papers and that should be good enough.' Jack advanced on the man as he spoke.

Taking one look at the determined face confronting him, Lionel backed away. 'Sorry to disturb you so early,' he muttered, the smirk back in place. 'You're probably right. I'll have another look around River House.'

'You do that.' Jack opened the front door and Lionel had no option but to walk through it.

'What a horrible man.' Flora felt the need for an immediate wash. 'How could Roger Gifford have a brother like that?'

'Everyone has relatives they'd rather not. He was talking about papers. What exactly was he after, do you think?'

'I thought when he first mentioned them he meant legal papers, a copy of the will maybe. But then he said something about his brother working here, and I realised he must mean the research Roger was doing.'

'Why on earth would he want that?'

Flora paused at the bottom of the stairs. 'I've no idea, but I have a feeling those papers are more substantial than we think – particularly if you consider what we found in Roger's library books last night.'

'I notice you didn't say anything about those.'

'The man made my skin crawl. I didn't want to tell him anything.' She stopped halfway up the stairs, turning to say, 'There's something about those signals centres that's important. Roger wouldn't have underlined those parts of the book if there wasn't.'

'If so, Lionel must suspect it's worth pursuing. Otherwise he wouldn't have landed on us at dawn, ready to grab anything he could.'

'It's way past dawn,' she pointed out, 'and high time we were both dressed. But I'd like to know what's in those papers or even where they are. Jessie might know – we must ask her.'

'Maybe, but this isn't the time to get sidetracked,' Jack said firmly, following her up the stairs. 'Research for the book is more important and we're starting on it today.'

'OK, but perhaps we could sidetrack just a little?'

He sighed. 'How?'

'Your father was here during the war and you said he served in a signals centre on the Lizard. Why don't you telephone him and find out more?'

7

Jessie arrived at the cottage as they were clearing the breakfast dishes.

'I'll be doin' those,' she scolded, bustling into the kitchen, apron in hand. 'It's what I'm paid fer.'

Flora was relieved their housekeeper seemed to have recovered her spirits a little, though she noticed there were shadows around her eyes.

'I'll make the beds first,' Jessie said, 'then put the floor sweeper round, jus' to tidy up. Then I'll be off to the village to get whatever shoppin' you need.'

'I think we're probably stuck with pasties for the time being,' Jack said, an apologetic look on his face. 'There won't be a lot of time for cooking.'

'You leave the cookin' to me. I'll be through the work soon enough. Plenty of time to shop and cook. Jus' tell me what you like to eat.'

'Everything,' Jack said cheerfully. 'Flora?'

'Everything,' she confirmed with a smile. 'It will be wonderful to have you cook for us. The casserole you left was delicious.'

'I'll think of somethin' tasty for tonight,' Jessie said comfortably, and dived into the sink cupboard for the washing bowl.

'I'm looking forward to it already!' Jack beamed. 'Right now, though, I'd better check the petrol gauge. Be back in a minute.'

Flora nodded and turned to her companion. 'Jessie, I wanted to ask you about the cottage, but it wasn't the right time yesterday.'

'Oh, yes?'

'Why is it called Primrose? From what I can see, the garden doesn't have a single primrose plant.'

The housekeeper gave a gentle snort. 'When Mr Roger bought the place, the outside were painted a pale yellow. That were before—' She stopped abruptly, her lips tightly pursed. 'His wife didn't like the colour, so he 'ad it painted white.'

'But kept the name?' she asked, wondering what it was that Jessie hadn't said.

'Everyone knew it as Primrose Cottage – it'd be too confusin' to change.'

'If we'd come a few months earlier, I'd have liked to plant primroses – beneath the windows, I think – but May is too late. They're already in full bloom along the roadsides. By the way, we had a visitor call this morning – early. He said he was Roger's brother.'

'Lionel Gifford?' Jessie's mouth was pinched. 'That no-good. What did he want?'

'He was after papers his brother was working on, he said. We took that to mean Roger's research.'

'Them notes'll be in the loft. Mr Roger always moved them there when he 'ad visitors in the cottage. You didn't give 'im nothin', I hope.'

'I denied all knowledge,' Flora said. 'I didn't like the man.'

'Nor should you. Lionel Gifford is a narsty piece of work. He were 'ere in the war. Drivin' tanks, he said, though you'd never credit it. Stayed back in this country, of course. He wouldn't have got near any fightin'. Then he got chucked out of his regiment. *He* said he were invalided out, but most folks round 'ere think he did somethin' bad. Moved to London, but couldn't keep a job fer more'n five minutes. Always arguin' with the boss, it seemed. Confrontational-like. *And* he drinks!' Jessie finished on a sepulchral note.

'He sounds the complete opposite of his brother. How did Roger get on with him?'

'Mr Roger were too soft. Lionel's 'is younger brother and he were always rescuin' 'im. Mr Roger were a saint. Time and again he got that layabout out of whatever mess he'd fallen into. Gave 'im money when he was in debt, which was most times, got 'im out of trouble when the police came callin'. Lionel Gifford were nothing but a rope round poor Mr Roger's neck.'

It was an unfortunate image, Flora thought, but aloud she said, 'He still lives in London?'

'Best place fer 'im.' For Jessie, London was evidently a cauldron of sin. 'But whenever he's in trouble, he turns up 'ere like a bad penny you couldn't get rid of.'

'Expecting Roger to help him?'

Jessie dried the last of the breakfast dishes. 'It's the way it's been fer years, but last month he said to me, "Jessie, I'm makin' a change. I'm goin' to live my life fer myself, look after number one instead of always runnin' around fer others."'

'So no more begging brother?'

Jessie nodded. 'That were the idea. Until Lionel got into trouble again. Some narsty people in London he owes money to. He came down 'ere a month or so ago and Mr Roger 'ad to put him up, but he refused to pay 'im the money he wanted. Lionel went mad, jumpin' we'd say, I 'eard him. Ragin' at poor Mr Roger about 'ow could he do this to 'is own brother? Mr Roger told me later, confidential-like, that he were changin' his will. About time, too.'

'Did he change it?' It seemed to Flora important.

Jessie shrugged. 'I don' know. I hope so, I hope he cut that no-good out fer ever. Anyways, whatever Mr Roger told his brother sent the man flyin' back to London and we 'aven't seen 'im since. I didn't know he were back in Treleggan.'

Flora paused at the kitchen door, deep in thought. If Roger had told his brother that he was about to change his will, it was a very strong motive for murder. But why didn't Lionel kill him at the time? The quarrel would have been the obvious moment, if the man were as enraged as Jessie painted... but he'd be suspected, wouldn't he? That was it. He was staying at Roger's house and no doubt there'd been plenty who'd heard the row between them. If his brother had been found murdered at that time, suspicion would have fallen on Lionel immediately. And it was possible that Roger hadn't actually changed his will by then, merely threatened to as a way of keeping his brother in order. If he stepped out of line again, Roger might have told him, he would go straight to his solicitor.

She walked up the stairs to her bedroom, taking a light jacket from the wardrobe and a pair of stout shoes – there could be a good deal of walking today – but all the time, her mind was busy. There was something she'd forgotten that was important. Of course, the letter she'd found. Roger's appointment! Roger had been about to visit his solicitor – to carry out his threat?

Had he telephoned Lionel in London and warned him what he intended to do? If so, Roger would have to be stopped. Would have to be killed, so... Lionel rushes back to Treleggan and lures his brother to the orchard. If no one saw Lionel arrive in the village, and from what Jessie said that seemed to be the case, he could pretend he was still in London at the time of the murder, only hurrying down to Cornwall the following day to play the grieving brother. Flora could understand his desperate need to stop the will being changed, but Roger's research? Why was Lionel so interested in that?

'Are you ready?' Jack called up to her from the hall.

Snatching up jacket and shoes, she padded down the stairs.

'Your limousine awaits, madam,' he announced grandly, retrieving his fedora from the coat stand.

'We're off to Helston today,' she explained to the housekeeper who'd emerged from the kitchen to say goodbye.

'Right on.' Jessie nodded. 'Enjoy your trip. I'll be back with supper a bit early today, if that's OK with you. They're showin' that *Dam Busters* in Falmouth and the Women's Institute 'ave hired a coach for us all. Fancy that!'

'Jessie told me something interesting while you were checking the car,' Flora said, as they drove out of Treleggan.

'More interesting than a dead body and an unsavoury brother?'

'It was about the brother. Apparently, he quarrelled badly with Roger when he was last in the village. Lionel is the proverbial bad penny, as Jessie called him, always turning up with a begging bowl. But this time Roger refused him money and told Jessie he was changing his will. She doesn't know whether or not he carried through his threat, but as a motive for murder you can't get much better.'

Jack half turned to her, his grey eyes darkening. 'If Lionel has motive, the police will pick it up.'

'Will they? They probably don't even know he's back in Treleggan. Jessie didn't. He turned up in the village unannounced and probably unseen. I'm wondering... what if he arranged to meet Roger in the orchard?'

'To persuade his brother not to change his will? A bit late for that.'

'It's possible that Roger never got around to signing the new will. Remember the solicitor's letter confirming an appointment? It might be worth a gamble on Lionel's part. He could manufacture an alibi. No one knew he was back in Treleggan and if the police asked for his whereabouts at the time, he could say he didn't arrive until after the murder.'

'How long has he actually been in the village?'

Flora spread her hands. 'Who knows, but it can't have been long. He's staying at his brother's house on the high street and someone would have seen him eventually.'

'Then that makes a nonsense of meeting Roger in the orchard.'

'No, it doesn't. He's not going to kill him in a house they share, is he? He would make a pretext of meeting him at Primrose Cottage.'

'What kind of pretext would get Roger out of bed at dawn to tramp to a wet orchard to meet a brother he's already living with?'

Flora turned it over in her mind. 'Say, that Lionel travelled down to Treleggan the night before and stayed somewhere else, a pub or a bed and breakfast, then telephoned that evening to say he wanted to meet his brother away from the house. Sort things out with him on neutral territory and in private – at a time when there wouldn't be anyone around.'

'Primrose Cottage isn't precisely neutral territory,' Jack pointed out.

'But nearly,' she urged.

'Well, it's a theory.'

'A good one, too,' Flora said spiritedly, though she wasn't feeling as confident as she sounded. 'The only thing I don't understand is why Lionel is so interested in Roger's research. Unless there's something there he can sell, since money seems his only interest, but what on earth could that be?'

'When you first saw him at the door, you thought he was after legal documents, and perhaps he was. Perhaps it's not the research he's interested in, though it makes a good cover. Whichever of Roger's wills is current, there'll be a copy of it somewhere, other than with the solicitor. If Lionel searched

River House and couldn't find the document, he'd assume it was in the cottage and, if he owes money again, as Jessie claims, he'd be desperate to get hold of it and know if he's inherited.'

'Desperate to know whether or not he's killed in vain?'

'If you like, or...' – Jack paused while he manoeuvred the car around a sharp bend – 'you could be right. There could be something in those papers that reflects badly on him.'

'Like what, do you think?'

'I don't know and I've no intention of finding out.'

'It could be inspiration for the new book,' she tempted.

Jack merely grunted.

The town of Helston was soon reached and, driving down the hill to the town centre, Flora was surprised to see a shining streak of water in the distance.

'I didn't know Helston was near water.'

'It isn't. Not any more. It used to be a busy port centuries ago, but then the river – it's a different one here, the Cober, I saw its name on the map – began to silt up and effectively closed Helston off. The sea is still there but too far away to be useful.'

'Even so, the town looks prosperous. Bustling.' Flora craned her head to take in the mix of Georgian and Victorian architecture. 'Beautiful houses, too.'

'They'll have been built courtesy of the tin trade.'

He steered the car into a parking space and looked around. 'The town seems much the same as when I was last here, though that was years ago and it was a special day. A day for celebration. I came with my parents. They were still together then and my father had this urge to see the Flora Dance. It's quite famous.'

'I've heard of it,' she said, climbing out of the car and stretching her limbs. 'What does it involve, exactly?'

'I remember the town being decorated from head to toe: greenery and flowers everywhere. Bunches of local bluebells in particular.'

'It must take place in May then. Around now.'

'It does. There's an amazing procession, a dance really, that snakes around the town, through the shops, through homes and private gardens, with the Helston band playing. I remember seeing gentlemen in tailcoats and women in beautiful dresses and children dressed completely in white. I reckon it's a remnant from pagan times, a dance to frighten away the devil! There's an amazing stained-glass window in the church my father took me to, depicting angels dancing on Flora Day along with the opening bars of the dance tune.' He smiled down at her. 'How does it feel to have a day of your very own?'

'Quite special, except I doubt I'd fit with the angels!'

He waved a hand at the street sign. 'This is the main throughfare, by the way.'

At Jack's direction, they walked the length of Coinagehall Street before turning off into one of the winding cobbled alleyways that led from it, and began a climb uphill.

'Are you sure the library is this way?' Flora was already out of breath. 'I don't want to have laboured to the top for nothing.'

'Look for yourself.' Jack pointed ahead. At the summit, a sturdy granite stone building had come into view and a steady procession of people were entering and leaving the main entrance.

She brightened at the sight. 'It's possible the library could have the answer to why Lionel might be keen to retrieve his brother's work. Roger must have spent a good deal of time here.'

'A nice place to spend it,' Jack commented, as they walked through the entrance into a high-ceilinged room, lit by a bank of long windows that filled one entire side of the building. Sighting the librarian's desk, he strode across to a young assistant who was busy cataloguing books. Her name badge read Miss Hodges.

She looked up as Jack approached. 'Good morning. You're wanting to return books?'

'Yes,' he said, 'but not ours.' He lined up the small pile of books on her desk. 'They were taken out by our landlord but I'm afraid he passed away yesterday. We found them in the cottage we're renting and thought we should return them.'

'Thank you. That's very good of you.' She glanced inside the first volume and her expression changed.

'Your landlord,' she said in a faint voice, 'he wasn't Roger Gifford by any chance?'

'Yes,' Jack said readily. 'Do you know him?'

'Very well.' The librarian sat down heavily and pointed to the book. 'I recognise this as a volume he borrowed a short while ago. And he's dead, you say? How very sad! He was a charming man, an old-school gentleman. Mr Penrose – he's our chief librarian – will be extremely sorry to hear the news. He's often out and about at the moment but when I see him, I'll be sure to tell him. He and Mr Gifford talked a lot together.'

'Mr Gifford came to the library often, then?'

'Oh yes, he was very keen on the research he was doing. But he was fine the last time I saw him. How—'

'It was very sudden,' Flora put in, not wishing to mention the murder, if news hadn't yet reached Helston. 'And quite unexpected. He seems to have been very interested in the last war and the part Cornwall played. Did he speak to you about it?'

'Only for advice on which books would be the most useful.'

'I glanced through them,' Flora said, tapping the pile of books with her fingertips, 'and was very surprised. I'd no idea how deeply Cornwall was involved in the preparations for D-Day. The event appears to have been Roger's main interest, along with the signals centres.'

'He'd only recently moved on to D-Day, I think,' Miss Hodges said, adjusting the neat bun at the nape of her neck. 'Before that he was looking into how rationing affected Cornwall, the social consequences of privation, that kind of thing. But I was able to tell him a little more about the signals centres. Or one of them, at least.'

Flora had begun to think it was time they left, but at this she held fast.

'I lived in Mullion as a child,' the assistant continued, 'and I remember the construction that went on. The men who'd worked the tin mines were drafted in to dig a tunnel into the cliff. We found out later, after the war, that it led inland to what was a bomb-proof cavern sunk into the heathland. Those men spent days blasting, drilling, digging. The authorities tried to keep it quiet but my mum and dad guessed what was going on, so did all the other villagers, I imagine. One of them asked some official who came down from the War Office what was happening and he told him the tunnel was a shortcut to the village pub from the beach. It gave everyone a laugh. As if anyone would believe that!'

'The bomb-proof cavern they built was a signals centre?' Flora pursued.

'No one knew for sure, but the whole thing was so hush-hush, it had to be. There was a rumour that whoever was working down there was involved with spying of some kind and linked to Bletchley Park – as part of the Enigma traffic.'

'That's impressive,' Jack said. 'And very interesting. Thank you.'

'Yes, thank you, Miss Hodges,' Flora seconded.

They turned together and made for the entrance, neither of them speaking. As they did, a man came bowling towards them and they stood back to let him pass. Flora caught sight of the badge on his jacket lapel – Saul Penrose. He must be the Mr Penrose who had known Roger well. She went to catch at his sleeve, but he was moving too swiftly, his sturdy body and short legs carrying him across the library floor, past Miss Hodges' desk and through an oak-panelled door in a matter of seconds.

Jack had seen her attempt. 'We can come back,' he said. 'Beard Mr Penrose in his den, if you're still interested. But how about a walk around town and a cup of tea before we set off for the Lizard?'

'We're going to the Lizard?'

'But naturally. Aren't you desperate to discover the secret tunnel?'

8

They spent the next hour or so exploring the town: the cobbled alleyways that led uphill from the main street, St Michael's Church, the Guildhall, Coronation Lake, all duly investigated, followed by a slow wander through the Penwith Museum. This proved more interesting than they'd expected and it was only the need to find lunch that persuaded Jack to leave at all.

'I'll have to come back,' he said, as soon as they were outside the museum doors.

'Another day,' Flora said firmly. 'I need some food and you promised me a secret tunnel.'

Lunch was a leisurely affair, Jack keen to try anything on the menu that was remotely Cornish. She shared the crab soup and bread roll with him but didn't follow suit when he ordered a giant pasty – the large pocket of flaky pastry came brimming with beef and vegetables. Then watched in fascination as he finished off with biscuits and a chunk of local cheese. 'It's an old recipe,' the waitress told them. 'The milk's from Friesian cows.'

'That was excellent.' He looked up from chasing the last morsel around his plate.

'Can you still move?' Flora asked, genuinely interested.

'I may have slowed a little,' he conceded, 'but watch me!'

When they finally emerged from the café, it was to find the streets a great deal busier. A crowd had gathered on the pavement outside and was clustered at the top of a flight of stone steps.

'What's going on? Can you see?' Flora craned her neck, but the crowd was too dense.

At nearly a foot taller, Jack was able to tell her. 'They're putting up decorations at the bottom of the steps. Stringing bunting from shop to shop and there's a ton of greenery fixed over the doors. Baskets of flowers as well. It will be for Flora Day, I guess, though it must be a delayed one. Normally it's on the eighth of May – so earlier this week.'

'I still can't see a thing,' she complained, and began jumping on the spot, trying for a better view. Catching sight of a woman's figure, she felt a jolt of familiarity. Surely, she'd seen the woman before. A face swam slowly into Flora's vision. An extraordinary face. Skin, weathered and lined, but shining brown, like a new-fallen nut. A head of hair that hung wild and eyes of piercing green. The woman stared hard at her and Flora felt herself shrink beneath the gaze.

'I need to wriggle forward to get a better view,' she said quickly. 'I'm small enough for no one to notice I'm pushing in!'

'Be careful, the stairway is steep,' Jack warned, but his voice faded in the air.

The crowd parted slightly, sucking Flora into its midst, then once more knitted together. For a moment her figure was lost to sight but, when Jack stretched tall, he could just discern, over the heads of the crowd, a tumble of reddish-brown hair. She was way out in front – the wriggle had been successful.

He was about to try to join her when there was a surge from within the crowd. A wave rippling through the spectators, a shuffling and a scuffling, and then he could no longer see her. She had completely disappeared.

In that moment, Jack forgot his manners and pushed himself roughly into the crowd, desperate to make sure Flora was safe. Pushing even harder, he broke through the final rank of people and stood aghast. She had fallen down the stone stairs and was lying awkwardly on a lower step. A man had clambered down and was helping her to her feet while a woman, who seemed to be his wife, began brushing Flora's skirt and tutting loudly.

Flora looked up as Jack hurtled down the steps towards her and tried to smile. 'Don't say it. You told me to be careful.'

He didn't say it, seeming too relieved that she was alive and talking.

'I don't rightly know how that happened,' the man said.

'People pushing from behind,' his wife offered. 'Dangerous thing to do. Are you all right now, my luv?'

'Yes, I'm fine, and thank you.' Flora's smile was strained. Her knee was throbbing and when Jack gave her his arm, she leaned on him heavily. Her eyes followed her rescuers as they climbed back up the stairs. The woman she'd seen earlier, the woman on the riverbank, was standing on the top step, her tall, thin figure motionless. She was watching again, staring with those astonishing green eyes that seemed to pierce Flora's very skin.

'Let's get you to the car,' Jack said. 'You're hurt and you need to be home.'

He walked her slowly down the remaining steps. She was trying not to hobble but finding it difficult.

'No Lizard today then?' she asked cheekily. It was a disappointment, but walking over heathland was not something she would manage.

Unrolling her stocking an hour later, she could see why. The knee had ballooned to twice its normal size, but since she could still walk it was unlikely to be broken. Jack hurried around fetching bowls of cold water and as many small cloths as he could find, then wrapping them, one at a time, around the swelling. As soon as one became warm, he substituted it for another, well-soaked in the cold water.

'You're fussing over me, but I know you're cross,' Flora said.

'Have I said so?'

'No, and for that I'm grateful, but you can say it if you like. You were right – I should have been more careful. I'll have to start listening to your wise words,' she said ruefully.

'That seems unlikely.' He spoke lightly but his face had the haunted look Flora had seen in Abbeymead, when he'd first shown her the anonymous letter.

'What's the matter? There is something the matter, isn't there?'

He sat back on his heels. 'I don't see how the crowd could have surged so much that it sent you flying down those steps. It would have needed a powerful force.'

Flora had her own reservations, not least why that strange woman had been in Helston, had stood at the very top of the steps and stared so hard at her, but when she spoke, it was an attempt to reassure them both.

'It's as my rescuer said, people were pushing, not thinking. They wanted to see the first of the decorations.'

'They didn't look as if they were pushing,' Jack countered, fetching yet another bowl of cold water. 'There was a shuffling around, a sense of movement, but the crowd as a whole budged very little. It's not as though it was an amazing spectacle they were about to miss. Just preparations for Flora Day. Who gets that excited?'

'Evidently the inhabitants of Helston,' she said, holding the wet pad to her knee. 'And me!'

. . .

The next morning, Flora walked down the stairs suffering only an occasional twinge. Jack's ministrations seemed to have been successful. He was already in the kitchen and greeted her with a grin.

'How's the wounded warrior?'

'Better. Much better.'

'I've made coffee – the proper stuff. The instant has been banished to the back of the cupboard, along with a very old bottle of Camp.'

'How did you find real coffee?'

'Aha! A secret stash, brought all the way from Sussex. Actually, from London when I was last in town.'

'The smell is wonderful. I don't think I've had proper coffee for years. It should set us up for our march across the Lizard.' She glanced through the kitchen window at a sky heavy with cloud. 'The weather's not looking too promising, though.'

'I'm thinking it might be better to forget the Lizard today and take a trip up the north coast. We'd be in the car for most of the time and you wouldn't be constantly using your knee.'

'The knee is fine,' Flora insisted. 'And I want to find that tunnel.'

'We could visit Tintagel.' He dangled the treat in front of her.

'Tintagel?'

'You know, Arthur and the Round Table stuff.'

'Yes, of course I know! But how is that going to help you write the book?'

'Absolutely no idea, but then how will a trip to the Lizard? To be honest, I'm beginning to feel a trifle desperate – my brain seems to have ground to a stop. Now, I don't even like the chapters I wrote in Abbeymead. And don't suggest I use Roger's murder to kick the story off. I can't – it's too near reality.'

Over the rim of her coffee cup, Flora looked at him thoughtfully. 'Tintagel might work, I suppose.'

'The landscape there is certainly stunning. Hugely dramatic. It might just trigger the imagination.' He didn't sound too optimistic.

'Landscape is all very well, but you need to speak to people. Have conversations.'

'There'll be people enough at the site. Some of them might even be Cornish.'

Flora chewed her lips. 'Let's hope so. You need something, someone, to get you started. Get *me* started as well. Give me things to do, places to explore.' She attacked her slice of toast, buttering it fiercely. 'At the moment, I feel a spare part.'

He looked across at her, frowning slightly. 'The idea was that you'd be around to help, but mostly that you'd rest. This should be a holiday for you.'

'I'm used to being busy, Jack, and apart from a few bus rides, there's not much I can do. It's not as if you have the time to chauffeur me around Cornwall.'

'You don't have to depend on buses. You can take a taxi anywhere you fancy and I'll put it down to expenses.'

'And end up paying yourself,' she retorted.

'You deserve a decent break and I want you to have one. I'm wishing now that I'd persuaded you to go to Paris.'

'Don't wish it. I'd rather be here with you.' The remark had been involuntary and Flora longed to bite back the words. 'I'm not taking taxis, that's for sure.' Her tone was severe to cover her confusion. 'If there's nothing I can do for you, I'll work in the garden. At least I can carry on taming the wilderness – I might even discover a primrose or two.'

9

They left immediately after breakfast, Jack finding his way cross-country to the road that ran northwards the length of the coast. Beside him, Flora was smiling, delighted to be making the surprise trip. Tintagel held a magic of its own. The few photographs she'd seen matched the romantic myths she'd read as a child, but she was pleased, too, that for a day at least she was leaving Treleggan behind for the freedom of the north Cornish coast. Helford was beautiful, there was no denying, but it had begun to feel just a little oppressive and Flora was pleased to escape.

The image of the strange woman continued to taunt her. The stare, cool, impassive, piercing to the heart, gave Flora the shivers, feeding the fear that she had been pushed – Jack evidently had his suspicions – and that it had been the woman doing the pushing. Had that curious figure been following them and thrust at Flora when the opportunity occurred? But why would she and why had she even been in Helston? And why by the river when they'd taken the boat? Who was she anyway? Could she possibly be the author of that anonymous letter warning them to stay in Sussex?

Flora's thoughts came to a sharp stop. This was getting ridiculous – she was constructing a fantasy. The woman had a perfect right to walk by the river and, in Helston, be just one of the crowd. It was only her appearance that made her stand out. She looked... different... but there was no crime in that. And her stare? Why that stare? Flora shrugged the question to one side. The woman might not even have been looking at her: by the river, enjoying the quiet beauty of the place and, in Helston, looking deep into the crowd at someone beside or beyond Flora.

She should ignore the mysterious presence and accept that she'd fallen by accident, since who else could have pushed her? Lionel's was the only name that came to mind. Flora hadn't forgotten him. He'd been refused something he clearly wanted very badly and it was possible he'd be prepared to cause harm to achieve his aim. Put her out of action, put her in hospital maybe, so that he could ransack Primrose Cottage at his leisure. *And* he could have been the one to send the letter. If he'd decided to rid himself of his brother before Roger could alter his will, he'd not want anyone near Primrose Cottage, particularly a writer of crime. Yet she'd caught no sight of him in Helston.

The incident must remain a mysterious blur and it was best she forgot it entirely. She knew herself guilty of leaps of imagination, leaps that had no logical foundation. Jack frowned on them and it was noticeable that he'd made no mention of yesterday's events as they drove northwards, instead carrying on a cheerful conversation.

Her first view of Tintagel was exactly as Flora had imagined: a deep green headland, dark grey rocks and a sea the colour of turquoise. Perched on the clifftop, the castle ruins commanded the landscape below, guarding its grassy slopes as they tumbled towards the rugged shoreline. She wound down her window and, in the distance, could hear the thundering swell of the ocean. The cliffs teemed with seabirds sheltering from the winds and, as they drew closer, Jack pointed out what he thought were seals playing in the wild seas below.

A thin strip of land divided the site into two, on one side the mainland and on the other an island, the castle lying on both sides of the chasm. A flight of wooden steps wound between the two.

'Centuries of erosion must have taken a good deal of the castle and its buildings,' Jack remarked, as he brought the car to a stop. 'There's not going to be a huge amount left.'

'Then we'll have to use our imaginations!'

'You'll be in your element.'

Flora pulled a small face and walked with him to the ticket office, collecting a leaflet from one of the castle's guardians. They seemed to be the only visitors this morning, the stormy day perhaps keeping people away.

'Let's start on the mainland,' Jack suggested. 'Then if you think your knee is up to it, we can take the steps over to the island.'

It didn't, in fact, require too much of Flora's imagination to visualise the mythical past: the castle's battlements and shadowy courtyards, its secret winding passages, the majesty of King Arthur and his knights, and the sorcery of Merlin, the enchanter, were easily conjured into being.

'This courtyard must have formed the entrance to the whole castle,' Flora said, as they wandered through what was left of a medieval gateway into the paved space beyond.

She looked out over the sea, brilliant blue even under louring skies, the constant lash of waves as they burst themselves open on the rocks below sending a bright, white spray into the air. It was a view that men and women had looked on for hundreds of years and Flora felt a tingle of connection. King Arthur, the legendary warlord, had led the fight against the marauding Anglo-Saxons from this windswept, rain-battered headland.

By the time they had sauntered through the ruins of both lower and upper wards, her knee had begun to throb, but she said nothing, keen to see more.

'The leaflet says that the remains of the Great Hall are on the island.' She looked at Jack hopefully.

'And you want to see it?'

'Naturally, I do. Just think, Arthur and his knights feasted there. Tristan and his Irish princess, Iseult, sat at that Round Table. Sir Lancelot and Lady Guinevere, too, before their ill-fated love affair.'

'You do know that never happened, don't you?' he asked, as they began their descent down the wooden staircase that was the only way of crossing the chasm. 'This place was a fortress for Cornish chieftains, true, but it was Geoffrey of Monmouth who first suggested the stronghold was the birthplace of King Arthur and that was five or six centuries later. Arthur may never even have existed and, if he had, there are numerous other sites that claim him for their own. Glastonbury Abbey for one.'

'I don't care. They are wonderful stories.'

Jack helped her down the last of the steps. 'I'm not sure we should have bothered with the island.' He sounded concerned. 'You'll have to climb back up and it won't be easy.'

'I'm fine. Don't fuss. Going up will be easier than coming down. Look.' She pointed to a diagram in the leaflet and then ahead. 'That's the Great Hall.'

'It's been built in a good place,' he remarked. 'A sheltered terrace, man-made by the look of it.'

The walls surrounding the wide, open space were crumbling but marked out clearly what must have been an impressive chamber; in the background, the sound of the sea, forever churning, forever hollowing at the rock. The modern world seemed a long way away on this island fortress, dark skies above, the wind whipping at Flora's skirt and the sea raging below.

'It is fabulous!' she exclaimed, forgetting her painful knee and twirling round and round, hair flying in the wind and her arms stretched to the heavens. 'Utterly and completely fabulous.'

Jack was laughing. 'Come on, let's go and see more fabulousness. There's a viewing platform at the northern end and we can see' – he took the leaflet from her – 'the Iron Gate. It guards a platform of slate, apparently the only landing-spot on the island.'

'Then can we go down to the beach?' Flora asked eagerly. 'And before you say anything, yes, I can climb up again.'

Jack shrugged his shoulders. 'You'd better hope so. I'm not carrying you – not after all those pasties you've been putting away recently.'

After the Iron Gate, they followed the cliff path as it wound its way down to the shore.

'Merlin's Cave!' she said, as soon as they reached the beach, and started towards a spectacular-looking hollow that had been carved out by centuries of ocean. 'It seems to go back a long way. I reckon the cave must pass right under the island. If it was low tide, we could have explored.'

'Just think how romantic that would have been, with the sea thundering above, below, all around us,' he teased.

But Flora was too excited to tease back. 'Do you remember that scene in Tennyson where Merlin rescues the baby Arthur from the crashing waves and carries him ashore to safety?'

'I do, but I also remember we haven't had lunch. And, apart from you, I haven't spoken to a single soul, which was one of the reasons we came. Let's make a start back.'

Climbing up the long stretch of wooden stairs tested all of Flora's endurance, but she followed in Jack's footsteps without a murmur.

'Just what we need,' he said, as they walked through the final archway, passing the first group of visitors they'd seen that day. Outside the entrance to the site, a stall had been set up, selling sandwiches and hot drinks.

It seemed to be doing little trade, which was hardly surprising. The wind had twisted its striped awning into several tight knots, and the stall itself rocked from side to side whenever a particularly sharp gust caught it full on.

'A crab sandwich?'

'Perfect.' She made herself smile. 'And tea please?'

They found a sheltered seat cut into the cliff, overlooking rocks and sea, and settled to enjoy an outdoor lunch.

'You been 'ere before?' The man on an adjoining bench suddenly asked.

They shook their heads.

'Champion place,' he said, his voice carrying loudly in the wind.

'It's one of the most beautiful places I've ever seen,' Flora agreed.

Jack bent his head forward so that he could see the man properly. 'I notice you're wearing overalls. Do you work here?'

'Tha's right. General handyman.'

Jack smiled. 'You must be kept busy then with so much of the site crumbling.'

'I don' do nothin' with the castle,' he assured them. 'Tha's for the archaeologists. No, I do the staff quarters.'

'There are staff quarters?' Flora was surprised.

'It's a bit grand to call 'em that. A shed really, toilets, kitchen, that kinda thing. Folks need somewhere to shelter when it gets rough up 'ere – the cashiers and the guides.'

'It must get very rough,' she said. 'It's pretty wild today.'

'You should see it in January. Them archaeologists 'ad to stop work this winter, it were so bad.'

'Are they still digging then? I would have thought the excavations were complete.'

'They don' do the castle. It's the old wartime stuff now.'

Flora sat up a little straighter. 'There's stuff from the war here?'

'Lots all round Cornwall. Old airfields, radar stations, signals centres. They 'ave to be careful when they're diggin', mind. They want to uncover it all – brings in the visitors, you know – but they daren't get too close to the castle.'

'There was a signals centre at Tintagel?'

'Jus' outside. A small one. You on holiday 'ere?'

She nodded.

'Where are you stayin'?'

'In a village on the Helford river.'

'Soft country, that is. There were a big'un down that way – Lizard Point, I think my dad told me.'

'You're talking about a signals centre?' She wanted to be clear.

'Real hush-hush stuff. Down Mullion way, if I remember right.'

By the time they had walked back to the car, Flora's face was pinched and white.

'You've walked too much,' Jack said. 'I told you—'

'—so,' she finished for him. 'I have, but I wouldn't have missed it for the world. And Mullion. We've got to go there. If that chap had heard of it, all these miles away, it must have been really important.'

'We'll go but not today. It's home and a sofa for you.'

'Yes, sir.' She gave a mock salute, but in her heart she wasn't sorry. Crab sandwiches and a cup of tea had been welcome, but even more welcome was the sofa waiting for her at Primrose Cottage.

They were back before the clock struck four. Jack went

straight to his bedroom and in minutes she heard him typing. Tintagel must have worked, she thought dreamily, her eyes closing against her will. To her shame, she fell fast asleep and didn't rouse until the front door opened and Jessie arrived to deliver their evening meal.

10

A day later and Jack seemed to have forgotten breakfast, the typewriter keys clacking furiously from the upstairs room as Flora poured her cornflakes.

'Mr Carrington's some busy,' Jessie said, when she'd taken off her coat and outdoor shoes, and tied an apron around her waist. Neither Jack nor Flora had persuaded her to call him by his first name. *Oh, I couldn't do that,* she'd said. *He's an important man. I saw 'is picture in a shop last time I were Falmouth way.*

'I won't disturb 'im,' she went on. 'I'll be workin' in the kitchen today.' From her basket, she unpacked a set of newly washed curtains.

'Can I help with those?'

'I were jus' gettin' ready to hang 'em, but yes, my luv, you can – afore you go into the garden. I saw what you did out there t'other day. I reckon you're fair burstin' to 'ave another go at that terrace. And it's a good day fer it.'

'Not exactly bursting.' Flora laughed. 'But I'm keen to finish clearing the paving.' Walking over to the kitchen table, she unfolded two lengths of bright blue gingham. 'Are these for the kitchen? They'll certainly cheer the room.' She held up one of the curtains for a better view.

'Tha's what I thought. Now bring that chair over and we'll 'ave a try.'

Several lost curtain rings and a wobble or two on the kitchen chair later, Jessie was satisfied and ready to plunge into a manic spring cleaning of the kitchen, making it clear to Flora that she needed space. It was with a clear conscience then that Flora slipped out of the back door and into the relative peace of the garden.

The tools she had discovered in the shed were old and rusted but they did the job she needed. With their help she had cleared half the terrace already. It was still only mid-May but the warmer weather would arrive very soon, and she was looking forward to spending her afternoons in this sheltered spot with a favourite book. A different impulse was at work, too, one not so easily explained. The garden held a magic for her that defied reason, and which, despite the hard labour, was pushing her on. It was back-breaking work – digging and scraping moss and lichen from the granite slabs – but she kept doggedly at it, only stopping to drink the cup of tea Jessie brought her.

'I'm off soon,' the housekeeper said, 'but I've left a couple of pork pies for your lunches.'

Flora thanked her effusively and spent the next hour or so imagining those pies, eventually persuading herself into an early lunch. She had finished washing her hands at the kitchen sink when stomping feet overhead told her that Jack had had the same idea.

The kitchen door was flung back and his rangy form filled the doorway. 'It isn't working,' he announced, screwing up his face so crossly that it almost disappeared beneath his mop of dark hair. The pair of black-rimmed glasses he clutched looked in danger of being splintered at any moment. 'I can't do it.'

Flora couldn't prevent a smile. 'Are you having an artistic moment?' she asked, tongue-in-cheek. It was not the most sensitive comment, but instead of an even more furious retort, Jack's shoulders relaxed and he burst out laughing.

'This bloody book! What can I say?'

'Say nothing but come and eat the pork pie Jessie has made you.'

'Pork pie? Really?' He sounded a good deal more cheerful.

'And when we've eaten,' she said cautiously, 'we could take the afternoon off and go adventuring.'

Jack groaned.

'Don't!' She held up her hand. 'Your book isn't working and, before you say a word, my knee is mended and well up to the rigours of walking on the Lizard.'

'We're going to Mullion, I presume?'

She beamed at him. 'I do hope so.'

He gave a long sigh before plunging his knife into the pie. 'I guess it's probably more promising territory for a crime novel. From the photographs I've seen, it's as tough a landscape as Tintagel, but one that's escaped the romanticising.'

'Is it far, do you know?'

'Not according to the map – I looked it up last night, after that chap had mentioned it. Mullion is less than ten miles from here, which is just as well since half the day has gone already.'

'We'll head for the village,' he said as they drove out of Treleggan. 'Mullion Cove ought to be signposted from there.'

'This is exciting, Jack!'

'I suspect it won't be as exciting as you think. The tunnel was built at least twelve years ago. It could have caved in by now, so be prepared for disappointment.'

Flora grimaced but, refusing to be daunted, she settled to watch the world go by.

As they drew nearer, the landscape grew flatter, the familiar high hedgerows disappeared and their place was taken by a heathland, carpeted in heather and strewn with boulders of serpentine rock that thrust from the ground. The day was mild and the sun had not completely disappeared behind banking clouds, but Flora felt her skin tingle with unease.

'This place must be so bleak in the winter.'

'How about springtime?'

'Today, it's beautiful, I grant you. A different beautiful than Helford. Just look at those wild orchids and violets. They're everywhere.'

'Here's the village coming up.' Jack pointed ahead at the signpost, then swung the car off the main thoroughfare into a much narrower road.

'I hope it's not far to the village.' Flora flinched as tree branches on either side of them scraped at the car. 'I hate to think what would happen if we met something coming the other way.'

'I'd have to find reverse gear, so let's hope not.'

Within half a mile, though, they were trundling to a halt outside a medieval church.

'St Mellanus,' Jack read, switching off the ignition.

'Mullion is larger than I expected.' As they'd driven into the village, Flora had spied several shops, in addition to a pub and a café. 'There's even an art gallery – there, on the corner.'

'This place must have plenty of visitors during the summer and all of them eager to buy a souvenir. Let's see.' He consulted his map. 'It seems we can drive to the cove from here – or there's a footpath down to the sea. What do you want to do?'

'We'll take the footpath,' she said decidedly. 'I don't want to drive down a lane that's even narrower than the last.'

The pathway was easy to find and it proved a pleasant walk

in the still of the May afternoon. There was a tang of salt in the air and, as they drew near to the sea, it fused with the smell of tar and rope.

'What a pretty harbour,' Flora exclaimed, as they rounded the last bend.

'A working harbour, too. The pilchards have long gone, I know, but there must be fishermen still making a living here.'

It was clear from the tackle left on the quayside that fishing boats would be returning with their catch that evening. It would be open sea, she thought, between Mullion and St Michael's Mount, but the stout walls of the harbour must offer boats good protection when the winter gales raged.

Jack's eyes were on the rocky cliffs that enclosed either side of the cove.

'It looks a dangerous coastline,' she said, following his gaze.

'Dad told me the Lizard was particularly hazardous for shipping. Several vessels went aground while he was serving here. I believe there used to be a lifeboat station, but that seems to have disappeared.'

Flora pointed upwards. 'The tunnel must be built into the cliff somewhere, but it could be either side of the cove. Miss Hodges wasn't specific.'

'Since there's only a footpath on one side, we best take that,' Jack said practically. 'Unless you fancy swimming.'

'And then scaling the rocks from the sea? No thanks.'

The footpath snaked its way from inlet to inlet. They walked in single file, their eyes fixed half on a sea that today stretched limpidly into the distance and half on the cliff side, scanning for the possibility of a tunnel. After a mile, when they'd encountered nothing more interesting than nesting seabirds, they turned as one, off the coastal path and onto a track that wound its way upwards to the heathland above.

'Are we looking for the start of the tunnel now?' Flora asked over her shoulder.

'It seems the best bet. There could have been a rock fall on the cliff that's blocked the tunnel exit, but the entrance should still be around. We might even stumble on what's left of the buildings themselves.'

It began to look, though, as if they were destined to find neither. As they moved further inland, more and more trees appeared and whole swathes of bushes.

'This is extraordinary,' Jack said, stopping to brush the flop of hair from his forehead. 'It's as though a plantation has been established in the middle of heathland. And what's this bush, tree, whatever, called? It's everywhere.' He pointed to the dark glossy leaves of a shrub at least twice his height.

'Rhododendron. They spread like wildfire.'

'So if there is anything to find, they could have covered it.'

Flora came to a halt beside him. 'Unless we're looking in the wrong place entirely. It's a vast area, isn't it, even just the land immediately around Mullion and the cove? I don't know how big this bunker was that Miss Hodges spoke of, but we could search for hours and not find a trace.'

'You're right and it was stupid of me to suggest coming.'

'You're as desperate as me to find a secret tunnel!' she teased. 'Like the Famous Five.'

'In this case, the Famous Two.' He gazed down at her and Flora felt her face flush and her body become uncomfortably warm.

'Let's make our way back to the car,' he said gruffly, turning and leading the way down to the coastal path.

They had driven halfway along the lane from Mullion village on their way back to the main road, when Jack suddenly lost control of the steering wheel. It was over in an instant and Flora had only a dim sense that something had been moving to one side of them. The churn of the engine was in her ears and, as if in slow motion, the car was veering off the narrow road and ploughing into the hedge. Later, she remembered thinking it was a good thing they hadn't travelled leftwards or they would have met the iron bars of a field gate.

For a moment, she sat utterly still, dazed by the impact and the sudden silence of an engine that had died. Turning to Jack, she was about to ask him what exactly had happened when she realised he was lying slumped forward, his head rammed against the wheel.

'Jack,' she called in a panic, grasping his arm. 'Jack, answer me.'

Trapped in her seat, it was impossible to help, but when she tried to climb out of the car, her door had become jammed against a hawthorn bush and she could barely open it.

Inching herself around so that she was half facing Jack, she tried to take hold of both his shoulders and pull him back against the seat. It took several attempts before she managed to shift him, only to see a dark wheal across his forehead, where the skin had been slashed by the hard surface of the steering wheel. Blood was dripping from the wound and, distraught, she fished a handkerchief from her pocket and mopped at his forehead.

'Jack!' She took hold of his arm again and shook him frantically.

There was no response and for one panicked moment she thought he might be dead but, calming herself, she reached for his hands and, though they were cold, his wrist had a pulse. Not dead, thank God.

A tap at the car window made her start and, twisting around, she saw a man's face. He was mouthing something to her. With difficulty, she wound the window down a few inches.

'Is 'e OK?' the man asked, nodding towards Jack.

'I don't know,' she said, trying not to sound desperate. 'He's not responding.'

'Best get you out of 'ere then,' the man said, unruffled. 'I'll go fetch the tractor.'

'Don't go,' she started to say, but he'd already disappeared. She didn't want to be left alone, not with Jack in such a frightening state. But that was stupid – a tractor was needed to lift them out of the hedge and, once free, she could get help for him.

The man did not return for fifteen minutes, minutes in which Flora's nerves were strained to breaking. Jack's face was white, his hands ice-cold and only the slow pulse beating in his wrist kept up her spirits. For the whole time, her clutch on his hand never weakened, as though by constantly holding him, she could keep him alive.

At last, the sound of a heavy vehicle approaching from the village and the man was back, with a companion this time, and a rope. Without speaking, the men attached the rope to the rear bumper and while one jumped back into the tractor, the other steadied the car.

With the first tug, the Austin heaved to one side so dangerously that Flora thought they would overturn completely. But the tug had at least brought Jack back to consciousness and he stared at her, wide-eyed.

'We're in the hedge,' was all she could think of saying.

With an effort he pulled himself upright, his hand clasping his head.

'You smashed into the steering wheel, and you've bled a bit. Here, have my handkerchief. I've mopped up the worst. Most of the blood is on the wheel.'

'Good to know,' he said, his tone ironic but his voice faint. He patted at the wound without any visible effect.

'How does your head feel?' she asked tentatively.

'As though World War Three is raging inside.'

'Your forehead looks quite badly cut, but I don't think you'll need stitches.'

He craned his neck to view himself in the driving mirror.

'It's spoilt my beauty, for sure.' He shifted further round in his seat and looked at her for the first time. 'How are you, Flora? Are you hurt?'

'No, I was lucky. Just aching. I guess tomorrow there'll be bruises galore.'

'Who are these chaps?' He gestured to the men who were about to make a second attempt at pulling the car free.

'I've no idea. From the village, I'm assuming. I'm grateful the man saw what happened.' There was a pause before she said, 'What did happen, though?'

'Search me. We were tootling along nicely and then suddenly, the wheel spun out of my hands and the world went black. It must have been a puncture. A pretty catastrophic one at that.'

On the tractor's third attempt, the car was finally heaved clear, sitting stranded in the lane like a duck that had lost its way to the pond.

Flora was able to force her door open at last while Jack staggered out of the car from the other side.

'Thank you so much,' she said to the men.

'Yes, thank you,' Jack echoed.

'We'll tow you back to Mullion. You won' be goin' far in this fer a while.'

'It's a puncture?'

One of the men squatted down. 'More'n a puncture. Both front tyres,' he said.

'Both?' Jack sounded mystified.

'Let's 'ave a look, Logan.'

The second man joined his companion. 'Two tyres,' he confirmed. 'But look 'ere.' He was pointing at the base of one of the tyres. 'Not just a puncture. Them tyres are shredded.'

Jack walked round to the front of the car and bent down, still holding his head with one hand. 'You're right, but how could it have happened?'

'Has to be somethin' in the road.'

'A spike belt, mebbe,' Logan suggested.

'I reckon you're right,' his friend said. 'Shreds tyres perfect.'

Logan got down on his knees and examined the ground beneath the car. He shook his head, then looked along the road for a few yards and then into the hedge. 'Nuthin' 'ere,' he said.

Jack had been trying to follow the conversation, his head clearly giving him pain. 'A spike belt?'

'It's like Logan says. The kinda thing the army uses to stop tanks. But you ain't got no tank there.' Both men gave a loud shout of laughter, before Logan said in a serious voice, 'It could have been the tractor that copped it. That'd bugger things up fer us.'

'Could have been any vehicle. Downright dang'rous.'

No, it couldn't, Flora thought, certain now that she'd seen a movement in the instant they'd crashed, not with true consciousness but with the fine sense that lies at its edge. It had been deliberate and they had been the target.

'Some tuss from Porthleven way, no doubt.'

Logan frowned at his companion. 'Ladies present, remember. Mebbe it were a kid,' he went on placidly. 'You know what boys are. Don' think it through, do they? Anyways, we best tow the car to the village, but it'd be easier if you both walk, miss,' he said to Flora. 'As long as the gent can manage it.'

'The gent can,' Jack said grimly.

They walked the relatively short distance back to Mullion in almost total silence. The tractor, forced to reverse all the way back down the lane, followed slowly behind, relinquishing its load when it reached the church.

Logan jumped down from the cab. 'Garage is Porthleven way. I'll phone 'em in the mornin' to come and collect.' He gestured to the car. 'Give us your phone number and I'll pass it on. They can ring you when the car's ready.'

'That's very kind of you,' Jack said, while Flora, though

relieved the car would be repaired, was wondering how on earth they were to get home that evening.

'Where you stayin'?' Logan asked.

'Treleggan,' Jack told him. 'I don't suppose there's a bus going anywhere near.'

A grin stretching from ear to ear filled the man's face. 'Only if you don' mind waitin' till Wednesday.'

That was in two days' time. 'Arsk at the Ship,' their new friend advised. 'Landlord's got a car and 'is boy drives. He'll take you back if you see him right.'

'We'll see him right,' Jack said gratefully.

They were home within the hour, battered and bruised, but delighted to be at Primrose Cottage again.

'I think we should get you to a doctor,' Flora said, as they let themselves into the tiny hall. 'You may not need stitches but someone should look at your forehead.'

'It's my turn to tell you not to fuss. I've got a bad headache, that's all.'

'If it gets worse...'

'Then I'll get help. Right now, all I want is a very large mug of tea and some food. Lunch seems an age ago.'

Flora walked into the kitchen. There was no sign of their housekeeper or their supper. 'I'm afraid Jessie must have been and left again when we weren't here.'

The thought of trying to concoct a meal from their limited resources was not a happy one. Wearily, she opened the larder door to scan the provisions that remained. Her eyes brightened. There, on the marble shelf, were two full plates of salad. Ham salad, by the look of it. Jack was in luck! With a few rounds of bread and butter, it would be perfect.

Taking the plates from the larder, she literally waltzed them to the kitchen table, humming a dance tune as she went.

'See what we have,' she said, as Jack walked into the room.

His face was a mirror image of hers. 'Ham salad,' he breathed. 'A life saver.'

11

Jessie had already cleaned the sitting room and was sitting having a cup of tea when Flora stumbled into the kitchen the next morning.

'My word, you don' look so good.'

'I don't feel it,' Flora confessed.

'Let's look at you.' The housekeeper stood up, taking hold of Flora's arms. 'What's 'appened? Bruises every which way.'

'We had an accident,' she said briefly. 'A puncture, and the car ended up in a hedge.'

'My goodness. And Mr Carrington?'

'Jack is OK. At least, I think he is. He hit his head on the steering wheel.'

'Jack is fine,' he said, coming into the kitchen. He was still white-faced, Flora noticed, and the gash across his forehead seemed darker.

'That looks bad, Mr Carrington. You should see a doctor.' Jessie shook her head at him. 'So where's the car now? It weren't out front.'

'A very obliging man is organising a tow to the garage,' Flora said, keeping the details of the accident sketchy. 'We can collect it in a few days' time.'

'Tha's a nuisance an' all. Mind, we do 'ave buses to Helston and Falmouth, if you fancy it. Or you can always walk!' She seemed to like the idea and gave a deep chuckle. 'I'll be off now to the village fer some shoppin'. Meat and two veg for you tonight, I think. A couple of nice pork chops if I can wangle them out of that rascal, Pascoe. You'd think we were still on rationin' the way he guards his shop.'

'I can smell those chops already,' Jack said, pulling out a chair and sitting down. 'But a cup of tea would do nicely for now.'

Flora walked over to the sink to fill the kettle. 'I don't know how you ever survived on ham sandwiches. You haven't stopped eating since we got here.'

'Must be the Cornish air. Thank you in advance, Jessie.'

Flora lit the gas and turned to her. 'You shouldn't have to come to the cottage twice a day. Jack and I will walk down to the village and collect our supper in future. It won't be any trouble.'

'And it won' be trouble fer me neither. I'm always leavin' things behind and 'avin' to pop back. It were my best slippers t'other day.'

'Talking about leaving things behind, I picked up a letter the other day and forgot to mention it,' Flora said, making for the door. 'It was in the sitting room – under a pile of library books that we took back to Helston. I'll fetch it for you. I thought it might be important.'

On Flora's return, Jessie scanned the sheet of paper, screwing up her eyes and holding it at a distance. 'Don' have my glasses with me,' she said. 'Did you read it?'

'I did take a glance,' Flora confessed, 'in case it was some-thing urgent. It mentions an appointment at a solicitor's and I've been wondering if the man who signed the letter knows what's happened to Roger.'

'Bound to,' the housekeeper said with certainty.

'Then we can safely ignore it.' There was a pause before Flora's curiosity got the better of her. 'Is the letter to do with Roger making changes in his life, do you think?'

'I dunno. Could be. He were gettin' there, poor man, gettin' rid of the rubbish. First his brother, then 'is wife, that Beatrice. Maybe that's what it's about.' She laid the letter on the kitchen table.

Flora's eyes opened wide. 'He was walking out on his wife?'

Jessie snorted. 'She were the one doin' the walkin'. Two year ago. Left him alone in that big house. Shockin'.'

'Where is she now?'

'I dunno and I don' want to. Plenty of rumours, though, and none of 'em good. It's enough we've got that no-good brother back in Treleggan kickin' up a row. Drunk and disorderly, that's what Will Hoskins said.'

'The Hoskins who was here when the detectives arrived?'

'Tha's 'im. He's the police round 'ere. Gifford spent the night in one of Will's cells, by all accounts.'

'Has he said how the inspector is getting on with his investigation?' Jack put in. To Flora's mind, he'd made the question sound deliberately casual.

'Nothin' you'd ever believe. I 'ad it from young Hoskins that Mr Roger's watch were missin' off the body, so what do the police say? It were a random thief who must've killed 'im. They've found no clues, don' know where to go next, so they say it's a mugger. A mugger in Treleggan – I arsk you! It's just an excuse to give up, you'll see.'

'They can't give up,' he protested. 'It's a major crime. It's murder.'

'I'm bettin' you that's jus' what they'll do. From Truro, in't they?'

'And?'

'Too busy to bother with a small village like Treleggan.'

'Truro isn't exactly huge,' Jack said mildly.

''Tis round 'ere. It's the big city! Make sure you 'ave your breakfast, Mr Carrington. You look like you could eat a dozen pork chops right now.'

'It's my scrawny physique that's to blame. I always look half-starved even when I'm full to brimming.'

'I'd say you've a nice figure fer a man. Wouldn't you?' she appealed to Flora.

An annoying flush crept its way upwards from Flora's toes. She wished she could stop herself doing that. To cover her embarrassment, she asked, 'Why was Lionel drunk and disorderly?'

Jessie shrugged her shoulders and began to pack up her wicker basket. 'The man can't keep out of trouble. And can't 'old 'is drink. Throwin' his money around, he were – and 'ow did he get that? – then started a fight in the Anchor. Normally Kenver – he runs the pub – just shrugs it off. Throws the troublemaker out and tha's an end to it. But apparently' – her voice lowered – 'this time it were more serious and Kenver called the police. Left it to Will to throw Gifford out.'

'Why was it more serious?'

'Lionel fell out with Farmer Truscott – accused 'im of spillin' 'is beer. Started 'ollerin' fit to bust and then punchin' 'im. When Truscott punched 'im back – tha's a man you don' tangle with – Gifford pulled out a knife and started wavin' it around.' Jessie was careful to emphasise the word 'knife'. She looked meaningfully from one to the other.

'You think—'

'I don' think nothin' but a man with a knife...'

'Mercy Dearlove has knives, too,' Jack reminded her, 'and at one time you thought she was responsible for Roger's death.'

Jessie sniffed and, picking up her basket, marched to the door. 'They were probably in it together.'

'How are the bruises?' Jack asked, crunching through his last slice of toast.

'Painful,' she admitted. 'And annoying. I'm suffering. You're suffering. But for what? The tunnel, the signals centre, are still secret.'

Jack brushed stray crumbs from the table onto his plate. 'I think I'll go to Helston again,' he said thoughtfully. 'Visit the museum. They had a whole room devoted to Cornwall during the last war. I can poke around for anything they have on the Mullion site but, at the same time, be looking for material for the book.'

Her eyebrows rose slightly. 'You're definitely plumping for a wartime murder?'

For a moment, Jack looked defeated. 'To be honest, I've no idea what I'm plumping for – my last effort turned out a complete waste of time. I've been debating whether or not to go back to my original chapters, the ones I wrote in Abbeymead, or maybe trash the lot and simply start over.'

'You might strike lucky today – an abandoned signals centre would make a brilliant setting. Mullion could be the very inspiration you're looking for!'

'Tintagel inspired me, but it didn't get me far,' he said gloomily. 'A hidden signals centre is intriguing, though, and, if I don't get anywhere at the museum today, I might brave a call to my father. It's possible he could pinpoint its location for us.'

Flora didn't respond immediately. In her mind, she'd travelled back to Mullion and yesterday's abortive search, skittering over the events of that afternoon, to settle eventually on the accident and the moment she'd thought Jack might have died. A cold hollow in her stomach was growing.

'You've not thought that maybe we should stop looking?' she ventured, despite fury that someone had set out to harm them. There was still a powerful need in her to track down whoever was behind the intimidation, but yesterday Jack had been badly hurt and it could have been even worse. It still might.

He frowned. 'Why stop?'

'Because of the stuff that's happened. It was after we visited Helston library and the museum that I fell down the flight of steps and, yesterday, it was after we'd gone looking for a wartime bunker that we ended up in a hedge. It's plain those punctures were deliberate.'

'Yes,' he said slowly, 'I agree the assault on the car has to have been deliberate, but the library? The museum? How would going to either place provoke an attack?'

'It's a rare visitor to the town who'd make their first port of call the library and their second, the museum,' she argued. 'It could suggest we were looking for something and, if someone was following us, they'd be suspicious. Don't forget the anonymous letter – you've already been warned off coming to Cornwall – so what if both the "accidents" were designed to make us go away, to stop us looking any further?'

'The chaps from the village, Logan and his mate, reckoned the slashed tyres were down to bored schoolboys. Or the local vandal,' he reminded her. 'And they could be right. We need to guard against getting paranoid.'

'But if someone has been spying on us,' she insisted, 'seen us go into the museum and the library, followed us to Mullion and watched while we searched the cliffs and took the track inland, they would almost certainly guess what it was we were looking for. And if they had a secret to protect...'

Lionel would have a car, she thought silently. Roger's car. He could easily have followed them, and it was possible he'd been in Helston the day she'd fallen down that steep stairway.

'I'd prefer to think it was someone in Mullion bent on

mischief, who didn't think it through properly,' Jack said. 'They couldn't have. They might well have killed us.'

'Maybe that's what they wanted.'

'You can't be serious.' He gathered up the breakfast plates and took them to the sink. 'A secret from the past, so important someone would kill for it!'

'I am serious,' she said stoutly. 'The murder may be about Roger's will but there's also something going on that involves his research, something to do with the last war.'

'Let's stick with the will. The war is a crazy idea. It's over, finished.'

'But not for some perhaps.'

'OK, answer me this. If someone was watching us yesterday, targeting us, how did they cause the accident? They would have had to position that spike belt in the lane at just the right moment or they'd risk hurting some other unfortunate, rather than us.'

'I believe that's exactly what they did,' Flora said calmly. 'There was a gate opposite to where we ploughed into the hedge. I remember sending up thanks that we'd veered in the other direction. The gate was a means of escape. Just for an instant, before we hit, I sensed a movement, someone moving quickly. When Logan pointed out that both tyres had been shredded by spikes, I knew definitely that I'd seen someone. They must have raced up from the village, then lain in wait. When they heard our engine, they dashed out and threw down the spike belt, then whisked themselves through the gate and hid behind the hedge. Afterwards, you were knocked unconscious and I was too dazed to go looking – even if I hadn't been trapped in the car.'

Jack thrust his hands in his pocket and studied his feet for what seemed a long time. He gave a small sigh before he spoke. 'It's still a mad idea, Flora. An action like that smacks of desperation and I can't think of a single person we've met in Cornwall who would be crazy enough to do such a thing.'

Two names came to Flora's mind – Mercy Dearlove and Lionel Gifford.

12

By silent consent, they spent the rest of the day quietly, Jack for the most part in his room reading through the chapters he'd written earlier, hoping to find a way forward, and Flora bent once more on clearing the terrace. Pulling a clutch of disorderly waves into a ponytail – a new style she'd seen in *Woman's Own*, a magazine her friend Kate had passed on – and wearing her oldest cotton skirt, she set to work on some of the hardest to remove lichen.

By afternoon, she was in need of a break and, when Jack suggested a walk, they strolled together to the village and then on towards the river. Yesterday's storm clouds had disappeared and the sun making a tentative appearance, sufficiently strong for Flora to bare her arms and enjoy its warmth as they walked along the riverbank. Wild flowers had begun to show their heads in the long grass, a pair of blackbirds sang from the trees, and alongside them the water gurgled, clear and fresh, over shiny, white stones.

'Treleggan is really beautiful,' she said. 'It's a pity Arthur expects you to chase across the county.'

'I'm not doing much chasing today, am I?'

'No, but you will. I saw the map you pinned on your wall. Land's End looks like your next trip.'

'I did put it on my list,' he admitted, 'but now I'm not sure.'

'Why not?'

'Every day I'm away from my desk eats into writing time. I've already planned to go back to Helston again, so a visit to Land's End? I'm not certain what I'd gain.'

'You won't know until you get there,' Flora pointed out. She was surprised at how disconsolate he sounded.

'I'll keep it in mind,' he promised, 'but it's another wild and windswept place and you might not want to come. After yesterday, you've probably had enough of rugged landscapes.'

'Of course I'll come. Wild and windswept is exciting and, if we're very good, the sun might even shine!'

That night, Flora went to bed happier than she'd been since their arrival in Treleggan, although she wasn't sure exactly why. Jack, it appeared, was still troubled by his book and for both of them the future appeared uneasy, but somehow the gentle tenor of the day had swept her along, encircling her with a comforting warmth and making her feel more at home – she hadn't realised until now how unsettled she'd been since leaving Abbeymead. How much she missed her own village.

When she woke the next morning, though, all comfort had vanished. Her body, still tender from the bruising she suffered, now felt as though it had been put through a mincing machine, her limbs stiff and unresponsive. It was as if she'd slept all night in a cage, curling herself tight in order to escape some terrible retribution. But what? It had to be Mullion continuing to play on her mind. The sickening moment when she'd looked across at Jack and seen him slumped and bleeding across the steering wheel. The moment she'd wondered if this was to be their end.

She was still concerned for him. He'd made a pretence of

being fine yesterday – working in his room, walking with her by the river – but the bottle of aspirins she'd left in the bathroom had been opened and a tell-tale trail of white powder indicated that tablets had been taken. He must still be in pain and head injuries couldn't be lightly dismissed. But he was a tough man, she told herself, a soldier who had been through all six years of the last war and survived despite a sniper's bullet in his arm. He would surely know to seek help if he needed it.

Reassured by the thought, she swung her legs out of bed and shuffled around in search of slippers, then somehow pushed herself to her feet, trying to stand tall. A loud groan came from somewhere deep inside her. Yesterday's gardening would be adding to her pain, she thought wryly.

Padding down the stairs, she made for the kitchen and a restorative cup of tea, only to be brought up sharply. The small side window in the hall had been smashed, shards of glass littering the wooden floorboards. Puzzled, Flora stood looking at the shattered window. Had there been a noise in the night? A very slight noise, she recalled, enough to wake her temporarily but not disturb her unduly. She'd felt chilled at the time, she remembered, and had responded by curling herself even tighter, too tired to investigate.

But why did they have a smashed window? A burglary? It seemed decidedly odd – there was so little to steal in the cottage. Best, though, to check that the wireless, the Lladró figurine and the ormolu clock, the only items likely to be sellable, were still where they should be. But when Flora walked into the sitting room, she was brought to a swift halt. Open-mouthed, she stood and stared. Every book had been hurled from the shelves, every small trinket thrown to the floor, the drawers of the bureau emptied and even the armchairs turned upside down.

She was still rooted to the floor, staring at the devastation, when a footstep sounded behind her. Jack appeared in the doorway, fully dressed and wide awake, his frightening pallor of yesterday thankfully disappeared.

'Did something upset you this morning?' he asked, looking over her shoulder at the mess beyond. There was a laugh in his voice.

'If I were that upset, it wouldn't be books I'd hurl around.'

'Someone did, though.' His gaze swept the room. 'It seems we had a night visitor – I saw the broken glass in the hall. What's missing?'

'Nothing as far as I can make out. Theft probably wasn't the object, at least not theft in the ordinary sense. It looks as though someone was searching for something, and doing it very roughly.'

'The someone being Lionel Gifford?'

'It has to be. Searching for those wretched papers, I imagine. He couldn't have believed us when we denied any knowledge of them and decided to collect them for himself by forcing his way in.'

Jack walked back into the hall and stood looking at the smashed window. 'Did he, though? Lionel isn't large, but I reckon that window is too small for any full-grown man to climb through. I wonder...'

He reached out for the handle and the front door opened. 'I locked this last night before we went to bed, and now it's unlocked. Someone has used a key and that probably means Lionel. He's the most likely to have one – Roger is bound to have had spare keys at River House. I should have thought of that and changed the locks.'

'We're only tenants,' Flora pointed out. 'We'd not be allowed to. But why break the window when he had a key? It could have woken one or both of us and he'd be caught red-handed.'

Jack's gaze was fixed on the bentwood coat stand and,

leaning over, he fished out a square of cloth tucked behind one of its curling arms.

He waved it at Flora. 'This is why we didn't hear anything. Lionel used it to muffle the sound of breaking glass.'

'I did hear something,' she confessed. 'A slight noise, but I was so tired I turned over and went back to sleep.'

'Just as well. You really wouldn't want to meet Lionel Gifford in a nightdress.'

'But why risk being caught, Jack? It seems stupid.' She shivered in the thin wrapper she'd donned. It was chilly in the hall at this time of the morning and she hadn't managed that warming cup of tea.

'Lionel probably *is* stupid, though he must have thought he was being extremely clever. I reckon he set up the smashed window as a decoy, to suggest we'd had a genuine burglar.'

'That seems pretty inept, even for Lionel.'

'He was probably drunk again. Or only partly sober. We didn't report the accident but should we call the police to report the break-in, do you think?'

Flora considered the question for a moment. 'We could,' she said, pursing her lips. 'But if nothing is missing, how interested will they be? Particularly as they haven't begun to solve the murder they have on their hands.'

She shivered again, this time badly enough for Jack to notice. 'You look perished. I'll put the kettle on.'

While he made tea, Flora tried to get her mind in order. Lionel was surely responsible for this break-in, but she'd become increasingly certain that he was responsible, too, for disabling the Austin and nearly killing them. Jack would disagree. He'd say she was allowing her fears to run away with her but, despite that, she needed to speak them aloud.

'I think it was Lionel who followed us at Mullion,' she began. 'He wants those papers badly. Either because Roger's will is among them or because they contain something that can hurt him and he needs to destroy whatever it is. He's searched River House unsuccessfully, and we've told him there's nothing here, but it's clear from this break-in he still thinks we have the papers. Maybe he suspects we've seen whatever he wants to hide and that's made him desperate.'

Jack turned from filling the teapot. 'He wants Roger's papers badly, I agree. He's broken in to find them, also agreed. But how would tracking us to Mullion help him in any way?'

Flora gave a little bounce. She could see exactly how it would help. 'Engineering an "accident" could have put us into hospital,' she said, 'or at the very least encourage us to leave Cornwall. He wants us out of the cottage so he can search the place thoroughly.'

Jack frowned. 'If he has a key, he could have searched any time we were out.'

'He needs space to do it properly and, if he broke in while we were out, he couldn't be sure when we'd be coming back. Then Jessie is here some of the day, too. This mess' – she waved a hand at the wrecked sitting room – 'is because his search was frantic. A last-ditch attempt, perhaps. If he'd managed to get us out of the cottage, he'd have had free rein.'

'You're saying that he was prepared to risk killing us. Do you really think he was desperate enough, given that he must already be in the frame for Roger's murder? Even Inspector Mallory will have him on his list of suspects.'

Flora took the cup Jack handed her. 'I think he is. If not kill us, then certainly put us out of action for a long time. And he was in the army remember – driving tanks, Jessie said.'

He gave a low whistle. 'I'd forgotten that.'

'And if he's mixed up with people from the London under-world, he'd know how to get hold of a spike belt.'

There was a pause, Jack evidently thinking hard. 'But where's the connection between the papers and Roger's murder? Is there even a connection? I can just about see that if

Lionel believes the papers contain the will, it could be important for him to get hold of them after his brother's death. Maybe to check where he stands and possibly try to alter the document or even destroy it. But that's a big "if", since the will could be anywhere – not necessarily in Primrose Cottage or the house in the high street. An even bigger "if", though, is the notion that these papers have anything to do with Roger's *actual* death.'

'I don't agree. They could provide a motive for killing,' Flora argued, 'and if they do, it explains why Lionel wants them so badly. We've plumped for Roger's changing his will as the reason for his murder, but it might not be. We don't even know if Lionel was a beneficiary. We're just assuming it from what Jessie told us. And there could well be others named in the will – Roger's wife, for instance.'

'Who could turn out to be a suspect, too.'

'I suppose, but the papers... whatever's in Roger's research could pose a threat – a different threat – to Lionel's inheritance, and that may be the connection.'

Jack slowly sipped his tea. 'But what is this threat exactly? As a motive for murder, it's pretty vague. Mind you, stopping Roger changing his will isn't much better. It's only a motive if Lionel believed his brother hadn't yet carried out his threat, and that's something we don't know. There'd be little point in killing Roger if he'd already done the deed. What if it was better for Lionel that his brother stayed alive?'

Flora put her cup down hard on the wooden table. 'How could it be better, if he's about to be disinherited?'

'Lionel is desperate for money, we're agreed on that. He believes he'll benefit from the current will and needs time to persuade his brother to reconsider any decision to change it.'

Flora interrupted. 'But that just reinforces his reason for killing. By murdering Roger before he can change his will, Lionel stops himself being disinherited and comes into the money.'

'Granted, he gets the money eventually and I imagine it's a substantial sum. But only after probate and that can take an awful long time.'

'He can wait.'

'But can he? Lionel needs the money now. He's being chased by some very nasty characters, according to Jessie, and could end up in rather a mess. Killing Roger wouldn't help.'

'It would if he could promise the nasties that the money was on its way.'

'Those kinds of blokes don't hang around. I'm thinking Lionel might want his brother alive, so that he can try again to pressure him into giving him money immediately.'

'Jessie says Roger was adamant he wouldn't.'

'What's your bet that he'd have stuck to that decision if his brother was facing a really bad end?'

Flora washed and dried their cups and hung up the tea towel. 'So if it's not Lionel, who's our murderer, Jack?'

She asked the question casually, but her spirits had taken a dip.

'I still favour Mercy as our villain,' he said, smiling. 'She's as good a choice as any.'

'I don't think you really believe that!'

'Why not? She quarrelled with Roger Gifford as fiercely as Lionel ever did.'

'True.' Flora tried to match his lightheartedness. 'And as Jessie said, they could be in it together!'

She walked back into the hall on her way to her bedroom to dress, but as her foot hit the first stair, she turned to say, 'Seriously, we need to keep an eye on Gifford. Make sure we know what he's up to.'

'Do you think he'll be making a return visit? Maybe come through the roof next time?' It was only half a joke. 'He hasn't searched the loft yet, after all.'

'No, he hasn't, but after what's happened recently, perhaps

we should have. There has to be something important in Roger's notes. Something linked to the war – after all, it's what Roger was researching. I did suggest you phone your father. It's possible he could help.' She looked at him expectantly. 'And now might be the right time.'

13

There was a deep reluctance in Jack to telephone his father – their relationship had never been easy – but it niggled him that Flora could be right about Roger's research. There just might be something in the man's notes that was worth uncovering, that might help to explain Roger's murder, as well as the bumpy ride he and Flora had endured since moving into Primrose Cottage.

He was still tussling with the idea of phoning when Jessie arrived at the house. He could hear her shocked voice from his bedroom where he'd retreated after breakfast. It seemed she was keen to report the break-in to the police.

'If you don' call that inspector, I'm goin' to tell Will,' Jessie declared. 'He should know. Things like this 'appenin' to decent folks, it's not right.'

'You said yourself that the police aren't interested in Treleggan.' Flora was trying to dissuade her, it seemed, but Jessie was stubborn.

'That's as mebbe, but Will's our local man and he needs to know, even though nothin's been stolen. Anyways, I doubt he'll come round too quickly – what with poor Mr Roger's murder – but I'll tell 'im all the same. After I get cleared up 'ere.'

When Flora murmured a reluctant assent, the two women moved off. To the sitting room? They would be putting it to rights, Jack thought, hearing the Nelson Riddle orchestra in full flow – Jessie's favourite programme, *Housewives' Choice*, was on the wireless – and steeled himself to walk down the stairs and pick up the telephone while he had the hall to himself.

He had never been close to Ralph Carrington, even though, as a fourteen-year-old, he'd moved in with him when life with his mother had become too uncomfortable. Ralph had made it clear from the day Jack walked into his flat that he had his own life to lead and a child was an encumbrance he wasn't going to allow to disturb it. It was a life of gambling, parties, women. Always the women. The constant shifting alliances had made the young Jack desperate for stability, developed a longing in him to find something, someone, to whom he could commit. In Helen, he'd been sure he'd found the right woman, only to have his certainty dashed, his love thrown back at him, the week before their wedding. The church had been ready, the reception booked, their tickets for the ship back to England waiting on the desk. And then she'd run off with his best friend.

His father had been pretty decent about it, Jack remembered, when the plans disappeared in a puff of air. Even sympathetic – until he'd quarrelled with Jack's mother over who should shoulder the burden of the wedding costs, now there was no wedding. The fragile ceasefire his parents had cobbled together to see Jack married had exploded into the familiar cat and dog fight that he'd thought he'd escaped for good. Since then he'd barely spoken to Ralph: a Christmas greeting, a desultory meal in London once in a while, a postcard from some palm-fringed shore where his father was currently enjoying the high life.

His son's success as a novelist seemed to have passed Ralph by. To his father, Jack had let his heart rule his head, allowed heartbreak to destroy a successful career in order to waste his time scribbling. When was he going back to a proper job, a return to quality journalism? That was the question on Ralph's lips on the few occasions they'd met since the abortive wedding. It was no wonder that Jack had held off telephoning. He would have to justify why he was in Cornwall, why he was writing yet another book when he could be doing something far more lucrative, not to mention the question, sure to be slyly posed, of who was with him.

He was surprised when Ralph answered the telephone immediately. He'd half expected, perhaps half hoped, that his father was out of the country or staying with one of his many women friends at some vast country estate in Yorkshire or the Cotswolds.

'Jack!' Ralph sounded almost as surprised to hear the voice of his only child. 'How are you, my boy?'

'I'm fine,' he said briefly, before remembering to ask the same of his father.

'Not so great this morning. Suffered a bad loss last night. But swings and roundabouts, you know.'

Minimal courtesies over, Jack plunged in. 'Dad, I'm hoping for some information.'

'Not about blackjack, I hope. I'm useless at it. Think I'll go back to poker – I've got the face for the game.'

'It's not about cards. It's about the war, in particular a signals centre on the Lizard,' he rushed on.

There was an eerie silence at the other end of the phone.

'Dad, are you there?'

'Yes, yes.' His father's breathing sounded harsh.

'You were in Cornwall, weren't you, during the war?'

'Yes,' his father admitted.

'On the Lizard?'

'Yes.'

'In a signals centre there?'

'Yes.'

'Where exactly was the centre?' Jack asked, determinedly.

'It's a long time ago, old chap.'

'Not that long, surely, that you can't remember. You must have spent several years there.'

'To be honest, Jack, I don't remember much about the war years. The whole ghastly business is best forgotten, in my opinion.'

'The place I'm thinking of was near Mullion, just up from the cove,' Jack pursued. 'You can't tell me anything about it?'

'Mullion... yes, the name rings a bell,' his father said hazily. 'I was only there a couple of years and then moved on.'

'You were there with Edward Templeton? Lord Edward?'

'Eddie? Yes, poor bloke. Died a couple of years ago, you know.'

'I do know,' Jack said, his teeth on the brink of clenching. 'I live in Abbeymead, half a mile from Lord Edward's family home. You know the village, don't you? You visited Lord Edward at the Priory, I remember you telling me.'

'I do recall it now, but Mullion I'm afraid has gone out of my head completely.'

Jack didn't believe him. His father was too studied, too deliberately abstracted. Flora was right. There was something here that needed investigating.

'It's good to talk to you,' he said, a lie that made clear the call was finished.

'Good to talk to you, too, old chap.'

Ralph put the receiver down before his son. Well, if his father wouldn't talk, maybe Roger Gifford's research papers would. It was time to climb to the Primrose Cottage loft.

∽

Having seen Jessie off to the village, Flora walked up the stairs to be confronted by a long pair of legs straddling the top of a ladder. Standing at its foot, she called up, 'Is this your idea of an escape?'

'It's my idea of a search,' came a muffled voice.

'For what?'

'You know what. Papers. Roger's papers.' Jack edged himself round on the ladder and looked down at her. 'My father was worse than useless. If we want to find this secret bunker – and it *is* amazingly secret – we need to go to the horse's mouth. Otherwise known as Roger's research.'

'It's a shame we're only looking now. Why didn't we think of searching before?'

'Possibly because seeing as much of Cornwall as we can is the reason we're here. Not spending our days sifting through a mountain of paper.'

'You never know, whatever you find up there could help you as much as travelling around Cornwall.'

'Highly dubious. But I'm irritated by the secrecy and I'm determined to get to the bottom of it, even if it takes the rest of our stay to go through these wretched papers.'

'There might not be too many boxes,' she said soothingly. 'Roger was an enthusiast but he may have done more reading than writing.'

Jack wriggled back to his original position and pushed open the hatch door, laying it to one side. Somehow he managed to fold his long legs into the aperture he'd revealed, kneeling just inside the loft and pulling from his trouser pocket a small torch.

'Does the loft have floorboards?' she asked, craning her neck upwards.

'I'm hoping so, but just in case, I'll stay on the edge while I have a good scan.'

Through the open hatch Flora saw the light from the torch flash intermittently as its beam wandered around the space. In a few minutes, Jack's legs were once more dangling, his feet feeling for a purchase on the ladder. Closing the hatch behind

him, he made his way down to stand beside Flora. She picked
something from his mop of hair.

'A cobweb,' she said. Then when he made no response,
'Well? Where are the boxes?'

'Well, nothing.' He pulled down shirt sleeves that had got
rucked by the effort.

'What do you mean?'

'There's nothing there. Like you said, Roger must have read
a great deal more than he wrote.'

'There has to be something – one box at least.'

Jack shook his head and took hold of the ladder, collapsing it
in a single stroke. 'I'd better take this back. I found it in the
garden shed.'

'Jack, this is stupid. Roger Gifford told us there were papers.
I've moved them, he said, so they don't get in your way. Jessie
confirmed it – she said that was what he always did. He put
them in the loft when visitors took over the cottage.'

'If he did this time, someone must have taken them out of
the loft.'

'No one has been here except for us and Jessie, and I doubt
she could manage to climb into the roof, apart from why she'd
want to. Our only visitor has been Lionel and he got no further
than the sitting room.'

Jack's face held an arrested expression. 'Roger said he'd
moved them, right?'

'As I remember.'

'And Jessie said they were always in the loft?'

Flora nodded.

'Maybe this time was different. Maybe he thought they
weren't safe in the cottage and decided they'd be better left elsewhere. So he moved them but omitted to tell Jessie of the
change.'

'But where would he move them to, do you think?' Creases
appeared in Flora's otherwise smooth forehead.

'We know he didn't store them at River House. We have his estimable brother's confirmation for that, and he didn't store them here.'

'If he was still a bank manager, I'd say the bank's vault.'

'But he isn't.'

'Jack,' she said suddenly, 'is it possible he really did discover something dangerous and decided to destroy what he'd found?'

'If it was a crime he'd discovered, he would have gone to the police. I can't see Roger being anything but law-abiding.'

'He did have that solicitor's appointment,' she mused. 'We've been assuming it was about the will, Jessie suggested it could be about his estranged wife, a divorce possibly, but what if he made it for another reason? What if he wanted advice about a discovery he'd made? He might even have left the papers at the solicitor's for safekeeping.'

'We'll never know.' He flicked a strand of dust from his trousers. 'The fact is there's nothing to help us in the loft, there's been nothing from my father, and we found nothing at Mullion.'

A sharp rap at the front door had them look at each other, surprised and a little wary. Leaving Jack to manhandle the ladder, Flora ran down the stairs to open the door, keeping a hand firmly on the latch. None other than Inspector Mallory stood on the threshold.

He lifted his trilby in greeting. 'Sorry to bother you – Miss Steele, isn't it? It's been brought to my attention that you've had a bit of a problem here.' He glanced to one side at the jagged edges of glass protruding from the small window. 'I see that you have.'

Jessie *had* been quick, Flora thought. She must have collared Will Hoskins on her way back to the village.

'Only a minor problem, Inspector. Nothing was taken and we intend to get the front door lock changed once the glass is replaced. Just in case.' It was a white lie, but she didn't want him involved. The mystery had grown too intriguing to be given up to the police. It was one that belonged to them.

'You've checked the whole house, I take it.'

'I have,' she said, ruffled. 'And with our housekeeper's help, we're almost back to normal. Mrs Bolitho is arranging for the window to be replaced.'

The inspector stayed rooted. 'I'd like to take a look, though, if it's OK with you, Miss Steele.'

'There's really no need—' she began to say.

'Inspector Mallory, good morning.' Jack had succeeded in losing the ladder. At least there wouldn't be questions about that.

'Good morning, Mr Carrington. I was just saying as I'd like to take a look around the cottage.'

To Flora's annoyance, Jack stood back and ushered the policeman into the hall. 'I imagine Will Hoskins told you of our break-in.'

'He did.' Inspector Mallory inserted himself into the small hall and chewed on his moustache. 'It's the kitchen I'd like to see.'

'The burglar didn't go into the kitchen,' Flora said sharply.

'The kitchen please, Miss Steele.' The inspector smiled affably and waited for her to move. More annoyed than ever, Flora led the way.

Inspector Mallory stood in the kitchen doorway and surveyed the room, taking time, it seemed, to familiarise himself with its contents. Then he walked across to the formica counter and gazed at the wooden knife block, shaped as a row of cricket bats.

'Unusual,' the inspector said. 'The knives are unusual, too. Did you realise you had several missing?'

'We never saw an inventory,' Flora was quick to point out. 'The rental agreement was signed by Mr Carrington's agent.'

'Quite so, but you might have noticed the knife block. It does stand out rather. Might even have used a knife.'

'We have,' Jack said. 'What is this about, Inspector?'

Mallory dug his hand into his raincoat pocket and removed a package which he carefully unwrapped on the kitchen table. A crooked-handled knife, its blade slightly rusted, lay in the folds of material.

Flora looked at it, puzzled. Then felt sick. The rust was, in fact, dried blood.

'The murder weapon.' The inspector beamed. 'One of my men found it buried deep in the orchard grass.'

'And it came from this kitchen?' Jack's expression was hard to read.

'Apparently so.'

Mallory turned back to the counter and slotted the knife into a space on the wooden block. 'Fits perfect, doesn't it?'

'But how...' she began, before thinking of Lionel. He could have stolen a key to the cottage *before* Roger died. Let himself in and taken the knife with which he'd murder his brother. The audacity of the plan took her breath away and for a moment she was speechless.

'The thing is,' the inspector went on, 'you seem to have lost a second knife, too. Now, was it missing when you moved in, or has it disappeared since?'

Flora felt her heart tighten. There had been a knife there. She'd noticed on their first night in Treleggan that only one had been missing from the block and now there were two yawning spaces.

'I used the knife that should be there the other evening,' Jack said gravely.

'So your burglar didn't leave completely empty-handed. Just needed to check.' Mallory wedged the trilby firmly back on his head. 'Thanks for your co-operation, folks. I won't take any more of your time, but best watch out for that other knife.'

When Jack came back from showing the inspector out, he was quick to say, 'Try not to worry. It might be Jessie who's taken the knife. Not Lionel.'

Flora shook her head and her voice wobbled slightly. 'You know she didn't. It has to have been Lionel and right now he's out there with a lethal weapon. We should have told the inspector what we suspected.'

'I'm pretty sure Lionel is on Mallory's radar. He's more clued up than you think.'

'And the knife? Why did Lionel take it?'

'He obviously likes knives. Remember, he got thrown out of the pub for waving one around.'

'Correction, he got thrown out of the pub for threatening to use it on someone. Will Hoskins would have confiscated that knife, but now Lionel has another. One stolen from here.' She paused. 'Jack... the murder weapon. The knife that killed Roger – that came from this kitchen as well.'

He nodded, looking grave. 'More than likely Lionel stole it, though theoretically, I guess, almost anyone could have got hold of it.'

'How? It has to be someone who had access to the cottage and that comes down to Jessie and Lionel Gifford again. I know who my money is on.'

'They're not the only ones. Roger's wife could have visited the cottage. A previous holidaymaker could have taken the knife by mistake, then abandoned it for someone else to pick up. Even the mysterious Mercy might have got her hands on it.'

'I can't see how.'

'Roger spent a lot of time in this cottage. If Mercy called on him here – that's more likely than bearding him at his house in the high street – to have one of their famous rows...'

'I see what you mean,' Flora agreed reluctantly. 'It's a long shot, though.'

'It's all a long shot. Look, I was going to Helston today, but I'll stay if you'd rather.'

'I don't think Lionel will be back just yet and I'm not that feeble,' she protested. 'Go!'

'If you're sure... I've probably missed the one bus this week. I'll have to telephone for what passes as the local taxi and travel in style.'

Flora's eyebrows rose. 'That *is* style.'

'You could always come with me.'

'No, I'll stay. You'll get on quicker at the museum on your own, and before the inspector called I'd decided to work on the terrace. I'm so close to finishing.'

'Then stay and enjoy the garden, but keep your eyes sharp. And don't open the front door!'

14

It took Jack several telephone calls before he located the local taxi driver. When he did, the man was more than willing to collect him immediately. A journey to Helston and back, plus a few hours idling in the town, all paid for, wasn't something to turn down.

For his part, Jack was happy enough to be driven. The Austin would be back in a few days, and that would be the time to return to the Lizard. Despite his earlier scepticism, the feeling had grown in him that the place was important, his father's hesitation on the telephone this morning convincing him, if he needed it, that he should investigate. He and Flora were caught up in this mess, whether he liked it or not, and the sooner Roger's murderer was found, the sooner he could get on with what he'd come to do. He was uncomfortably aware of the three foolscap sheets currently sitting on his desk – suggestions by the tourist board for where the book they'd commissioned should go – and, so far, it had gone nowhere.

From the beginning, Jack had felt uneasy about this novel, but the Roger problem, as he termed it, had derailed him completely. He'd always known writing the book would be difficult – now, though, it had become almost impossible. He felt himself constantly worried, distracted, unable to focus.

Not so Flora, of course. From the moment she'd discovered the body, her mind had been busy constructing a story that would get to the bottom of the mystery. He was usually quick to dismiss her fantasies, but had to admit that most often she'd been proved correct, and this time, too, it looked as though she was on the right track. He really should trust her instincts, particularly as his own were hinting at the same message. There were too many occasions when the hairs on his neck had risen in warning for him to arbitrarily dismiss the idea of something lying hidden in the depths of the past, and worryingly about to erupt beneath their noses.

The anonymous note he'd received in Abbeymead had given him a jolt, but hadn't alarmed him unduly – not at the time. A local crackpot could have read one of his novels and decided he didn't want a crime writer in his village. The murder of Roger Gifford had come as a far bigger jolt, followed by Flora's tumble down the Helston steps. That could easily have been an accident, Jack recognised, but the spike belt on the road? Yes, he could explain that away as an accident, too, if he really tried. Individually, each event made only a small noise, but it was the accumulation of incidents that gave him pause.

The driver dropped him outside the Penwith Museum where there was already a small queue forming at the ticket office. The museum itself was spacious and relatively uncrowded and Jack was able to wander at will, passing quickly through rooms dedicated to Cornish mining, to fishing and farming, and several brilliant displays of home life in the eighteenth and nineteenth centuries. It was the wartime room he was intent on finding.

Once there, he spent over an hour going from display to display: reading extracts from diaries and letters, absorbing military orders, viewing uniforms and weapons, gazing at photographs of barricaded ports.

Mullion Cove was alluded to once or twice but always in passing and without mention of a signals centre. He read through a good deal on the work of such places – identifying targets, deciphering the results of bombings, supplying information on enemy troop and armour movements. It was fascinating stuff, yet too general to be helpful. But if a centre was top secret, he guessed, there would be very few records kept and no visible plans of the original site.

He left the museum feeling more frustrated than ever. It was as he was crossing the road that the idea of returning to the library came to him. He'd paid a considerable sum for a taxi so why not make good use of the time he had in the town? When Flora and he had last visited the building, it had been only to return Roger's library books and they hadn't lingered, yet when he considered it properly, it was where their former landlord must have spent a great deal of his time.

The reference section, Jack decided, that's where he'd go – they hadn't given it a glance on their earlier visit. Miss Hodges had said that Roger had been borrowing books for a long time so the collection must be extensive, and there would be volumes on the shelf that were not available for loan and had to be read within the library. It might be worthwhile retracing the dead man's steps, for a short time at least. He might even get to talk to the chief librarian – what was his name – Penrose? A Cornish name if ever there was. Penrose and Roger had talked frequently, according to Miss Hodges.

He was in luck. Miss Hodges must have taken the day off and the figure at her desk appeared to be the man that Jack had seen briefly as they'd left the library. Closer inspection proved him right. Saul Penrose, the name badge announced.

'Good morning,' Jack began.

Mr Penrose looked up expectantly. He had a pleasant face,

soft and smudgy in the English fashion, rather than the dark colouring of the Cornish.

'Can I help you?' He asked the question so quietly that his voice was barely above a whisper. A reminder, Jack thought, that they were in a library. He modulated his own tones to comply.

'We – my friend and I – called in a few days ago, to return several library books for the man whose cottage we're renting.'

Mr Penrose tried to look interested, while fiddling with a list he'd been compiling.

'His name is Roger Gifford,' Jack pursued. 'I believe you knew him.'

The librarian's face fell. 'Yes, indeed. Miss Hodges told me the news – quite terrible.'

'Mr Gifford came to the library frequently, and I believe he often talked to you. I'm trying to discover more on the research he was conducting.'

'Really?' Penrose looked slightly fazed. 'Why is that, Mr...'

'Carrington. Jack Carrington. I'm writing a book and I think it's possible that Mr Gifford's research could be useful to me.'

'Unless you're writing a genre that's never been heard of, I doubt it.' The librarian allowed himself a wintry smile. 'Roger was an inveterate researcher. It gave him an interest after he retired. But as with many older people who no longer have work to sustain them, he found it difficult to find focus.'

'How is that?'

'His interests were a little wide-ranging, shall we say.'

When Jack continued to look puzzled, the librarian said frankly, 'His mind was all over the place. First, he looked at tin mining, then it was monasteries and how the dissolution affected those in Cornwall, then the social effects of two world wars on the people here.'

'It's the war I'm most interested in,' Jack interrupted. 'The

Second World War, that is. What aspects of it did he discuss with you?'

'I can't honestly recall much of what was said. He'd been in the Home Guard and was extremely proud of it. He talked quite a bit about that.'

Mr Penrose appeared not to rate Roger's research very highly. 'Nothing about army deployments here?'

'He mentioned the number of Americans stationed around the county. That's always a topic that engages our older residents. And the way the ports were so heavily defended.'

'Nothing specifically about D-Day, for instance?'

The librarian shook his head. 'Sorry. As I say, Roger was a trifle eclectic. Now, if you will excuse me, I am rather busy this morning. Miss Hodges is unwell.'

'I'm sorry to have kept you.'

Jack knew he sounded abrupt, but his visit to the library had been a failure. If Penrose couldn't remember a single thing of any note, what use would it be to trawl through the reference section? Walking back into the street, he told himself he'd been a fool to consider for one moment that a wartime secret might be responsible for their landlord's murder. Had allowed himself to be led down a path that was spurious, if not silly. Most likely his father's vagueness was due to having drunk too much and lost a good deal of money the previous evening. The accident they'd suffered at Mullion was probably just that, an accident. The spike belt had been the idea of someone out to cause mischief. A car bearing a 'foreign' number plate announced an 'emmet' and, for some, the Austin would have been fair game.

Jack's irritation increased the more he thought of how he'd wasted a perfectly good morning and a large sum of money on what was clearly a fool's errand. Desperate for distraction from a book he already hated, he'd allowed himself to be influenced too readily by events in Abbeymead this past year, when he and Flora had been plunged into very different mysteries and emerged triumphant. But their landlord's death was something else. It offered no easy answers and should be left to the police. Roger's research, if it existed at all, was a blind alley. Flora would have to accept that whatever was going on in Treleggan, it had nothing to do with papers that had mysteriously disappeared.

15

Flora stood up and stretched her newly tanned arms to the sky. Every muscle ached, but she had scraped the very last piece of moss from the paving slabs and tugged clear the very last wisp of grass. Gazing down at her handiwork with pride, she considered whether it was warm enough to eat lunch on the newly restored terrace. Jessie had left four large slices of ham in the larder and a fresh loaf in the bread bin. A chunky sandwich with plenty of Cornish butter, along with a much-needed cup of tea, would go down well. She might even make Jack one of his beloved sandwiches if he returned from Helston in time. Picking up her tools, she started along the path she'd made through the long grass, intending to return them to the shed and bring back with her a couple of chairs.

But then she stopped, her limbs stiff and hard, her knees locking. The wasteland was no longer empty. A figure was standing in the middle of what had once been the lawn. The figure of a woman. *That* woman. Flora caught her breath and wondered if she should make a bolt for the kitchen door. Then she steadied, telling herself not to be such a coward. What could this strange creature do to her in the middle of a garden?

She had marched halfway towards the woman when she remembered Roger and what had been done to him.

'You done a proper job there,' the woman said, as Flora approached. She pointed to the terrace behind them. 'A proper job,' she repeated.

The comment was so banal as to be comic. 'Thank you,' was all Flora could stutter.

When the woman said nothing, she decided to grasp the nettle and hope it didn't sting too fiercely. 'I think I saw you – the other day in Helston.'

The woman nodded. 'You did.'

'And on the riverbank.'

'Tha's right.'

'You've been watching me?'

'I 'ave.'

'But why?'

The creases in the weathered face deepened. The woman was smiling now and her teeth shone like a neat row of white pearls. With her tanned skin and long tangle of black hair, she looked serene. Beautiful, almost. In that moment, Flora lost her fear.

'Who are you?' she asked.

'Name of Mercy Dearlove, my 'ansum.'

So this was the fabled Mercy, the witch of Treleggan and the scourge of Jessie Bolitho. 'It's good to meet you, Miss Dearlove,' Flora responded. 'I am—'

'Oh, I knows who you are, Miss Flora. And call me Mercy. Everyone does.'

Flora walked closer and felt the woman's green eyes watching her. Sharp eyes, intelligent eyes, though close up, they seemed kinder.

'May I ask why you've been watching me?'

'You got nice manners. I like that. I been watchin' out fer you.'

'Watching out for me,' Flora stammered. 'In what way?'

'There's danger, my luvver. Real danger, for you and that nice-lookin' chap you're with. Is he your 'usband?'

'No, a friend.'

'A friend who should take better care of you, I'm thinkin'.'

Flora was shaken. Meeting the woman who had featured frighteningly in her dreams of late was disturbing enough. Being told by a witch that she was in danger, even more.

'What kind of danger?' she asked at last.

Mercy looked at her, those green eyes probing, seeking, it seemed, to uncover whatever Flora might be hiding. 'I can't tell. Not at the moment. But it's there.'

'That day in Helston – was I pushed?'

'Mebbe you were, mebbe you weren't.'

Flora felt a twinge of annoyance. What use was a witch if she couldn't tell you that? 'Did you see anyone who might have done it?'

Mercy shook her head very slowly from side to side.

Flora changed tack, giving up the unequal struggle. 'Do you often come to Primrose Cottage?'

Jack's suggestion that Mercy Dearlove could have stolen the murder weapon was sharp in Flora's mind, the bloodstained knife the inspector had shown her a vivid image still.

'I don' come to the cottage, jus' the orchard.'

The fear was back, Flora's hands clammy and her stomach hard with tension. For a moment, she was rendered dumb. Then she said as boldly as she could, 'Did you see Roger Gifford the morning he died?'

'See 'is body, you mean? I did. He were past 'elpin'. I left him in peace.'

'It wasn't you, was it?' Flora ventured, a tremble in her voice.

'Me kill Roger Gifford?' Mercy gave a loud crack of laughter. 'He were cut' – and she mimicked a knife slicing at her neck – ''ere to 'ere. Why would I do that?'

'You have a knife.'

'Plenty, as it 'appens, my luvver, but if I wanted to kill Roger, I'd not need a knife.'

It was the very same thing that Jack had said.

'I quarrelled with 'im, but I wouldn't kill 'im. He were a mistaken man,' Mercy went on, 'not a bad 'un. He listened to bad folks, though, ignorant folks, that was 'is problem, folks that don' like me. He shoulda been braver.'

'Why don't they like you?' Flora had already been told, but it was Mercy Dearlove's opinion she wanted.

'I'm a peller. These days some of us call ourselves pagans. Less threatenin', you know, but pellers is what we are.'

'It's an unusual word.'

'Repellers of hexes! See? Pellers ain't well-liked, though folks use 'em plenty – farmers paying to protect their beasts, spells bought to ease folks' pain. People use pellers but no one likes 'em.'

She paused, the green eyes shrewd and watchful. 'I best be off now, afore them police come trampin' round 'ere again.'

'They haven't been near the place since Roger was murdered,' Flora said tartly. 'Well, hardly,' she amended, thinking of the inspector's visit that morning. 'But don't go. I'd like to talk more to you.'

Mercy raised a pair of thin dark eyebrows.

'Lionel Gifford – what do you know about him?'

The peller spat on the grass. ''im!' she said, in a voice charged with disdain. 'Why are you arskin'?'

Flora decided that honesty would be best. 'He came to the cottage asking for Roger's papers and last night I think he broke in, looking for them. I'm not sure why.'

'It'll be to do with money, maidy.' Mercy nodded knowingly. 'What else? Money is all that 'im and that trollop know.'

Flora ignored the trollop and said quickly, 'He was on his own both times.'

'Course he was. He and the trollop 'ate each other's guts.'

'Who *is* the trollop?' she asked, bewildered.

'The wife, though she's 'ardly a wife now. Beatrice, that's 'er name. A posh name for a narsty bit o' work. She wants Roger's money – been after it ever since she left. I've seed her 'ere plenty, pleadin' with 'im, then shoutin' fit to bust when he wouldn't listen. If he 'ad any sense he'll 'ave left it to the dogs' 'ome. She were 'ere in the garden the day before he died, doin' the same thing. Only went when she 'eard the car outside – when you and your young man turned up.'

Flora greedily stored this piece of information away, but was careful when she spoke to sound casual. 'Beatrice and her brother-in-law – Beatrice and Lionel – don't get on?'

'When that will's read, it'll be a battle to the death between those two, you'll see.' Mercy gave a small laugh.

'I've been worried about Lionel,' Flora confessed. 'Worried that he might be trying to harm us.'

Her ploy didn't work as she'd hoped. Mercy said nothing.

'Why do you say we're in danger?' she asked again, in desperation. She seemed to be getting nowhere.

'You been stirrin' things up. Things best left in the past, mebbe.'

'Such as?'

Mercy straightened her thin shoulders. 'Come with me,' she commanded.

Without waiting to see if Flora was following, she turned to walk back through the wilderness and into the orchard. In single file they pushed their way through thigh-high grass, zigzagging a path around the gnarled trunks of apple trees towards the gate that Flora had found on the day Roger was murdered. Mercy's legs were long and lean and Flora was soon breathless in her effort to keep up. Avoiding the spot where she thought she'd found Roger, she reached the rear gate. But Mercy didn't go through it. Instead, she turned sharp left and walked towards one corner of the orchard.

'There,' she said, pointing to a fallen tree.

When Flora drew near, she saw that, in toppling, the apple tree had unearthed a granite slab. The side of the slab that was uppermost revealed several faint lines of carving, eroded over many years.

Flora was curious but uneasy. 'Why do you come here?' she asked. 'Why did you bring me to see this?' She pointed down at the slab of granite that lay between them. 'What is it?'

'A witch's grave, that's what it is.'

Flora gave a gasp.

'Witches weren't buried in churchyards, you know. Their graves were hidden in sacred places.'

'This is a sacred place?'

'To us, 'tis. Near running water, and a place rich in sprowl.'

The running water Flora understood, the river flowed just beyond the gate, but sprowl?

'This sprowl...' she began, but Mercy had closed her eyes and begun swaying on her feet, at first only slightly but gradually gaining momentum.

As Flora watched, the woman's figure transformed, in some way growing in stature. It was as though a curtain of energy had risen from the earth and surrounded her, a vibrant force passing through her from her toes to her head. Mercy's breath sounded loud and harsh in the silence of the garden.

Flora stood stupefied, then as she was about to turn and run, Mercy began to speak. Her voice was as changed as the rest of her, low and deep, as though travelling from a far distance.

'There's a body lyin' there,' she said.

'Yes?' Flora whispered.

'Dead afore 'is time.'

'Roger Gifford?'

'No. A young man.'

'Who?'

Mercy gazed sightlessly into the distance. 'No name, jus' a number. Everywhere numbers.'

'Where is this young man?' Flora leaned eagerly forward.

'Not far. There's earth. Mountains of earth. And trees, so many trees. There's blood – blood-red petals.'

'Yes?' she whispered again.

But Mercy had stuttered to a close. Opening her eyes, she looked at Flora with a puzzled expression.

'You were talking about a body among earth and trees. What more?'

'No more, my luvver. I ain't strong enough. I need 'elp from others.'

'Can you get help?' Flora asked, not understanding what the woman meant, but craving to know whose body she had seen. Could it have been someone connected to Roger? Was this the reason behind his murder?

'If I'm in danger, if Jack is in danger,' she pleaded, 'you could help us understand who's threatening us.'

Mercy remained motionless, her face impassive. 'Sprowl is the Earth's life force and this place 'as power. But not enough. If you want to know the danger that threatens, find a place where the magic is strongest. A place that guards more'n one witch.'

'And you know such a place?'

Mercy gave a throaty chuckle. 'I do.'

'Can we go there?' she asked eagerly.

'I like you, maidy. I'll take you when it's right – wait for me to call. Till then, take care.'

16

Jack needed space to think and, rather than returning to Treleggan immediately, he asked the taxi driver to take him to Helford village. He'd seen from the map there were long walks to be had and a long walk fitted his mood precisely.

Some miles out of Helston, the road dropped to run alongside the river as it wound its way around tiny coves and past slate-roofed cottages, barely visible through the trees. The journey turned out to be brief and, when they came to a halt, he saw they'd pulled into a large parking area at the top of a hill.

'Can't go no further,' his driver informed him. 'No cars in the village. You 'ave to walk.'

'That's fine. You'll wait?'

'I'll wait.' The man took out a packet of cigarettes. 'Fer as long as you pay me.'

A creek lay below them, a deep gully of water, overhung by trees on either bank with several small boats drawn up on a sandy beach. Jack started downhill, eager to explore.

Helford village, when he reached it, was as idyllic as the water it stood beside. Thatched cottages, boat houses, an ancient wooden footbridge, a village stores and a public house, the Shipwrights Arms, were picture perfect. This was the softer edge of the Lizard, it seemed, a secluded backwater of gentle weather and plentiful gardens. It was hard to imagine that such a quiet settlement had once been a bustling port with trading ships from Europe regularly docking here.

Once past the pub, the paved road petered out, and Jack branched off to take a footpath that ran behind one of the white-washed cottages. He walked, hands thrust deep in his pockets, feeling the peace settle around him, yet troubled within. He was flailing, that was the truth. One plot idea after another had been abandoned. He'd thought Tintagel would do the trick, had written a full synopsis, even the first chapter, before tearing the paper from the roller and throwing a morning's work into the wastebin.

He should never have agreed to this contract. If Arthur Bellaby, whom he'd always trusted, hadn't been so keen on the project, he would never have signed. But why *was* it proving so difficult? True, he was governed by boundaries, the need to hone his story to fit the wishes of his paymaster, but surely he was an experienced enough writer to overcome this disadvantage? Yet he hadn't been able to. Words had always flowed for him and he couldn't understand why now they refused to come.

That wasn't strictly so, he admitted. When he'd first met Flora, he'd been struggling with another book, one he'd had to rewrite several times before Arthur deemed it acceptable. At the time, he'd silently blamed Flora for interrupting his work, for demanding that he help her find whoever had dumped an inconvenient body in her bookshop. At the same time, though, he'd been glad to forget the struggle to write and join her in her quest – and they'd been successful, working together. Though not before she'd faced extreme danger and he'd been driven half-mad with fear for her.

Was Flora the problem again? When, at last, she'd had the chance to travel, to leave behind a village that at times he knew she found suffocating, she'd chosen to accompany him here. He should have encouraged her to go abroad, to the cities she'd always dreamed of visiting. Why hadn't he? Why had he invited her to Cornwall? And why had she accepted his invitation so readily? They were questions he hadn't wanted to answer – and still didn't.

The pathway had widened, he realised, and suddenly through the trees, he saw water again. He'd reached a cove, small and silent and secret, sheltered from the world by close-packed trees growing thick and dense, their branches trailing in the water. Penarvon Cove, if he remembered his map correctly, and entirely magical. The word brought Flora back into his mind and he wished she were here with him.

He hadn't wanted a woman in his life ever again, yet it seemed he had one. He enjoyed Flora's companionship, was grateful for the way she'd helped him back into the world again, the way meeting her had thawed feelings and emotions frozen by Helen's betrayal. Perhaps that was the problem. That unless he hid himself away, as he'd done at Overlay House for so many years, he couldn't write. It was a frightening prospect and he didn't want to believe it.

For a while, he stood and watched the herons feeding. Bird life was all around and he was soothed by the whirr of wings, the rustle in the trees, the occasional note of song. Setting off once more, he followed the creek as it flowed from the cove, past a large farmyard, through woods, negotiating a muddy track, until he was back in Helford village. A drink at the Shipwrights Arms would go down well before he climbed back up the hill to find his taxi. The fare would be astronomical, but the time it had given him to walk, to think, was worth every penny.

Completing his circular tour, he'd jettisoned, one by one, every approach he'd been working on, every idea he'd had for the book, and very slowly had felt his head clear. He would forget Tintagel. Forget Roger's murder and mad witches. Forget signals centres and their secrets. Instead, he'd keep the place and the period, the Lizard and the war years, and from those bare beginnings wrangle a fearsome, blood-soaked mystery that had its origins in a small Cornish village. Talking to Jessie would be a good place to start. Their housekeeper had lived in just such a place for all six years of the last war. She would have a tale, or several, to tell.

When Jack walked through the door of Primrose Cottage, Flora bounced out of the kitchen to meet him.

'You've been a while – you must have had a successful day. Jessie's here. She's brought supper.'

The words were tumbling out and his heart sank a little. Flora was in a state of suppressed excitement, he realised, and he dared not think what she had been up to in his absence.

'The day was OK,' he answered briefly, walking into the kitchen where Jessie was hanging up a pair of oven mitts.

'Been to Helston again, I 'ear,' she said by way of a greeting.

'Tired myself out, Jessie, but supper smells delicious.'

'It is delicious.' Flora followed him, bouncing back into the kitchen. 'A real treat, chicken and mushroom pie. Jessie has been organising the veg. She was just leaving.' He could see she was keen the housekeeper didn't linger.

'I don't want to hold you up, Jessie,' he said, 'but I'd like to talk to you when you have a moment – about wartime here. What it was like in Treleggan.'

The housekeeper looked surprised.

'I think it might be useful for the book I'm writing,' he explained.

Jessie took a deep breath. 'Well, now,' she said, untying her pinafore and dropping into a kitchen chair, 'it were a massively busy place back then. Same as where you come from, I reckon. All along the south coast, really. Lots of new airfields, I remember, and a lot of them bombers settin' off. Anti-aircraft stuff, too.'

Jack pulled out a chair and sat down opposite. 'Cornwall was well-defended, you'd say?' he asked, leaning forward.

'I dunno about that – mebbe. Though we 'ad a load of Spitfires crash over the sea. My mum and dad were that upset, those poor boys, drowned if they went down too far out. But lots of planes,' she repeated. 'There were Canadians 'ere, well everywhere, I 'spect, and the Americans, too, comin' and goin' all the time.'

Flora was getting impatient. He was aware of her foot tapping a tattoo on the kitchen linoleum. Ignoring it, he asked, 'Where were all the troops accommodated?'

'In tents, mainly, 'cept the officers who got the big 'ouses. Camps full of tents sprang up all over the place, sometimes overnight. And there were tanks and lorries parked along the lanes – under camouflage nets so they wouldn't be seen. You can't imagine the noise and commotion, not now it's so quiet.'

There was a long silence. Jessie appeared to have said all she was going to but it seemed she'd only just got into her stride. 'Come D-Day, it were incredible. The build-up, jus' amazin'. It were all done secretly, mind. The phone boxes disconnected, all the letter boxes sealed up weeks before. You weren't supposed to know anythin' – jus' the police and the ambulance, the ARP, those kinds of people. There were ammunition stored everywhere, tonnes of it. It went on the ships on D-Day, but if any of those dumps had been hit, they'd have blown Cornwall off the map!'

'Thank the Lord that didn't happen. You must have been praying hard.'

'We were that.' Jessie's gaze was distant. 'It were a strange thing, you know, D-Day. Like a play, really, that had come to an end. The music kinda stopped, the words disappeared, the actors went off stage. Jus' the audience – that were us – left behind. It were real strange. But then we 'eard on the news what was 'appenin'. How all the tanks and the men were in France. Jus' fancy, goin' over the Channel with all that stuff, and it was some rough that June. But they were there and they were fightin' and we thought we're goin' to win. We're goin' to live free. Goin' to get our life back again.'

He might not use any of this, Jack thought, but to hear first-hand how it had been for those left at home, even in a rural paradise such as Helford, was humbling. When you'd seen war from only one perspective, it did you good to realise what the reality of life for millions of your fellow countrymen had been.

Jessie gave a faint sigh. 'They were difficult days all right, but we pulled together. Now, where'd I put my basket?'

When she'd packed away her apron and house slippers, Jack accompanied her to the front door. 'Stew all right fer you tomorrow?' she asked.

'Perfect.'

Walking back into the kitchen, he saw Flora, arms folded and looking peevish. 'What was all that stuff about the war?' she demanded.

'I thought you'd be interested.'

'I'm interested in Mullion, not how many troops flooded the county or how good American toffee apples tasted.'

'That's a thought – Jessie didn't mention toffee apples.'

'Stop teasing and tell me how you got on today.'

'I've nothing to report. I drew a complete blank.'

'Nothing? But you've been gone an age. I thought you were never coming back.'

'I went for a walk,' he admitted. 'After Helston. The museum didn't turn up anything useful, nor the library.'

'I didn't know you were going back to the library.'

'I didn't either. It was a spur of the moment decision. I met the chief this time, Mr Penrose, for all the good it did me. His recollection of Roger and his scholarly dabblings was precisely zero.'

'You couldn't have been in Helston for long,' she said accusingly. 'You must have taken a very lengthy walk.'

'I did, but I needed it.' Flora looked unconvinced and he added quickly, 'I know you're bursting to tell me something, but I need to wash and change before we eat. Can you bear to wait ten minutes?'

'I've waited longer already, so why not?' Flora's response verged on the sharp.

When Jack walked back into the kitchen, feeling a good deal fresher, she was warming their supper plates.

'Go on,' he said. 'Tell me the worst.'

A wide smile filled her face. Pushing a stray wave behind her ears, she took a seat, her elbows resting on the table. 'We have a new suspect,' she announced.

Jack groaned.

'Don't groan. It's true. *And* I've met Mercy Dearlove. And finished clearing the terrace,' she said as an afterthought.

'Dearlove? The witch?'

'She is wonderful, Jack. Terrifying but wonderful.'

'I take it she's not your new suspect.'

'Of course not. She was on my list originally, but now she's not a suspect at all. She showed me a witch's grave – in our orchard, would you believe? It's why she comes so often to the garden.'

'And yet she's not a suspect?'

'She saw Roger's body. She was quite straightforward about it. Saw him dead and left him in peace, they were her words.'

'And you believe her? The woman who quarrelled bitterly with Roger and, on her own admission, frequents the orchard where he was found with his throat cut?'

'She said what you said. If she'd wanted to kill him, she didn't need a knife to do it. Which was kind of chilling, but true.

And though she quarrelled badly with Roger, I don't think she disliked him. She called him a mistaken man.'

'He certainly made one mistake in agreeing to meet his murderer.' Jack tipped his seat back, stretching his legs. 'That walk has given me an appetite. Do you think the pie could be ready?'

Flora jumped up and opened the oven door. 'It should be OK and it smells wonderful. Jessie is a marvel.'

'You were keen to get rid of her,' he remarked mildly.

'Only tonight. I was dying to tell you about Mercy and she's definitely not a favourite with Jessie.'

Flora donned the oven gloves and carried a large white china dish to the table, then returned for bowls of peas and carrots. 'Can you bring the potatoes? They're keeping warm on the hob. I think Jessie's wrong about Mercy,' she went on. 'Now I've met her, I trust her. I did have my doubts – I never mentioned it, but I saw her in Helston just before I fell down those stairs – but I'm sure now that she means no ill.'

'You're sure it was Mercy in Helston?'

'You can't mistake her. She is... striking. If you saw her, you wouldn't forget,' Flora said confidently, cutting slices of pie for them both. 'And I'd seen her before Helston, too – on the riverbank.'

'Did she see you fall?'

'No, but she warned me we could be in danger. I think she's watching over us.'

'She wasn't watching over us too closely when we were in Mullion, was she?'

Flora put her head on one side. 'Somehow, I can't see her driving a car, can you?'

'Definitely not a car. A broomstick, maybe.'

'If you're going to mock, I'm not telling you any more.'

'Sorry. There's more to tell?' He took a mouthful of pie. 'Hmm, this is delicious. So who's the new suspect?'

'Beatrice Gifford,' she announced exultantly. 'Roger's wife, or once-upon-a-time wife. I know she's come up in conversation before, but not seriously.'

'And now she is serious?'

'Beatrice, Mercy said, likes money as much as Lionel. She would be as anxious as he to stop Roger changing his will. And, remember, Jessie told us that Roger was turning a new page, which means that if he'd previously left money to his wife, he was about to cut her out. She was for the chop.'

'Where is this Beatrice? We've not met her.'

'I'm not sure where she lives, though I'm fairly certain it's not Treleggan. Mercy said Beatrice was here the day we arrived. The day before Roger died. She and Roger were in the garden together and she was shouting abuse at him. Mercy overheard her. It only stopped when we turned up in the car. He looked a bit frazzled when he came to greet us, didn't he? I thought at the time it was because we were late and he was one of those men who insist on military timekeeping, but now I see it was the row with his wife.'

'So Beatrice yells at him, disappears when we arrive, and then some time between then and the next morning, contacts him to meet her in the orchard?'

'Or the rear lane.'

'Wherever you're suggesting, it's hardly feasible.'

'Why not?' Flora demanded, scooping another spoonful of chicken from the dish. 'She could have telephoned Roger to apologise for her outburst and then asked to meet him.'

'Why would she apologise and then want to meet him still?'

'Maybe she had something for him – something with which to say sorry – or she thought they should try to talk again, but more reasonably. She might feel she'd made a fool of herself and wanted to meet him as quietly as possible. I'm sure Mercy wouldn't have been the only one who heard her shouting. Meeting her husband very early in the orchard is pretty private, if Beatrice didn't want the whole village to know.'

'Your imagination is incredible. Fertile isn't the word. Really, you should be writing these books.'

'My incredibly fertile imagination tells me we should speak to Roger's solicitors. Now that I know him so much better, I really want to help him. I need to find his murderer. *And* the person who's threatening us. They're one and the same. The police have done nothing so far, just as Jessie said they wouldn't.'

'We don't know that, and why go to the solicitors?'

'The letter, Jack. Roger made an appointment to see them. I want to know what it was about – if we go to their offices, we might find out.'

'You won't learn a thing. Solicitors are sworn to confidentiality.'

'They might let something slip and it's important we try. If Roger was about to discuss a divorce, or cut his wife out of the will, it means we definitely have another suspect. We can look around Falmouth at the same time.'

This was supposed to tempt him, he thought drily. 'We don't have a car,' he reminded her.

'We don't need a car. There's a regular boat that goes from Treleggan – I asked Jessie.'

Jack pushed back his chair and collected their empty plates. 'I can't win, can I?'

'You can't, so give up now!' She gave him a gentle poke in the ribs.

'Beatrice could be another of Jessie's prejudices, like Mercy Dearlove. You know nothing about her, except what you've been told, but she's now your quarry. It seems unfair.'

'It's not only Jessie who dislikes her. Mercy was scathing about the woman. But I agree, it could be prejudice on both their parts. I don't know Jessie's personal circumstances –

whether there's a Mr Bolitho or not – but I feel she rather carried a torch for Roger.'

'Then he was a lucky man,' Jack said, turning on the hot tap. 'For a while, at least.'

'You're just thinking of Jessie's pies.'

'And why not?' he said dreamily. 'They're perfection.'

The washing-up done, they finished stacking the china in its rightful place and had just settled themselves in the sitting room when the front door knocker sounded.

'Are you expecting anyone?' Jack asked.

'Hardly. Are you?'

He was already at the front door before she called out, 'Jack – be careful.'

Ignoring the warning, he prised the door open a few inches. Then stood back, dumbstruck. He was looking at his father.

'Hello, my boy. How are you?'

17

Jack stood motionless, staring at the figure in the doorway. 'What are you doing here?' he said at last, his voice edged with annoyance.

'Not much of a welcome, Jack. Do you think I could come in? Getting a bit parky out here.' A pair of amused blue eyes looked directly into his.

He stood back to allow his father to squeeze past into the small hall. Ralph shrugged off his navy wool blazer and launched it at the coat stand, then smoothed down an already immaculate head of silver hair.

'You better come into the sitting room,' Jack said reluctantly, and gestured to the open doorway. Flora looked up as they came into the room.

'Who—' she began.

'This is my father, Flora.' Jack's introduction was terse. 'Dad, this is Flora Steele. She's helping me with research.'

'Really?' There was a gleam in Ralph's eyes and doubt in his voice.

Flora held out her hand. 'How nice to meet you, Mr Carrington.'

'At least someone's pleased to see me!' He lowered himself into one of the high-backed chairs.

'Tea?' she asked.

His father beamed. 'Wonderful!'

Jack sat, his gaze doggedly fixed on what had once been the jewelled colours of a Persian rug, while from the kitchen the sound of running water, the flare of gas, the clink of cups, only emphasised the silence that stretched between them. He had no idea what Ralph Carrington was doing in Treleggan, but his father had been right when he'd said his arrival was unwelcome. It was the last complication Jack needed, just when he'd cleared his head sufficiently to make a new start on this wretched novel.

Once Flora returned with a tray of tea, Jack weighed in. 'Well? Why *are* you here?' he asked abruptly.

His father looked uncomfortable for the first time since he'd arrived. 'Your phone call, old chap. It sounded urgent and I didn't give you much to go on, so I asked that agent of yours where you were and thought I'd look you up.'

'You gave me nothing.'

'My war was over long ago, but I did remember more than I said,' Ralph confessed. 'The thing is, what happened at Mullion was a painful business and you caught me on the hop rather. It's not always a good idea to go raking up stuff that's best forgotten. Why is Mullion so important to you anyway?'

'The man who rented us this cottage was murdered the day after we arrived,' Flora put in.

'Good grief!'

'We think – I think,' she corrected herself, 'that the murder might be connected to the research he was doing on the war. In particular, on the signals centres in this area. We discovered that Mullion was the largest of them and the most secret and Jack remembered that you'd been here at the time.'

'I see.' Ralph paused. 'But surely, if there's been a murder, the police will be dealing with it?'

'They should be, but they don't appear to be getting very far. Mr Gifford's watch is missing and the police are keen to pursue the theory that it was a random mugging, though why they should think somewhere like Treleggan has a mugger roaming the village, I can't imagine.'

'Sparky little lady, isn't she, Jack?'

Jack ignored him and brought the conversation back to where he wanted. 'Have you changed your mind then, about talking?'

'I suppose I have. I'd like to help you, and to be honest I thought it might be good for me if I got it off my chest. But I didn't want to telephone – a lot of party lines in the countryside, you never know who's listening in – and you were down here in Cornwall and I haven't been back since...' He trailed off.

'So you thought you'd lay a few ghosts?'

'Got it in one!' His father gave a loud shout of laughter. 'The Mullion business put a damper on my career and I was glad to leave the army as soon as the war ended. Broke a decent friendship, too. A very good friendship.'

'Yours and Edward Templeton's?'

Ralph nodded. 'When I was first posted to Mullion and discovered that the officer with whom I'd share responsibility was a Lord Edward Templeton, I expected some half-witted aristo who'd got his position through pulling strings. That I'd be doing all the work and he'd take all the credit. But Eddie wasn't like that. Not at all. He was conscientious, highly intelligent and very skilled at his job. A true comrade.'

'I knew Lord Edward,' Flora put in. 'He was a lovely man. So what led you to fall out with him?'

'We fell out together. It was the Martin affair.'

'Thomas Martin?' she asked.

Ralph looked surprised. 'You've heard of him?'

'I come from Abbeymead, the same village as Lord Edward, and a friend told me about the Martins losing their son.'

'Ah, I see. Thomas was a good chap, at least we all thought so. Came to us in 1943. Diligent, willing to learn. He was in one of the units that dealt with Bletchley Park.'

'Units?' Jack interrupted. 'Wasn't Mullion a single centre?'

'It was and it wasn't. The centre was pretty big, most of it built underground and stretching a fair way towards the coast. There was a tunnel leading to the beach – just in case we had to get out quickly.'

Flora stared hard at Jack, but neither of them spoke a word about their abortive search.

'The centre was big,' Ralph repeated, 'but divided into smaller units. It was thought to be a better way to safeguard secrets, and there were plenty of those. We were dealing with highly confidential material every day, so working in restricted teams made sense. Eddie and I were in overall charge, one of us taking over from the other when we were due a break, otherwise working together. We each had a number of teams reporting to us and we'd meet regularly to share how things were going.'

'And Thomas Martin?' Flora asked.

'He was in a team working on particularly sensitive material and there started to be problems.' Ralph paused, looking down at the teacup he was nursing, then raised his head and began again. 'There was a new airfield on the Devon border, just completed and ready for the planned invasion, whenever that happened. Knowledge of the location was strictly limited, but the day after the builders moved out, the place was bombed and completely destroyed. Then a few weeks later, a convoy of Canadian soldiers, en route to relieving their fellows, was targeted by German fighters. A lot of the men died. The movement of those troops was supposedly secret, Martin's group the only signals unit privy to that information. Suspicions were growing that someone in that team was passing information to the Germans. Bletchley Park were hopping. If we had a spy in our midst, we couldn't be part of any final invasion plans and they were counting on us. Counting on dozens of signals centres, it's true, but we were pivotal. We had to discover if we had a mole.'

Both his listeners had their eyes fixed on Ralph, their tea growing cold on the table beside them.

'Eddie and I devised a plan between us, but before we could put it into action the corporal in charge of the unit came to us – can't for the life of me remember his name – and told us more or less what we'd been thinking. He wasn't at all happy about it, but he did his duty and gave us a name. Thomas Martin.'

'Why was he so sure it was Thomas?'

Flora sounded indignant and Jack, noticing her flushed cheeks, realised how difficult this must be for her. Martin was a boy from Abbeymead and the son of Alice Jenner's friends.

'The chaps in the unit worked in shifts,' his father explained, 'and Martin always made a point of staying behind when his shift finished. Occasionally, there'd be a few minutes when he was on his own in the unit. Not very often or for very long, but he was the only one who was ever alone. The corporal had him down as a keen worker, but when it became clear there were problems, he began watching the lad closely. He reported his findings to us, and I agreed with him. Martin was the guilty one.'

'And Lord Edward?' Flora asked. 'Did he agree?'

Ralph's face was shadowed. 'Eddie refused to believe it. Martin came from his village, from a decent, honest family, he said. Martin's father had been Eddie's tenant for thirty years. He'd known Thomas as a child – even paid for him to go to the local grammar school. He wouldn't hear a word against him, said there was no real evidence, and the lapses in security could have been accidental. While we were arguing about how best to proceed, Martin disappeared. Simply walked out of the centre one day and never came back.'

'No one saw him go?' Jack asked incredulously.

'Not a soul. But, after he went, the intelligence was never again compromised, so we drew our own conclusions. Martin was the guilty one, all right, and hopped it before he could be court-martialled. But Eddie would never accept that... and so we fell out,' he ended forlornly.

'Couldn't it have been someone else in the unit?' Flora was still fighting for Thomas, Jack thought.

'There were only three others and Martin was the one acting suspiciously, watching his fellow workers very closely, monitoring their comings and goings, making notes he never showed them. It all came out in the investigation.'

'He might have been trying to find the culprit himself.'

'You're from the same village, my dear, you know his people, and you're bound to be partial, but everyone came to the same conclusion, even the high command when the case was presented to them. It was Thomas Martin all right.'

'But not Lord Edward.'

'Whom you continued to see,' Jack reminded him, recalling the school he'd attended on Lord Edward's recommendation and thoroughly hated.

'We tried to keep up the association. For old times' sake, really. Occasionally, we'd meet in London for a whisky and soda, but it was never the same. Eddie never accepted what had happened. But tell me,' Ralph brightened suddenly, 'how is Mullion going to help find your landlord's murderer?'

Flora was quick to answer. 'If Roger discovered someone's guilty secret while he was researching the war, that someone might need to get rid of him.'

Ralph gave a bark of laughter. 'Bit of an imaginative stretch, wouldn't you say?'

'I'm very good at imaginative stretches,' she answered serenely.

'I'm sure, m'dear, but if you're looking for a murderer in the unit I've talked about, none of the chaps I knew would fit the bill. The Canadian – I do remember his name, it was strange to an English ear – Randy Paradis. He went back to Canada after D-Day, transferred to a regiment there. Retired now, I imagine. And poor Ronnie Brooks, he was killed by a stray V2 while we were dismantling the camp in 1945. He'd popped out to have a ciggie – dashed bad luck. I remember his name well. I had to write to the poor blighter's parents to tell them, just when they thought he'd come through the war unscathed.'

'And the corporal?'

'A teacher originally. From London. He really missed the city and went back there after the war. Back to teaching, I believe.'

Ralph sat back in his chair and smiled expansively. It was as though telling his story had restored a peace that he'd previously lost. 'I've not been much help, I'm afraid, but unless there are suspects you haven't mentioned, I'd say the police have probably got it right – a random mugger.'

'We have other possibilities,' his son said briefly. 'Mr Gifford has a brother and an estranged wife, both of whom seem to covet our landlord's money.'

'There you are then. Mystery solved. Isn't murder always about money? If it's not about love.'

'Can you take us there?' Jack asked out of the blue. 'To Mullion. To the site of the signals centre?'

'It will be a complete ruin by now,' Ralph protested, 'and why would you want to go?'

He decided on boldness. 'Cornwall is the setting for my new book and I'm thinking of writing a wartime story. Getting a glimpse of where a signals centre once stood would help me build atmosphere.'

His father pulled a wry face. 'You still churning out those books?'

'I don't churn them out,' he snapped back. Then feeling guilty, he said in a more conciliatory tone, 'I'm afraid we can't put you up for the night, Dad. There are only two bedrooms in the cottage – unless you fancy the sitting room floor.'

'No problem, old chap,' Ralph said easily. 'I booked myself into the local pub before I knocked at your door.'

'You have your car with you, I imagine?'

'Naturally.' His father looked shocked. 'Wouldn't trust British Rail to bring me this far. But what about you? You can't have embarked on a research trip without a vehicle.'

'There's been a slight accident,' Jack hedged. 'The car will be back on the road in a few days, but in the meantime...'

Ralph nodded. 'If we must. A few more ghosts to lay, I suppose.'

18

Jack and Flora were outside the Chain and Anchor well before nine o'clock the next morning, Jack impatient to get back to his typewriter and Flora convinced that today's outing might begin to unlock the mystery of Roger Gifford's death.

Ten minutes later, when there was still no sign of Ralph Carrington, Jack proposed they go into the pub and prise his father out. They found him in the low-beamed dining room leisurely making his way through a large English breakfast, a newspaper spread across the table.

'You said nine o'clock.' Jack was brusque.

Ralph looked up from his paper. 'Good morning, Jack. And you, Flora.' He looked at his watch. 'Dear me, is it that time already?'

'Yes, it is. And nine o'clock outside the pub is what we agreed last night.'

'True, true. Just let me finish my coffee, old boy, and I'll be with you.'

Jack swung round and marched towards the door, Flora feeling forced to follow. These last few hours, it had become very clear how troubled a family Jack's was. She wondered if his relationship with his mother was as difficult – probably more so. It almost made her glad she had so few recollections of her own parents.

'You're not exactly polite to your father,' she said, once they were outside again.

'Does he deserve it?'

'He *is* driving us to Mullion, and he's willing to show us the signals centre, if he can.'

'*If* he can. And, really, what's the point of it?' Jack asked irritably. 'The Mullion thing is a distraction. I know now what I'm going to write and it's not about spying. I must have been mad to ask him to drive us.'

'This isn't all about you,' Flora said tersely. 'Or your writing. We should be thinking more of Roger – he deserves justice and he isn't getting it.'

Jack didn't respond, but seeing his changeable grey eyes darken and his mouth set firm, she tried to coax him into a better mood. 'The story your father told us last night was quite a tale, wasn't it? No wonder the Martins won't talk about their son. I don't suppose the army ever charged him officially, but rumours are bound to have reached them. To have a son spoken of as a traitor. That's horrible.'

Jack gave only a brief nod but, at that moment, Ralph emerged from the pub's front entrance and strolled towards them. 'Sorry about that, folks,' he said, hoping, it seemed, to placate his visitors with a wide smile. 'The breakfast was so damn good that time ran away with me.'

He waited for a response but, when it didn't come, murmured, 'The car's round the corner. The car park is minuscule but I managed to squeeze a space for the old banger.' The old banger turned out to be a vintage Bentley, which brought a smile to Flora's face. At least this time she'd be travelling in comfort.

The journey to Mullion was accomplished in almost total

silence, Jack still too grumpy to talk and Flora deep in thought about what they might find today. Ralph drove fast but skilfully and within half an hour they were pulling into the village.

'There was a footpath down to the cove. If it's still there, I suggest we take that,' he said, climbing from the car and stretching his long legs. No wonder Jack was so tall, she thought.

Beginning their traipse along the bramble-strewn path, Flora sent up a prayer that they wouldn't meet Logan or his friend. It could make for a very awkward conversation, since neither she nor Jack had mentioned having been to Mullion before. Hopefully, the men would be busy riding a tractor in one of the fields they'd passed on their way to the village.

It felt strange to be retracing their footsteps of a few days ago, even stranger when Ralph took exactly the same route along the coastal path. What had they missed that day? Something, for certain, since when Ralph stopped to look up at the cliff face, a signal they'd reached the tunnel entrance, it was a good way short of where she and Jack had walked.

'The tunnel was here, I'm pretty sure.' He sounded puzzled. Glancing back at the harbour, he nodded. 'Yes, definitely here. I remember how the harbour wall looked from this point, and the way the cliff turns a sudden corner ahead.'

Jack was gazing at the cliff, too. 'Nothing to see here, Dad,' he said, his tone laconic.

'Has there been a rock fall?' Flora walked closer to the cliff.

'That must have been what happened.' Ralph joined her, and both stood for some time peering upwards. 'See that overhang? That was never there. I reckon a great chunk of cliff has come away and blocked the tunnel.'

It was no wonder they'd not been able to find the entrance – but neither had Jack's father. For a moment, she felt crushed.

Ralph smiled down at her. 'I can see it means a lot to you, but don't fret. We may be unable to get into the tunnel, but that doesn't mean we can't find the site. There are several pathways to the cliff top, but one in particular should take us where we want.' He walked to one side and parted the overhanging bushes, revealing the narrowest of tracks. 'Still here. It was sometimes quicker getting back to base this way than through the tunnel. More private, too, if you were out of camp when you shouldn't be – for an illicit swim or two.'

He gave a wicked laugh and Flora wondered whether it was only the swim that had been illicit. Jack rarely talked of his parents' marriage, but it was plain it had been anything but happy.

In single file they clambered up the track, pushing bushes aside, fielding low-lying branches from their faces, and avoiding the rocks that here and there had encroached on the track. They made slow progress but, when they finally reached the top of the cliff, it was to see that they'd arrived at the outer edge of the plantation of trees that she and Jack had discovered on their previous visit.

Ralph stood, his arms folded, gazing to left and right, clearly baffled. 'There were never any trees,' he said. 'And all these bushes.' He turned in a full circle, evidently trying to orientate himself. 'The village was a mile to the left of where we joined the track, the sea is half a mile south from here – you can just glimpse it through the trees – so, I think... I think for the centre we should walk down the hill a way, maybe veer to the left a little.'

'That sounds pretty woolly,' Jack muttered.

'Bound to be, son. The place looks entirely different. Who the hell planted all these trees?'

It was a question that Flora had asked herself. It might, she supposed, have been an attempt to bury memories of the war. To smother the landscape in greenery, hoping to blot out the recent past. People's feelings about the war were often conflicted. They could be proud of what the country had achieved, what as a people they'd suffered and come through, yet many were also desperate to forget those six long years of hardship and sorrow.

And the young men who had served at Mullion, what would they wish to remember of those years? Their recollections would surely be mixed. Their job as signallers and spies had been to protect the country they loved, and they would have understood all too well how much depended on them, how many lives were in their hands. Yet at the same time, through the long years of conflict, their own fate must always have been in the balance. It could only be a hope that as serving soldiers they would survive.

As Ralph led the way downhill, the sun, which had been growing ever fainter, disappeared altogether, throwing the landscape into deep gloom. Flora shivered in her thin cotton blouse. The weather had changed for the worst – it was amazing how quickly it could. Foolishly, she'd been tempted by what she'd thought was a warm day to leave her cardigan at the cottage.

But the shiver came from somewhere else, too. She wasn't sure whether it was the place itself – the dense thicket of trees cutting out the light, the shadows thrown by gaping hollows in the surface of the cliff, the glossy clamour of dark green leaves – or her own foreboding of what might have happened here, but she was conscious of an oppression. A sense of simmering threat. Of being watched, she realised. But, surely, there was no one here but the three of them? Yet, she couldn't be entirely certain. The trees were too numerous, the bushes too prolific, and every so often mounds of earth, the spoil perhaps from when the site was first excavated, provided endless opportunities for concealment.

They had gone only a short way in the direction Ralph had indicated, when through the trees she glimpsed fragments of a building, of concrete sullied and begrimed by the encroaching greenery. Drawing closer, a large oval shape emerged from the forest of trees that stood guard. The hump of a whale, Flora thought, or the carcass of some prehistoric monster.

'That's it! That's the roof!' Ralph said excitedly. 'A few more yards and we'll be at the entrance.'

He was right. In less than a minute they were facing a corridor, long and narrow and made of concrete, that sloped downwards from the surface and disappeared into a pool of darkness.

'Lucky I brought this.' Ralph produced a torch from his jacket pocket. 'Always carry a torch when you're travelling. Be prepared is my motto.'

'A regular boy scout,' Jack remarked acidly.

Really, Jack was being tiresome today. She, for one, was grateful for the torch, being eager to explore but not at the expense of breaking bones. She followed Ralph down between the corridor's echoing walls and into the main building. A warren of small rooms linked by cramped passageways greeted her, grass sprouting through the floors and clumps of damp moss dripping from the ceilings. The earth smelt dank, rotten, corrupt. Flora tried not to think about it.

'This was my room. I recognise it!' Ralph stood in the doorway of a small square box, his head almost touching the ceiling. 'My God! How many hours I spent here! And here,' he darted past them to a room on the opposite side of the passage, 'This was Eddie's.'

'Where did the unit you mentioned live?' Flora asked.

'Bletchley One? Down the corridor to the left.'

But setting off to find the fatal room where Thomas Martin had supposedly turned traitor, she was stopped in her tracks. A fall of earth had completely blocked the far end of the passage and it was impossible to go further.

'Sorry, folks.' Ralph came to stand beside her. 'That's it, I'm afraid. Time has done its worst. Got enough atmosphere, Jack?'

'My nose certainly has. Let's go, unless you're keen to linger, Flora.'

There was no point in staying longer; there was nothing more to see. Disappointed, she took herself silently to task. What had she expected? Some kind of revelation?

On the way out, she stopped to look at the graffiti that had been carved into the concrete of the corridor wall. There were several artistic portraits amid the usual hearts and initials.

'Strictly forbidden,' Ralph said, coming up behind her, 'but the chaps still did it. Relieved the boredom, I guess.'

'Were you bored?' Flora was surprised.

'For much of the time not a lot happened, but when it did, it was all hands on deck.'

'Who's SP?' Among the forest of initials, this one was etched more strongly than most.

Ralph peered at it. 'I can't – yes, hang on a minute – that was Lofty's artwork. Lofty Price – the corporal. His name has just come back to me. He should have known better.'

'With a name like Lofty, however did he cope with that maze of low-ceilings?'

Ralph chuckled. 'He was short, my dear. A little man. The nickname was a joke. Wonder if he's still teaching? There was a huge demand for teachers at the end of the war. A different chalk face, though, eh?' He laughed good-naturedly.

Flora wondered it, too. Lofty Price would be in his forties by now. If he was still working as a teacher, would it be possible to trace him? she wondered. Ask him if he knew of anyone in the signals unit who was still living in Cornwall, someone who might be defending a terrible secret by murder. But this was fantasy land again and she gave herself another scolding.

After the claustrophobic network of passages and cell-like rooms, it was a relief to breathe fresh air once more, and all three of them stood for a while, savouring the feeling, before starting on their way down to the coastal path.

Ralph was ahead, winding his way through the plantation of trees to regain the track that led back to the sea, but he'd gone only a few yards when he suddenly stumbled and fell. In an instant, Flora was at his side, but it was Jack's strength that heaved the older man to his feet.

'Sorry about that.' Ralph's smile hinted at embarrassment. 'I must have slipped.' He peered down at the ground. 'The earth's a bit uneven here. I didn't see that ridge.'

'No wonder with all this mush around.'

Flora looked where Jack was pointing. Fallen petals from the rhododendron bushes had lain there all winter, through every kind of weather, and formed themselves into a spreading puddle of scarlet.

As the others moved off, Flora stood motionless. There was a thought, barely formed, pushing its way into her mind. Words that were close, yet deep in darkness. Words she must have heard but drifting out of reach in her struggle to catch hold of them.

'C'mon, Flora, we need to get back. I've a book to write.'

Jack really was in a bad mood today.

19

Flora glanced over her shoulder through the rear window. There was a car following them. Ralph driving, and Jack in the front passenger seat, seemed unaware, but she had seen the black Humber pull out of a lane shortly after they'd turned onto the main thoroughfare, and it was still there even as they turned off again into the country road that would take them back to Treleggan.

As they passed the first outlying cottages of the village, she made a decision.

'Can you stop at the village stores, Mr Carrington? There are one or two things we need for the kitchen cupboard.'

Jack half turned his head. 'What are we missing? Jessie's bringing supper and we've plenty for breakfast.'

'Just a few extras I thought of,' she improvised. 'I don't want to ask Jessie for more shopping.'

Stopping in the main street of the village meant the Humber would have to pass them, and Flora was hopeful she would get a good view of whoever was in the driving seat. He or she could be the murderer they were seeking. It was too much of a coincidence that the vehicle had pulled out of a lane close to Mullion the moment after they'd passed, then hugged their tail all the way back to Treleggan.

As Ralph swung the car into a space outside the village stores, the Humber at last overtook them, but in the end too fast for Flora to catch sight of the driver. She bit her lip in frustration. Then, miraculously, having swept past them, the vehicle swerved to a halt yards up the road and she watched as a man's figure emerged. Even from this distance, she could see that it was Lionel Gifford. He must have been at Mullion, must have followed them to the ruined site and spied on them. The persistent feeling she'd had there of being overlooked, of a spectator within that tangle of trees, was explained.

She watched now as he adjusted the wing mirrors on what looked to be a new car. Her suspicions that he was their villain and that Roger's papers lay behind the trouble in Treleggan were stronger than ever. Could Beatrice now join Mercy on the innocent list? It was Lionel who had come calling the day after his brother's death, Lionel who had broken in to Primrose Cottage, and Lionel who could easily have been behind the earlier attack at Mullion. On the surface, his motive was clear. In debt to some very unpleasant people, he must be desperate to find the will, to know there was money coming his way. Quite possibly desperate enough to attempt forgery, if the document disappointed. After murder, forgery would be a minor problem.

But there was a more intriguing possibility, wasn't there? That Lionel was searching for those documents out of fear, that he needed to suppress something, a dangerous secret buried deep in Roger's research. Had he followed them today to try again to stop them discovering that secret? What was it at Mullion that was so important?

'Will you excuse me one moment?' Flora opened the car door and clambered out.

'I thought—' Jack began, but she was already out of earshot.

Lionel looked up as he heard her approach, the customary

smirk on his face. 'Good afternoon, Miss... Steele, isn't it? Come to admire my car?'

He had his hands latched into his lapels. A brand new jacket by the look of it. Harris tweed, the favoured wear of the country gentleman. Was this the role he was adopting now?

'Why a different car?' Flora asked. 'You have your brother's to drive, surely.'

For a moment, the man's face held a surly expression, but was almost instantly replaced by a smile that didn't reach his eyes. 'I'm not allowed to drive Roger's car. Blasted formalities, eh? Not allowed to touch Roger's possessions, not until the will is settled. You should know the law, Miss Steele.'

'*You* couldn't have known the law or you wouldn't have come to Primrose Cottage asking for Roger's papers,' she pointed out.

'Oh, those.' He gave the suggestion of a sneer. 'Enough to send you to sleep, I'm pretty sure. Bound to be if Roger wrote them. Never knew such a boring fellow. I'm glad to say they hold no interest. The only paper I need is right here.' He patted his top pocket.

The remark was cryptic, but he didn't elaborate and was walking away towards the Chain and Anchor when Flora, keen to keep him talking, said, 'I hope the will can be settled soon. It would help us to know who owns the cottage and whether or not they wish to continue the lease. If they want us to leave, we'll have to start looking elsewhere. You haven't heard anything, I suppose?'

He stopped and walked back to her, the smirk back on his face. 'You'll have to learn patience, Miss Steele. The solicitors are dragging their feet, as they always do – spinning it out to grab a bigger fee. And that bitch is helping them.'

'I beg your pardon?'

'No need to beg. The woman *is* a bitch.' He moved closer to Flora, his eyes narrowing in spite. 'She's employed an expensive lawyer, you know. The fancy man must be footing the bill. Intends to fight the will, if it doesn't go her way. She's after inheriting the lot, always has been, but I'm crossing my fingers that she's going to be very, very disappointed.'

'I take it you're talking about your sister-in-law?' Flora couldn't pretend she didn't know to whom Lionel was referring. 'It's an unpleasant way to speak of her.'

'But more than appropriate. Beatrice Gifford *is* an unpleasant woman. She's a harridan. A man-eater. Beatrice, the man-eater,' he said with satisfaction. 'She left poor old Roger high and dry for some tuppenny ha'penny bloke and now she hasn't the wisp of a claim on him. She'll be lucky to get a cent.'

A crease marred Flora's forehead. 'If Mrs Gifford was still married to your brother when he died and he hadn't changed his will, then she'll be entitled to claim a share of his inheritance, if not all of it.'

'Changed his will?' Lionel looked taken aback. 'Who said anything about changing the will?'

'Your brother did, I believe.'

'Nah. He wouldn't do that. He may have threatened to, but he'd never have done it.' *Because you killed him before he could?* she asked herself silently. 'Any case, whatever the will says, I'll fight her all the way. In the meantime, things are OK with me. I've got this beauty to keep me company.' He slapped the bonnet of the shining black Humber.

And just where, Flora wondered, had he got the money for that?

Ralph was leaving for London the next morning and they said goodbye to him a short time later outside the Chain and Anchor, Flora having decided that she didn't after all need to buy from the village shop. There had been a half-hearted invitation on Ralph's part for them to join him at the pub for dinner, but Jack had said rather too quickly that Jessie would be at the cottage very soon, bringing their supper with her. Ralph had looked relieved, and that was that. Flora guessed that father and son had seen sufficient of each other for quite some time.

Walking into Primrose Cottage, she felt its walls close protectively around her. She was happy to be back. Jessie must have already visited and a casserole was in the oven. Flora lifted the lid and peeped, allowing herself to savour the contents.

'Beef stew with dumplings,' she called out to Jack, who was busy discarding muddy shoes and hanging his jacket on the curly coat stand that filled much of the tiny hall.

'Good.' He came into the kitchen. 'Ooh, yes, that smells delightful. Nearly ready, do you think?'

Flora nodded, her mind busy with the telephone call to Abbeymead that she'd decided she must make. That shadow of an idea she'd had at the site this afternoon continued to drift in and out and around her head, but still wouldn't quite form. It might have something to do with Lionel Gifford, though she was unsure. All she knew was that somehow it was connected to the ruins they'd explored today, connected to an event at the signals centre all those years ago that might have been discovered and recorded by Roger, unaware of the danger it contained.

Flora's only lead was the story of Thomas Martin and Alice was the one to talk to. She had known the Martins most of her life and, if there was anything to tell, to confess even, she would know. For years, she must have been the recipient of Mrs Martin's woes and, though Alice would be circumspect, Flora was certain she could prompt her friend to confide.

When to make the call was the problem, since she'd no wish for Jack to overhear her conversation. At best, he would make fun of her and, at worst, insist on her forgetting Mullion and erasing the place from her mind. It was obvious he'd done just that. He'd been peevish all day, showing little enthusiasm for the site they'd discovered. A secret signals centre and the possibility of a spy in the camp was of no interest to him, now that he'd decided to set his book in a Cornish community.

Was he right to dismiss Mullion from his mind? Jack's father had seen no mystery, had felt only nostalgia. For Ralph Carrington, the ruins they'd found meant only regret for a lost friendship. And Lionel? Flora wanted very much for Mullion to mean something to *him*, something that would implicate him, but she had to admit he might simply have been driving in the countryside this afternoon, enjoying his new acquisition.

Over supper, Jack had suggested she was in danger of letting spies become an obsession, and she supposed real life events might be colouring her view. In recent years, a huge spy scandal had rocked the nation: two of the Cambridge Spy Ring as it became known – Burgess and Maclean – had fled England only to reappear days later in Moscow. The dreadful news had been splashed across the newspapers for months. There might be an element of truth in Jack's accusation, she acknowledged, but it wasn't a Russian spy she had in mind. *Her* spy was definitely German.

It was after she'd decided she would have to pretend the need for a walk and use the telephone box on the village green that Flora had a stroke of luck. Instead of retiring to the sitting room after supper to read a book or listen to the wireless as he usually did, Jack made for the stairs.

'Do you mind if I work this evening?' he asked. 'I've wasted a whole day and I'm so far behind that I really can't afford to lose more time.'

'That's fine.' She tried to keep the eagerness from her voice. 'But you shouldn't consider it a wasted day. Not entirely. Think of all the atmosphere you soaked up.'

'I'm not just thinking it, I have it for company.' He gave his shirt sleeves a theatrical sniff.

'Go and work,' she encouraged. 'There's a programme I want to hear.'

As long as he never questioned her for details, she could telephone Abbeymead without discovery.

Alice answered immediately, delighted to hear from her young friend. 'How are you gettin' on, my love? What's the cottage like? What's the village like?'

Flora held up her free hand as though to ward off the barrage. 'Fine, Alice,' she said laughingly. 'All fine. Cornwall is beautiful and we're getting around – we've rowed on the Helford river, walked on the Lizard, seen Tintagel.' She was careful not to be too specific.

'And Mr Carr— Jack? He's doin' all right?'

'Jack is working upstairs at the moment.'

'The book goin' well, then?'

'It's been a slow start but I think he's on his way now.'

'And you're still good friends, I hope.'

Alice was fishing, Flora knew, and she was quick to shut the subject down. 'Why wouldn't we be?' she countered. 'But how are you?'

'Well enough, my love. No work at the Priory since you left, but I'm still helpin' Kate out at the Nook. Doin' a lot of bakin'. It keeps me busy and it means she don't have to work so hard.'

'She must be delighted to have your help.'

'I hope so. The girl's gradually comin' to terms with bein' a widow, but it can't be rushed.'

Bernie Mitchell had been a wretched partner, Flora reflected, yet that made little difference. Kate's sadness went deep.

'Alice,' she began tentatively, 'I need to talk to you about Abbeymead.'

'Are you missin' us already?' She could hear Alice's rumble of laughter.

'You know I am! But tell me, how's the All's Well doing? Is Sally coping?'

'More'n copin'. You've nothing to worry about, Flora love. The shop is doin' really well. That niece of mine has a head on her shoulders, I will say that. She had a leaflet printed and delivered round the village sayin' the bookshop is fully open and she'd love to see the villagers if they'd care to come in and meet her. And she held a tea and cake mornin' last Tuesday to entice the waverers. She says that sales have been excellent.'

Flora felt a stab of jealousy.

'You'll be real pleased with what she's done, I know, when you get back,' Alice finished hopefully.

'I'm sure I will.' Flora managed to sound as though she meant it. 'Please thank her for me.' She paused for a moment, then plunged in. 'There was something else, Alice. I wanted to ask you about Thomas Martin.'

There was a silence at the other end of the line. 'Why's that?' Alice asked eventually, sounding cautious.

'You mentioned him – do you remember? – just before we left Abbeymead, and his story stuck in my mind. I believe we're very near where your friend's son was stationed.'

She made a pretence of vagueness, not wanting Alice to guess the true reason behind her request.

'Well, I never! I'm not sure, though, what I can tell you about him. He was a lovely lad, clever, too. Passed his scholarship for the grammar school. Lord Edward helped with the fees, leastways that was the rumour in the village. When the war came, he didn't wait for conscription but volunteered. Barely eighteen he was. He was that kind of young man. Honourable, upstandin', you know what I mean. The army soon cottoned on to how intelligent he was and trained him in signals. That's what his mother said. She was so proud of him. Broke her heart when he disappeared. Still breakin' her heart, if you ask me.'

'The Martins had no idea where he might have gone?' She could imagine Alice shaking her head at the question.

'No idea whatsoever. Not that Lily Martin has ever given up hope, poor lady. She's sure that he's still alive. Says it all the time. I don't say anythin' back but I can't believe it. Thomas was a good son, he loved his mother dearly. He wouldn't have let her grieve unnecessarily. If he was still alive, he'd have made contact, no matter what the rumours said he'd done. Not that I believe he did anythin' bad,' she ended firmly.

'Did the Martins never think of making enquiries?'

'How d'you mean?'

'By employing a private investigator, for instance. I'm sure Lord Edward would have helped pay for it.'

'They wouldn't do that!' Alice sounded shocked. 'It would be makin' private things public. Sayin' there was something to investigate.'

Flora didn't follow her friend's reasoning, but said gently, 'It would have been a way of giving them certainty. An investigator could have interviewed people who knew Thomas in the army, who worked with him just before he vanished. But it's not too late to do it. Some of those men must still be alive and maybe could throw light on his disappearance.'

'I dunno about that. Mrs Martin don't want the army mentioned, won't think about Thomas's time in the war. I don't believe the soldiers were kind when they visited to tell her that Thomas had gone missin'. She wants to remember her son as he was before he left home, and you can understand that.'

'He must have written to his mother during his years in the army,' Flora tried. 'It seems strange that he never mentioned the men he was working alongside.'

'I don't think he wrote that often. Leastways, not many letters got through. But who do you mean?'

'He worked very closely with someone called Randy Paradis – he was a Canadian – and a Ronnie Brooks. There was a Lofty Price, too. He was the corporal in charge of the operations unit where Thomas worked.'

She hoped Alice wouldn't ask how she'd arrived at these names – having to confess that Jack's father had told her, that he'd worked in the same signals unit as Thomas, could give the game away and lead Alice to guess that Flora was once more involved in something she shouldn't be. Fortunately, her friend was too engrossed in marvelling at the Canadian's exotic name to ask.

Eventually, Alice said, 'I've not heard tell of any of these.'

'Could you perhaps ask Mrs Martin?'

Alice sounded doubtful. 'I don't like stirrin' up painful memories, Flora.'

'I understand, but if you could do it casually, it might not be hurtful. You could say that you'd seen a newspaper article about the work of signals centres in the war and that Thomas's unit was singled out for special praise. If you mentioned a few names, you could see if Mrs Martin recognised any of them from Thomas's letters.'

'But I haven't got a newspaper article.'

'I know, Alice,' she said as patiently as she could. 'I'm suggesting you make it up. Mrs Martin will either recognise the names or she won't. One or other of those men could have appeared in his letters home, and could still be around to throw light on what happened to Thomas. If we had more details, we might be able to trace them.'

'Why do you want to know, Flora?' There was an edge to Alice's voice as well as curiosity. It was the question Flora hadn't wanted to answer.

'I feel sorry for the Martins,' was all she could say.

20

Jack worked late that evening; Flora could still hear the tap of typewriter keys as she made ready for bed. Snuggling beneath the covers, she realised how weary she felt, tired not so much by the expedition to Mullion but by the sheer tension of the day. Tomorrow, Ralph Carrington would be on his way to London and hopefully Jack would be in a better mood.

He was, it seemed, when he appeared in the kitchen the next morning just as she was reaching to the top shelf for a box of cornflakes.

'Here, let me do that.'

She turned at his voice, taking in the fresh shirt and trousers, enjoying the smell of cedar and lime as he came close.

'How are you?' Her question was tentative.

'Good,' he said shortly, then seemed to relent. 'I'm well on my way with the book – and sorry about yesterday.'

Flora looked directly into a pair of grey eyes that were no longer stormy.

'I was a grump.'

'You were,' she agreed, rattling bowls and plates onto the table.

'It's my father,' he said awkwardly. 'He has a bad effect on me.'

'No, really? I'd never have guessed.'

Jack gave a puff of air. 'Let's forget Ralph Carrington. He'll be on his way to London by now, or will be very soon. If my memory serves me right, we're off to Falmouth. And the sun is shining.'

'So it is. And there's hardly any breeze. I won't get seasick on the ferry.' She looked out of the kitchen window at the meadow of grass where hardly a blade moved. 'Any plans for when we get there?' She tried to sound indifferent.

'We can explore – but nowhere near Roger Gifford's solicitors.'

Flora gave up. She couldn't fool him and was reduced to pleading. 'Only a brief call, I promise. Please.'

'It's pointless. They won't tell you a thing and in any case why are you still interested? I thought Roger's research was now the hot topic rather than the will.'

'They're both hot topics, as you call them, and either could be the reason for Roger's death. The solicitors could be holding everything that's important – everything that might finally unmask our murderer. You were interested once,' she pointed out, taking two slices of toast from under the grill and lopping them onto a plate.

'Maybe, but it's become a distraction now and I need to get on with this book. Today's visit to Falmouth is the last jaunt I'm allowing myself for a while. When I'm a bit further on, I'll prob-ably take a trip to the villages around Land's End, but as for this investigation, it's officially parked.'

'But not by me,' she said stubbornly.

He sat down at the table, fixing her with a severe look. 'Why is it so important to you?'

'Because Roger Gifford seems to have been a decent man

and he's dead and no one has been charged with his murder, nor likely to be at the pace the police are moving.'

'You can't be certain. You've no way of knowing how they're getting on.'

'We've given them only the briefest of statements, but have they come back to interview us again? Have they spoken to Jessie, Roger's housekeeper for years? Have they interviewed the people likely to benefit from his will? Have they talked to anyone in the village? There's a big loud "no" to all those questions.'

Jack pushed his cereal bowl to one side and reached for the toast. 'That's unfair. We don't know what's going on behind the scenes.'

'I can hazard a very good guess. And it's not just Roger, is it? Someone is out to hurt us, too. Don't forget the letter you received.'

'I haven't forgotten, but there's been nothing since. And if there *is* someone targeting us, it's because we've been poking around instead of leaving matters to the police.'

You been stirrin' things up, Mercy Dearlove had said. *Things best left in the past, mebbe.*

She had spoken truly and Flora recognised the danger, but it seemed to her cowardly not to meet it face on. 'The solicitors?' she asked again.

'OK, if it makes you happy we'll make a brief call. Once they tell you what I know they'll tell you, that's it.'

'Which is?'

'That they don't divulge a client's business, that Gifford's affairs are confidential. Once you've got the message and believed it, we'll explore the town. Did you check on the times of the ferry?'

'I forgot to ask Jessie.'

'That's where you're lucky. I did check,' he said smugly. 'They're listed on one of the leaflets Roger left for his visitors.

We saw the quay when we rowed down the river and, if we're quick, we'll catch the ten o'clock boat. Eat up!'

The *May Queen* had already docked when they arrived on the quayside, Flora still buttoning her cardigan and fastening her handbag. Jack rushed to the booth to buy their tickets and they managed to skip aboard just before the barrier came down, shutting off the gangway. The ferry was busy, the fine weather having tempted people out and about, but they found a quiet bench at the rear of the boat and settled to enjoy the thirty-minute trip north, along the coastline and into the Fal estuary that formed a large navigable channel all the way from Falmouth to Truro.

Flora gazed around her with appreciation. Beneath a cloudless sky, the world was filled with colour this morning: green hills tumbling towards a bay of deep blue, small boats riding at anchor, their sails every colour of the rainbow, charming fishing villages with whitewashed cottages that shimmered in the sun.

'Why have we changed direction?' she asked, suddenly aware of the boat veering to the right. 'And what's that?' She pointed towards the hill they were steaming past, a ruined building at its summit.

'The ferry crosses the Carrick Roads to collect passengers from St Mawes before it goes on to Falmouth. And that's St Mawes castle, or what's left of it,' Jack said authoritatively. 'If you look back across the estuary to where we'll be heading, you can see Pendennis Castle. Both of them built by Henry the Eighth for defence.'

'Where do you get all this?'

'From books, Flora. Remember them?' he teased.

She would have enjoyed sailing for longer but very soon they were pulling into the square of Falmouth harbour, the

ferry weaving its way to the pier where people were already
forming a line to board for the return trip.

Once they'd disembarked, she walked straight to the ticket
office, pulling out the letter she'd stored away and showing the
address to the man behind his glass partition.

'Market Street,' he read aloud. 'Easy enough. Walk straight
on until you get to the main road, then turn left. Dunno the way
the numbers run, but you'll find it OK.'

Jack caught up with her as she was thanking her informant.
'I'd like to visit the fortress,' he said. 'I reckon there'll be some
wartime stuff to see. Maybe my first victim could take a day trip
to Falmouth and meet his death on the ramparts.'

'Before he does, we need to walk to Market Street.' She
linked her arm in his.

Jack looked resigned but fell into step with her, a short walk
along Market Street taking them to the number that appeared
on the firm's letterhead. The ground floor was home to an opti-
cian's, but a side door sported various brass plaques announcing
the offices above. Sadler and Sadler was on the third floor and,
without the benefit of a lift, they puffed their way up the stairs
and, slightly breathless, walked through the glass door to the
office.

A young woman with a head of ginger curls was at the
reception desk, talking on the telephone. Her conversation
finished, she flashed them a professional smile.

'Good morning. Can I help you?'

'I hope so.' Flora stepped forward, leaving Jack to hover in
the background. She gave the girl what she hoped was her
warmest smile. 'Could we speak to' – she consulted the letter –
'to Mr Alan Sadler please?'

'Do you have an appointment?' The receptionist looked
puzzled.

'Well, no, but we're happy to wait. It's important we see Mr
Sadler.'

'I'm afraid he's out of the office today and his diary for the rest of the week is very full.'

'Perhaps *you* can help then.' Flora was undefeated. 'I imagine you must know a good deal about the business.'

'I'll certainly try.' The girl looked gratified.

'We have a problem,' Flora began. 'We're renting a cottage from Mr Roger Gifford, or we were renting it. You'll know that Mr Gifford has died and, as he was one of your clients, we're hoping you can give us some information.'

The ginger curls shook a little. 'I'm sorry, but I don't understand.'

'It's quite simple. We rented a cottage from Mr Gifford and we're naturally a little concerned for the future. The new owner of Primrose Cottage may wish to retain it for their own use, in which case our tenancy agreement will be void and we'll be forced to look for other accommodation. Do you know who the new owner is? Has the will been read yet?'

'I'm afraid I'm not at liberty to say.'

Flora battled on. 'I understand you have to maintain professional discretion, Miss' – she searched for a name, but drew a blank – 'but we do need to know. You won't realise, of course, but there are rumours in the village – in Treleggan – that Mr Gifford changed his will at the last moment. If that's the case, it could affect us badly. If, for instance, the new heir turns out to be someone who knows nothing about the cottage being rented out.' She was improvising wildly. 'As I say, we're concerned.' It was a limp finish.

Ginger curls stared at her but said nothing.

'Well, did Mr Gifford change his will?' Flora asked bluntly.

'I'm sorry but I'm not at liberty to say.'

'So this appointment' – she waved the letter under the girl's nose – 'wasn't to change his will? Was it perhaps to arrange storage for certain papers?'

'I'm sorry, I'm not at liberty to say.'

'That's not too helpful.' Flora's smile tightened. 'Still, while we're here, perhaps you can tell us where we can find Mrs Gifford? We'd like to offer our condolences. You'll have her address, I imagine.' She looked pointedly at the brand-new Rolodex sitting squarely on the reception desk. 'No, don't tell me, you're not at liberty to say.'

The girl gave a sheepish smile. 'Thank you for understanding.'

'Told you,' Jack whispered in her ear, as they walked towards the door.

Halfway there, Flora stopped, clutching at her stomach and emitting a loud groan. The girl started up. 'Are you all right?' she asked anxiously, leaning across the desk.

'No,' Flora panted. 'I'm sorry. This bug – I thought I was clear of it or I'd never have ventured out today but... do you have a bathroom I could use? Could you take me there?'

'Yes...' the girl had begun to slide around the desk, 'but really I shouldn't leave reception.'

Flora gave another loud groan. 'Please, help me...' She reached out a hand for support and ginger curls took it.

Flora had been conscious of Jack watching her performance with an amused look, but she needed him to do something. She waggled her eyebrows as she passed him and glared fiercely at the Rolodex.

Minutes later, she reappeared, seemingly restored to health and talking effusively. 'Thank you so much. I feel so much better now. It must have been the bug's dying gasp that got me.'

'Don't mention it.' Hastily, the girl opened the glass door for them and ushered them towards the staircase as quickly as she could.

Once back on the pavement, Flora asked urgently, 'Did you get it?'

He nodded. 'I think what I've just done is illegal.'

'Probably, but no point in fussing. At least we have an address.'

'*You* have an address,' he corrected. 'I don't want to know what you intend to do with it.'

'We'll walk up to Pendennis Castle,' she said placatingly. 'You can look for Henry and I'll decide about the address.'

'I have a horrible feeling I know exactly what that will be.'

Her hazel eyes sparkled. 'I imagine you do,' she said saucily.

It was a long walk through the town to reach the grey stone fortress that dominated the grassy headland, but once they'd climbed to the castle entrance, the panorama below made the effort worthwhile. Castle Beach was immediately beneath and, further afield, large swathes of sand stretched into the distance, the most prestigious hotels in the town clustered around a series of bays.

Flora shielded her eyes, pointing to the ferry pier they'd left. 'Look how far we've walked. The harbour is on the other side of the town.'

'Can I tempt you to walk a bit further and climb to the keep? It's the oldest part of the fortress – I'd say, its very heart. It's a fair climb but we can stop halfway for a breather. There's an exhibition that looks interesting.'

'What exhibition? I didn't see any notice.'

'We passed a board at the entrance. You were too busy gazing around. It mentioned a reconstruction of what life in the castle was like over the ages, including during the last war. It could be helpful.'

Flora nodded. 'Especially if your victim is to die on the ramparts!'

She was happy enough to climb the long, winding staircase that took them past various gun rooms, in and out of turrets, and into the exhibition that Jack had mentioned.

'I didn't know a lot of this stuff,' he said, after studying a large exhibit for some time. 'And I'm surprised. The castle was rearmed at the beginning of the war with long-range artillery. I guess it was important in the run-up to the invasion. It would be a defence against E-boats. German fast attack craft,' he added, when Flora looked puzzled.

Stifling a small yawn, she drifted to an earlier section of the exhibition, finding the founding of the fortress and its beginnings more absorbing. When Tudor life began to pall, she waited patiently for Jack. He had a real interest in the castle's more recent history and it was good to see him so much happier today.

Eventually, though, she was moved to ask, 'Can we carry on now?'

He turned and grinned at her. 'Am I being a bore?'

'A war bore,' she confirmed. 'But let's go. It will be lunch before we know it.'

They were in for another long climb before they reached the keep and its large grassy expanse. Walking through the final archway, Flora spread her arms, savouring the welcome freshness after the cramped, dank interior. She strolled over to what she thought must once have been a gun platform and looked out across the town: it was a busy scene. A cluster of roofs, the several harbours and their adjoining docks, the small boats, the large ships, and always the magnificent backdrop of the sea.

'This is a wonderful view,' she said to Jack who'd joined her on the platform. 'One that's been here for centuries. It's amazing, isn't it, to imagine the Falmouth Packet setting off from the harbour down there, to deliver mail around the world?'

'It's certainly a thought.' He was taking in the view, but she could feel him fidgety beside her.

'Would you mind if I nipped back to the exhibition to check on something?' he asked.

She shook her head. 'If you need to, go. I'm happy enough here.'

'I won't be long,' he promised, and disappeared back down the stone staircase.

Flora's gaze rested on the beach below. Several families had set up camp on the sand, and, though it was only May, there were a few brave souls who had taken the plunge and were swimming in what must still be very cold water. But the sun shone, the sea glittered, and children danced in and out of the surf.

Flora was smiling at the happy scene below when she sensed a movement. Then felt hot breath touch her neck. She tried to turn round and see who was behind her, standing far too close, but found herself pushed against the parapet, blocked in the narrow gun embrasure with no way out. Looking down over the waist-high wall, she saw the granite ramparts fall sheerly to the beach.

Her knuckles turned white as she gripped the wall's stone coping, and small drops of sweat broke out on her forehead. Stay calm, she counselled herself. Push back hard and whoever this is will give way. But when she forced her body backwards, the intruder pushed her even harder against the wall and, despite her determination not to panic, a snake of pure fear broke loose and slid a pathway through her body.

Struggling to speak, she began, 'Don't—' but could manage only a whisper before her voice died altogether.

There was silence, but for the sound of breathing. Harsh, guttural breathing. The moment could have lasted only seconds, though it felt a lifetime, before a familiar sound drifted towards her. Jack! Thank God!

'I'm glad I went back,' he was saying. 'I managed a chat with the chap on duty – he was here during the war – and told some great stories.'

His voice released her from the spell in which she'd been

caught and turning, she almost ran at him, hardly registering the fact that they were alone.

'Hey, what's the matter?' He put his arm around her. 'What's got you scared?'

She was about to answer him when, looking over her head, Jack said in an entirely different voice, 'Mr Penrose! Fancy seeing you in Falmouth.'

Flora moved to one side and turned to look. A man was rounding the keep wall. Was this the man who'd threatened her? He couldn't be. Jack would have seen him when he emerged from the staircase. Would have seen him forcing her against the rampart. At times, her friend could move like a cat and the man walking towards them would not have had time to move to the shelter of the keep. Had there been another figure, perhaps, another man? Could she ask this Mr Penrose if he'd seen someone? Or had she dreamt the whole encounter?

The stranger was looking puzzled. 'Mr...'

'Carrington,' Jack supplied. 'We met at the library. Have you left Miss Hodges in charge today?'

Penrose smiled. 'I have – I've escaped. I'm afraid I couldn't resist this wonderful spring weather.'

'Flora, this is Mr Penrose from Helston Library. I don't believe you ever met him. Mr Penrose, my friend, Flora Steele.'

He held out his hand and she took it with only the glimmer of a smile.

'Officially, I'm on library business,' Penrose confided. 'I have a meeting with my colleague – head librarian here in Falmouth. But on this occasion duty and pleasure coincide. I hope your stay in Cornwall is going well.'

'We're enjoying it very much. Aren't we, Flora?' Jack asked meaningfully.

'Yes, it's brilliant,' she murmured.

'That's good to know. And good that you've come to Pendennis today. The castle is a wonderful example of Tudor engineering.' He beamed at them. 'I must be off, though. Duty calls. I'll leave you to enjoy the view. It's nice meeting you again, Mr Carrington.'

Flora watched him as he disappeared down the stone staircase, then realised that Jack was looking at her with concern.

'Are you all right? You were very short with him and your face looks ghostly. Your freckles have almost disappeared.'

'I had a shock, that's all.'

'What kind of shock?'

'Someone... someone came up behind me. I didn't hear them until they were standing inches away. I felt trapped in that enclosure. I couldn't seem to move and the only way out was down.'

'Now, there's a thought.'

'What?'

'The book. My victim could be corralled in one of the gun embrasures.'

'You really take the biscuit, Jack. I'm scared half out of my wits and all you care about is your story.'

'You're being silly. What was there to scare you? You've obviously been reading too many crime novels!'

When she said nothing, he took her hand and pulled her towards the stairs. 'I'm starving. Fancy finding a pasty?'

21

Jack might make light of her fears, but Flora couldn't. She had felt ambushed, squashed into a confined space and pushed hard against a retaining wall that barely covered her thighs. Below, a dizzying drop to the rocks and the beach beyond. It would have been the easiest thing in the world for a predator to pick her up – she wasn't the most solidly built female – and tip her over that wall. Yet, when she'd finally managed to wriggle free, there had been only Jack standing feet away and, appearing around the side of the keep, Mr Penrose, Helston's chief librarian and pillar of the community. They must have arrived within seconds of each other, and there had been no one else in sight. Was it possible for the man, whose breath she'd felt on her neck – and she was sure it had been a man, she'd sensed his bulk, felt the force of his body – to have disappeared before Jack and his companion spotted him?

And if he had, who was he? Lionel Gifford again? The man had the transport and could easily have got to the castle. Could it have been him or was she going mad? It wasn't a question she asked herself lightly. It seemed that every day since they'd arrived in Cornwall had brought a new test for her nerves.

Walking back into the town in search of a café, Flora's eyes scanned every face they passed, hoping one of them might be Lionel's. Then she would have her answer. There would be too much circumstantial evidence to suggest anyone else was behind Roger's murder and the subsequent threats that she and Jack had faced.

Intent on watching faces, she felt confused when Jack pulled her to a stop and pointed to a bookshop they were passing. Dougal's Cave, she read. He was smiling at her and she could see why – it was one of the quirkiest shop windows she'd ever seen. A replica of a seaside cave filled the entire space, with books displayed on various ledges, or springing from false rock pools or laced to lengths of rope hanging from the roof – standing in for stalactites, she supposed. Shrimping nets had been placed in each corner and beside them a collection of buckets filled to the brim with what looked like glossy travel guides.

'Give you any ideas?' Jack asked.

'It's certainly novel,' she conceded, 'though I can't see it working in Abbeymead.'

No ideas, but what Dougal's Cave had done was waken a painful homesickness, made far worse by the fear she'd experienced. She was suddenly desperate to be back in Sussex. Back at the All's Well, following her daily routine: unpacking parcels, arranging bookshelves, greeting customers, tweaking window displays. Flora wanted to be home.

'Let's have a quick lunch,' she said, tugging at his arm, 'and find Mrs Gifford.'

Beatrice Gifford might be the key to solving the murder and allow her to enjoy what remained of their stay in Cornwall. Her eagerness to speak to the woman grew stronger with every step. Lionel's sister-in-law would know every last discreditable detail about him and would likely be glad to share it.

Don't get carried away, though, she counselled herself.

There was the inconvenient truth that Beatrice herself was a suspect. She stood to gain from her husband's will as much as Lionel and it was a fact that the woman had quarrelled badly with Roger the very day they'd arrived in Treleggan, hours before Flora found his body in the orchard.

Jack was halfway through his second pasty before he said, 'If you're really still intent on bearding the ghastly Beatrice, Wendron Gardens was the address on the file. It sounds a posh neighbourhood.'

Flora put down her teacup with a clunk. 'I definitely want to speak to her. More than ever. Wendron Gardens shouldn't be difficult to find. The waitress will probably know the road.' She looked around for a black dress and white pinafore, then got to her feet ready to walk to the counter.

Jack put out a detaining hand. 'Sit down, I'll ask the girl. You look washed out.'

At last, some acknowledgement of the fright she'd had.

On enquiry, Wendron Gardens was found to be in the newer part of town, a fair stretch from the harbour area but, after a substantial lunch, they were glad of a brisk walk. It got them there in record time. Turning the corner into the road, Flora thought the street glowed with newness: flawless brick-work, fresh-smelling paint, shining slate roofs and, in front of each box-like dwelling, a manicured square of grass.

'Our landlord must still have been putting his hand in his pocket,' Jack observed. 'A house like this wouldn't come cheap, even if Beatrice is only renting.'

'Have you considered she might actually earn her own living?' Flora asked crossly. It was annoying that Jack automati-cally assumed a married woman was there to be kept.

'Somehow I doubt work has too much appeal for Beatrice,' he said.

In truth, Flora doubted it, too, and in a burst of honesty,

said, 'She has a fancy man – according to Lionel. Perhaps he's the one who pays.'

'Flora Steele, have you been consorting with the enemy?' His eyes were alight with amusement.

'Only for a few minutes, in the high street on our way back from Mullion, and it was a useful consorting. Lionel hates his sister-in-law. He called her a harridan and is convinced she's after Roger's money for herself.'

'That makes two of them.'

'Except that Lionel has money, hasn't he? Apparently out of the blue. That was a brand-new car he was driving.'

'Robbery maybe? Doing a bit more breaking and entering?'

'Nothing went missing at the cottage, apart from a single knife, and somehow I can't see Lionel as a serial burglar. It would require too much effort.'

Jack glanced at the house numbers they were passing. 'Forty-seven must be on the other side, a little way up.'

'There was something else that Lionel said, after the diatribe about Beatrice. Something odd. He's been searching for Roger's documents, right?'

'And not found them.'

'Exactly, but yesterday he told me he had the one piece of paper that mattered and the rest didn't interest him. He called them boring.'

'Which is probably correct.'

'But why, out of all of those papers, is this one piece significant?'

'Perhaps the former Mrs Gifford can tell us. Here's the house. Will you ring or shall I?'

'She's still Mrs Gifford, as far as we know,' Flora warned.

Beatrice Gifford came to the door on the second ring.

'I don't buy from the doorstep,' she snapped, her hair a rigid puffball framing a face that was trying too hard. Flora noticed a smudge where the woman's make-up had run. She seemed to

have been crying, but looking into those hard eyes it was difficult to imagine a tear ever issuing from them.

'We're not selling,' Flora said quickly, as the woman went to
shut the door in her face. 'We wondered if we could talk to you,
Mrs Gifford, about the cottage we're renting in Treleggan –
Primrose Cottage.'

The information had Beatrice look uncertain. 'The solicitors—' she began.

'We've called on them, but they weren't able to help.'

'They're never able to help,' she snapped again. There was
an ungracious sigh. 'You'd better come in.'

She led the way into a sitting room drowning in beige,
except for a small footstool that had dared dress itself in a
vibrant green.

'Well?' Beatrice stood and glared at them. There was no
offer to sit down.

'This is a beautiful room,' Flora said, steadfastly ignoring
Jack's grimace, 'and your garden. What an array of spring
flowers!'

'It's not mine. The house. The garden.' She looked as if she
was about to say more, but then demanded abruptly, 'What
exactly do you want with me?'

'The house we're living in isn't ours either,' Flora
responded, trying to establish a smidgen of communality, 'and
we were hoping you might set our minds at rest. Our tenancy
agreement was signed by Mr Gifford, but now that he's—'

'What on earth do you mean? Set your mind at rest?'

'As the future owner of Primrose Cottage. At least, we
presume so,' Jack said. 'We realise it's early days and there's the
matter of probate, but if you already know what you intend,
whether you'll want to continue having tenants or you'd prefer
to sell the cottage, and that would be quite understandable,' he
added smoothly, 'it would help us enormously. We'd know
whether or not we need to start looking for somewhere else.'

Beatrice wore a stony expression. 'I have absolutely no idea who will be the owner of Primrose Cottage, let alone what they'll want to do with it.'

'But surely—' Flora began.

'Except,' Beatrice continued in the same expressionless voice, 'that it won't belong to me. Nor the beautiful Georgian house I personally chose when I married. Nor anything that Roger ever possessed.'

Flora frowned. 'If you're certain, though it seems a little... odd.'

'Not if you knew Roger Gifford. A vindictive man. Even more vindictive than that spiv of a brother. Roger has made quite sure that I inherit nothing.'

For an instant, Beatrice's mask slipped, and eyes weary of the world looked out of a face that was crushed.

'I'm so sorry.' Flora felt a moment of true compassion. 'The solicitors have definitely confirmed that's the case?'

'Solicitors? They confirm nothing. They're like the three wise monkeys. I had it from Roger himself. At Primrose Cottage, strangely enough. He wanted to meet me there as it was neutral ground. I ask you, what ground that Roger owned could ever be neutral? He told me to my face. I won't divorce you, but I have the right to leave my possessions where I will.'

'Was that the day we arrived in Treleggan?'

'It must have been. Yes, it was. Roger got into one of his neurotic panics when he heard a car outside. Forced me to make myself scarce by lumbering through that ridiculous wilderness to the rear gate. You weren't to see me, weren't to know what a complete and utter heel he was. You won't go without, that's what he claimed. You'll have an easy enough life. Someone else can take care of you now. Ha! As if Derek ever took care of anyone but himself.'

Derek, Flora presumed, was the fancy man.

'I've changed my will, that's what he told me,' Beatrice

continued, 'as calmly as though he were announcing the weather forecast. I've changed my will and you are no longer part of it. Then what does he do,' she finished bitterly, 'but die before I can persuade him to think again.'

'Would he have thought again, do you think?' Flora was engrossed in this story of marital anguish.

Beatrice considered, her head to one side, the puffball of hair unmoving. 'In time, maybe, when he saw what a wretched state I've been reduced to. But not then. Not at that moment. He was adamant.'

'He must have told you the day before he died,' Jack put in.

'Ironic, isn't it?'

'Forgive me for asking, but this house,' Flora said cautiously, 'it's very smart and this seems to be a good neighbourhood. You don't look exactly wretched.'

'Don't I? What does wretched look like, little girl? I have until the weekend to pack my bags. I'm being thrown out for a younger model.'

Flora was truly shocked. 'Have you nowhere to go? Will you be homeless?'

'That's the general idea,' Beatrice said bitterly.

'I know you aren't the best of friends...' – Flora sounded even more cautious – 'but couldn't Lionel Gifford help? For a few days, at least. There must be a spare bed at River House.'

'That creep! I wouldn't ask him if I was down to my last sixpence which, as it happens, I am. But if he's still occupying River House, he won't be for much longer. Sadler and Sadler are hopeless at getting anything done, but they do know how to say no. Gifford will be made to leave – until the will is proven.'

'If Roger changed his will before he died, as you believe, would it have favoured his brother, do you think?'

Beatrice shrugged. 'Lionel and he were always at odds. You couldn't have had two more different people as brothers.' Her mouth twisted horribly. 'But who knows? I had a blazing row with Roger that last evening and he wasn't going to make me privy to the will's contents. I've hired a decent lawyer, he'll be paid on results, and whatever this new document says, I'll fight it all the way. I may not benefit from Roger's money, but I'll do everything in my power to ensure that little rat, Lionel, doesn't either.' There was venom in her voice.

'And your immediate plans?' Flora dared to ask.

'I have a sister in Exeter, not that she's anything like a true sister. But, grudgingly, she's offered me her spare bedroom. I'm catching the train there tomorrow. The new little tart is eager to move in, I understand, and I wouldn't want to spoil Derek's pleasure.'

These last words were almost spat and, instinctively, Flora turned towards the door, desperate to shake herself free of the woman's coruscating presence. A hasty word of thanks from the hallway and she and Jack let themselves out of the house.

'Phew!' he said, as they retraced their steps along Wendron Gardens. 'Lionel was right about one thing. She is a harridan. A spitting viper of a woman.'

'But sad, too. She'd been crying and I bet she's crying now. A spare bedroom in an unfriendly house in Exeter doesn't sound much fun.'

'The wages of sin.' He wagged his finger at her.

'Don't you have any finer feelings?'

'Not for women who betray their husbands, I don't.'

'Or women who betray their fiancés,' she said knowingly, and felt him glare at her.

'So what did we learn?' His question was terse.

'That Roger had already changed his will when Beatrice had the stand-up row with him, which means there was no point in her killing him.'

'Unless she met him early the next morning, hoping to persuade him to think again, and she was so furious at what he'd done that she killed him.'

'She would have had to be carrying a knife,' Flora said. 'Highly unlikely if the meeting was supposed to cajole him into changing his mind. It would be in her interest to keep Roger alive.'

'She had less reason to kill than Lionel, certainly... I think we turn here if we want to get back to the ferry.' He steered her into an adjoining street. 'She definitely knew the will had been changed, while Lionel probably didn't.'

'When I spoke to Lionel in the high street, he was adamant his brother would never do such a thing. Yet, he must have had an inkling he was in for bad news. Wouldn't Roger have hinted at some point that he was about to change his life and, along with it, his will? And it's possible Lionel knew about the solicitor's appointment. If he put two and two together and assumed the appointment was for Roger to sign a new will, he'd want his brother dead before that day came round.'

Jack nodded agreement. 'It's looking more and more as though it's the will that's key to this killing. You might have to say goodbye to Roger's research.'

'Such a pity! It's far more interesting as a motive for murder than common or garden will-changing.'

'At least,' Jack murmured, as they retraced their steps to the quayside, 'we know your Mercy Dearlove was telling the truth when she said she heard Beatrice quarrelling with her husband the day we arrived.'

'I never doubted her and neither would you, if you'd met her. But it still begs one very important question.'

Flora came to a halt outside the ticket booth she'd stopped at earlier.

'The solicitor's appointment I found in that letter wasn't to set a divorce in motion because Roger didn't intend to end the marriage – we've just heard Beatrice confirm it. And it wasn't to change the will because we know now that it had already been changed. So why *did* Roger want to see his solicitors?'

22

They arrived back at Primrose Cottage to find Constable Hoskins at the front door. He turned as he heard the garden gate click, his face clearing.

'Afternoon, folks. I were just about to give you up.'

'I hope not – if you're bringing us news,' Flora said.

Jack found his key and ushered the young man over the threshold. There was a momentary hustling and scuffling as they manoeuvred around each other in the narrow space, hanging up jackets, slipping off outdoor shoes, but then Jack fought himself free and showed the policeman into the sitting room.

'Have you caught him then?' he asked. 'Or her?'

Will looked blank.

'Whoever ended Mr Gifford's life,' Jack prompted.

Will's fresh face brightened. 'Ah, I see. Not yet. Sorry. Maybe soon, though. I've to call on everyone in Treleggan – and beyond.'

'There's been a development?' Flora asked eagerly.

The constable shifted from one foot to the other. 'I s'pose

you'd call it that.' He screwed up his face, as though thinking it through.

'So what is it?' she asked. 'Why have you been asked to call?'

'I'm not s'posed to say much – it's Inspector Mallory who's in charge.'

'In charge!' Flora gave an audible snort. 'It's not what I'd call it. The inspector is as speedy as a tortoise and once you let the trail go cold, you might as well give up.'

Will began nervously to finger the helmet he had taken off and Jack took pity on him.

'Of course, you can't tell us everything,' he said soothingly, 'but perhaps why you called today?'

The boy look relieved. 'I were arsked to make a list of anyone from round 'ere – that's Treleggan and the farms and the small 'oldings – who's been in the army or navy. I've to call on every one of 'em and find out what they were doin' when poor Mr Roger... passed away.'

'Right, I see.' Jack looked slightly puzzled. 'You know that we aren't from around here,' he reminded the officer gently.

'No, sorry. It's Mr Gifford I'm lookin' fer. Mr Lionel, that is. He's on the list but he weren't at River House when I called and I thought mebbe he were 'ere.'

'Well, he's not,' Flora said shortly. 'And why on earth are you calling on people a week too late? To ask them what they were doing on a day they no longer remember?'

Jack couldn't blame her for sounding exasperated. This investigation was beginning to look half-baked. True, they were getting only scraps of information from a police constable who had little to do with the murder hunt, but still... progress seemed painfully slow.

'Let's hope when you get to ask your questions, they produce a result,' he said mildly. 'Before the next body appears.'

Jack showed the boy to the front door, exchanging a few

words with him before he returned to the sitting room and found Flora staring out of the window at the meadow beyond, arms wrapped tightly around her body.

'You were a bit harsh on him,' he remarked. 'He's just a boy.'

'What's the point of interviewing local men just because they've been in the services? It will take forever and yield, what, precisely?'

'What you don't know is that the police have the pathologist's report now. The chap reckoned that Roger's throat was cut by someone who knew what they were doing. Someone who'd had training in warfare.'

'Will Hoskins told you that?'

Jack smiled slyly. 'Sometimes, Flora, you need subtlety.'

'It's still rubbish. How subtle is calling on half of Helford? Nearly every man in the country under fifty was in the services.' Flora's voice filled with disappointment.

'It's possible it might turn up something.'

'"Possible", "might", "something" – the words themselves suggest how hopeless it is. They should grill Lionel Gifford, not just speak to him, that's what they need to do. And after him, Beatrice.'

'Beatrice is back in the frame then?'

Flora sank into a fireside chair. 'I was thinking about it on the ferry back. Money is what links them, money they won't have if Roger really has changed his will. But we've only Beatrice's word that, when she quarrelled with Roger, he'd already carried out his threat. What if he hadn't? The quarrel could easily have been over his plans to do so. Beatrice isn't a trustworthy woman – she'd happily lie, I'm sure, to save her skin. And lie to implicate her brother-in-law. To my mind, they're both credible suspects, so why is the inspector and his team wasting time searching for a man who knows how to cut throats? I can't imagine it's that difficult.'

'You'd be surprised.'

She looked up, staring at him. 'Have you—'

'Mallory's probably still got it in mind that the murder was a random act,' Jack said swiftly. 'Someone trying to steal from Primrose Cottage who was disturbed by its owner and went on to kill him.'

'A random murder – that's such nonsense! Roger's killing has to have been premeditated. He was in the orchard very early that morning, and he wouldn't have gone there unless he was lured. And why lure him? You can dredge up an explanation – it was neutral ground in which to talk reasonably, patch up the arguments he had with either Lionel or Beatrice. But then why go to a meeting armed with a knife? Why choose dawn when no one else was around, unless you had the clear intention to kill and wanted to ensure you wouldn't be disturbed? The anonymous letter you received – we tend to forget that, but it's important. It shows the same premeditation. The killer wanted the cottage empty, not occupied, and particularly not by a crime writer, though I think that exaggerates your prowess rather.'

'I think it does, too,' Jack agreed. 'Particularly as you seem to be making all the running.'

She jumped up and walked to the window and back. 'That's because I care. Really care.'

'Me, too,' he said mildly, 'but I'm here to work, not chase criminals. Personally, I thought Beatrice was telling the truth, probably the only time in her life that she has. If you trust Mercy Dearlove and discount Mallory's idea of a random mugger, all we're left with is Lionel. He has a clear motive. He could have come down to Treleggan the night before without anyone seeing him, telephoned his brother and arranged to meet him in the orchard, bringing with him a knife he'd stolen earlier from the cottage. It makes sense, but it's entirely circumstantial. There's not a shred of real evidence to support the charge and no jury would ever convict on those grounds.'

'Then we need to find the evidence,' she muttered, 'and if you're too busy and the police won't look where they should, *I* will.' She tugged at her hair, looping it severely behind her ears. 'By the way, did I tell you it was Jessie's day off today? We'll need to shift for ourselves tonight.'

'Is it the thought of cooking that's making you fizz like a Catherine wheel?'

'I'm frustrated, Jack, and it's making me bad tempered. The police are bumbling around while someone is getting away with murder. Probably Roger's brother. And getting away with money that isn't his, I'm certain. Why doesn't the inspector look at that? Roger is bound to have had a safe at River House. Is that where Lionel is getting his new-found wealth? Charging him with theft would be a start.'

'If he's broken into a safe and stolen from the house, it will soon be discovered and Lionel will be number one suspect. Once they start investigating him, a murder charge could follow.'

'He could have skipped the country by then. It's all too slow. Action is what's needed. Now.' She chewed at her lip. 'Couldn't you ring your police friend?'

'Inspector Ridley?'

Flora nodded. 'He came up trumps before.'

Jack was startled. It was the last thing he'd think of doing. 'I can't involve him,' he protested. 'He's in Brighton police, it's a different force. Toes would be most definitely trodden on.'

'I don't mean he should come here and start interviewing people. He could pick up the phone, speak to Mallory, suggest a line of enquiry to follow, one that involved Lionel.'

Jack shook his head. 'Ridley wouldn't dream of interfering in another force's investigation and I'm not going to ask him. Why don't you switch off for a while? Sit and read a book while I make supper.'

'Ham sandwiches?'

'There are worse things. I can poach eggs if you'd rather.'

'I would rather. And thank you.' She touched him lightly on the arm and, in response, he grabbed her hands and clasped them tightly between his.

'Sometimes you care too much, Flora.'

Inclining his head, he looked searchingly into her face. An insane desire suddenly took hold, to pull her close and make things right.

'Go on.' He nudged her towards the sofa he'd just vacated and made for the kitchen. 'Eggs will be served in—' he said over his shoulder.

'Best not to promise,' she called after him.

Flora laid her head against the sofa cushion, her book untouched, trying to make sense of the jumble of emotions Jack could inspire. She wished she could sort it out. She wished he could. Despite his denials, he was still smarting from a disastrous engagement, it was plain – it showed in the barbed comments that sometimes escaped him – yet he'd allowed himself to grow close to her. He hadn't wanted to, she was sure, but somehow it had happened. He cared for her in all kinds of small ways, though never once stepping beyond simple friendship. Flora wasn't even sure she wanted him to.

She had reached for her book in an attempt to stop the noise in her head, when the telephone rang.

'I'll get it,' she called out.

'Hello, Flora.' It was a voice she should be able to place, but struggled to. 'It's Sally,' the voice prompted.

'Sally! How are you?' Then caught her breath in a sudden panic. 'The All's Well?'

'Relax, the shop is fine. More than fine, in fact. I'm ringing about something else.' There was a pause. 'Alice told me of the conversation she had with you.'

'Yes?' Flora said guardedly.

'Auntie isn't keen on speaking to Mrs Martin. I'm sure you gathered that, but if you really think she should, she'll go ahead.'

Flora wondered where the call was leading. She'd no wish to pressure Alice unduly if that's what Sally was hinting at, and was about to say that her aunt should forget the conversation completely, when Sally went on, 'It was the names that Auntie mentioned. I thought maybe I could be the one to help.'

'You? But how? You hardly know Abbeymead.' The stab of jealousy was back. Had Sally so ingratiated herself in the village that she knew the most private details of the Martins' tragedy?

'It may take a while to explain. Are you able to talk?'

Flora forgot about Jack's poached eggs. 'Yes,' she said eagerly. 'Go on.'

'If you remember, I worked at the British embassy in Bonn until a few months ago. Several of my colleagues there had worked in the embassy when it was based in Berlin. When Alice mentioned the name Price, it rang a bell. I'd heard some of them mention him.'

'There was a Lofty Price in Berlin?' Flora's brain was working furiously.

'There was. I never met him, of course – before my time – but his name was well known in Bonn. Written large in embassy history, as it were. Disgrace doesn't visit the diplomatic service very often and, when it does, it's remembered for a long time.'

'Go on,' Flora urged again, leaning into the telephone.

'Lofty Price – Lofty was his nickname – was part of a team that worked in the Treasury and was dismissed for false accounting. He was never prosecuted, but he was definitely a thief, embezzling thousands of Deutschmarks. He was sent packing in the most ignominious fashion and later on stripped of the medals he'd won in the First War.'

Flora thought for a moment. 'But he'd couldn't be the same man. He'd be too old to be a combatant in World War Two.'

'That's what I thought, but then I remembered what Cookie had told me – she was a dear, a secretary who'd been at the embassy since the Boer War – only joking – but she told me about Lofty's son. Stephen was a nice lad, she said, who attended the International School in Berlin and was a very good student, by all accounts. He was a happy boy, plenty of friends, then his father was disgraced and he had to leave the school and leave Berlin. According to Cookie, it broke his heart.'

'And the son had the same nickname as his father?'

'That's it,' Sally said excitedly. 'A bit annoying for them both, I imagine, but if you're shorter than average, you're prob-ably destined to go through life with a stupid label. But what does he have to do with Thomas Martin?'

Flora couldn't answer the question. She felt too confused. Instead she asked, 'How old was the boy when he had to leave Berlin?'

'Sixteen, seventeen – around the time Hitler came to power.'

'Do you happen to know if he spoke German?' Another thought was slowly forming, tentatively unfurling its wings, and sending Flora's mind hurtling back to Mullion Cove and the site of a lost signals centre.

'Bound to have. His father was fluent and the boy was brought up in Berlin. The school he attended would probably have used German as their teaching language.'

There was a long silence, while Flora tried to stop her brain from racing.

'Does any of this help?' Sally enquired.

There was a loud crash from the kitchen and a stream of curses that Flora shut her ears to.

'It will, I'm sure, Sally. I can't see how just yet, but it will. Thank you so much. You've been wonderful.'

And Flora meant it. Sally's news had reignited her old suspicions that a secret from the past was at the bottom of this mystery.

23

Flora peered cautiously around the kitchen door. The room had come to resemble a battlefield, Jack having worked his way through almost a tray of eggs, the remains of which were scattered across the formica counter. But a plate of buttered toast and two perfectly poached eggs were waiting for her on the table and Jack wore a pleased smile.

'Supper is served,' he announced, waving her grandly to her seat.

'Just think how well you'd do at the Ritz!' she teased.

'I am thinking. I've started my application already – in case this book comes to nothing!'

'These are good,' she said after the first few bites. 'Thanks for taking charge.'

'No reason why I shouldn't.' He sat down opposite and salted his eggs generously. 'I might try my hand at something more adventurous next time.'

Flora quailed at the thought. 'You don't want to upset Jessie.'

'I'd only cook on her day off,' he said cheerfully. 'By the way, who was that on the phone?'

'Sally Jenner. She rang to let me know how well everything is going at the shop. To reassure me I'd no reason to fret.'

Flora felt very slightly guilty that she'd not mentioned the information on Lofty Price, but then dismissed the feeling. In time, she must tell Jack, but right now she needed to ponder what Sally had told her. Think it through before he bulldozed apart any theory she might advance. And he surely would.

Jessie's rhubarb tart and custard provided a satisfactory encore and, once his bowl was empty, Jack leaned forward, a conciliatory look on his face. 'If you don't mind...'

'I don't. Go and warm up the Remington. I'll clear the dishes.'

'If you're sure.'

'You have a book to write and I have *The Talented Mr Ripley* to read – once I've restored this room to looking half-decent.'

'Yeah, sorry about that,' he said, making for the door.

It was a good half hour before Flora had the kitchen ship-shape. Taking a cup of tea into the sitting room, she put aside her book to contemplate Sally's words, allowing them to float free in her mind, to circle, to linger, trying to make sense of what she'd been told. Was it likely that the boy whose father had left Berlin in disgrace was the same Price who had been the corporal in charge of Thomas Martin's unit? And, if he had been, what bearing, if any, did it have on Thomas's disappearance?

The corporal had been the one to point the finger at Thomas, she remembered Jack's father saying. He'd done it reluctantly. He hadn't wanted to believe the young man guilty, but had come to the sad conclusion that the mole in their midst had to be Thomas. On what grounds, though? The fact that it was Thomas who stayed working late, who'd been seen scribbling notes he never divulged, who watched his fellows closely? Seen from this distance in time, the reasons appeared flimsy.

Ralph had assumed that at the end of the war the corporal had returned to teaching – there had definitely been a very large demand for teachers – but there was no certainty that he had. If Price had indeed gone back to the schoolroom, had he taught German? Flora wondered whimsically. His command of the language would have been a huge asset to the army and it was no surprise that he'd ended up in a signals centre that was highly secret. It would have been his role to oversee the translation of messages garnered from the German airwaves and make sure they were passed securely to Bletchley Park. Maybe sending messages himself – decoy communications to deceive and disorientate the enemy. In his supervisory role, it was possible he'd been the one to discover messages that should never have been sent, messages typed from Thomas Martin's desk.

On and on Flora's mind travelled, trying to find coherence in what she'd been told, until she looked at the clock and saw that it was nearly eleven, and well past her bedtime. Upstairs, Jack was still typing, only pausing when she craned her head round his door to say goodnight.

His usual flop of hair was standing up in tufts where he'd harrowed it through fingers, a pencil was stuck behind one ear and a cigarette burnt in an ashtray.

'I've never seen you smoke before,' she said, surprised.

'I don't.' When she pursed her lips, he waved the smoke to one side. 'It's a prop – just for now.'

'You better not let Jessie smell it. She was complaining yesterday that her husband – I've discovered there *is* a husband – is never without a pipe in his mouth. *Sucks it like a baby*,' Flora mimicked.

Jack laughed. 'I brought cologne with me. I'll spray the room before she gets here.'

'Cedar and lime?'

'How did you know?'

'I have as good a nose as Jessie,' she retorted, and shut the door.

She wouldn't admit – to him or to anyone – that the smell of cedar and lime had come to make her happy.

The next day saw a huge change in the weather. Jack had mentioned the possibility of hiring a taxi and going to Land's End that morning but, hearing the rain thrash against the kitchen window, Flora thought it unlikely.

'Land's End will be wilder than ever,' he said on cue, walking into the room to stand beside her at the window.

'You'll not go today?'

'You're right. I won't. It's a day to hunker down.'

The next morning, too, saw them forced to stay at home. Once again, they stood together at the kitchen window, peering wistfully through streaming glass as the rain bounced off the granite stone of the terrace.

'This weather! It's messed up my schedule completely,' Jack said glumly. 'It looks as though we'll have to forget Land's End altogether, just when I'm in urgent need of another dangerous setting – I've a minor character I need to bump off. Usual breakfast for you?'

'I guess so. If the rain would only ease, I'd go to the bakery and buy some crumpets.'

'Crumpets are for tea.'

'Why not for breakfast, too? They'd make a change. So what are your plans for the rest of the day, or need I ask?'

'I'll have to write. There's no escape. And you?'

Flora's spirits deflated. 'No idea. Reading, I suppose. The garden is hopeless in this weather. By the way, did you notice I'd left you notes on the books you gave me?'

'I did, and read them, too. A tour de force! But if you're really at a loose end, I could use more help.'

'How come?'

'I've a couple more volumes tucked away. They could do with a quick scan.'

Her expression, reflected in the window, was dispirited. Jack must have seen it, because he went on without pausing, 'I packed them on the off-chance they'd be useful, and what do you know? They're actually spot on – accounts of Cornwall in the last war. If you fancied it, you could give them a swift read and mark up anything you think might add background.'

'I trudged through those huge tomes on the Helford river,' she reminded him, 'and for absolutely no reason, as it turns out.'

Jack sat down and poured cornflakes into a large bowl. 'I was still looking for a focus then, but these books are different. I'll definitely use anything interesting you can dig up.'

She looked sceptical and he tried to convince her. 'No, truly. I'm well into the novel now and I could weave in any unusual descriptions, personal anecdotes, that kind of thing.'

After breakfast and still reluctant, Flora collected the two books Jack had mentioned and took them to her bedroom, making herself comfortable in the one easy chair the room contained. Both sported the unexciting title of *Cornwall at War*. At least they made no bones about their subject. The same title, but two very different approaches, Flora decided, flicking through one book and then the other. The first appeared to be a straightforward history of the county from 1939 to 1946, while the second was a collection of people's memories of the time, along with letters and extracts from various parish magazines. This looked to be far the most interesting and Flora settled to read.

The book proved fascinating and by lunchtime she had filled several sheets of foolscap with page references for Jack to consult. Absorbed in her task, she hadn't noticed a change in the weather, but a beam of sunlight falling across her lap made her look up in surprise. While she'd been deep in parish magazines – and from her life in Abbeymead it was clear they hardly varied from county to county or from period to period – the world outside had transformed.

'Jack,' she called, walking out onto the landing and pausing at his door. 'The sun's shining. How about lunch on the terrace?'

Footsteps tracked their way across the wooden boards. He opened the door, the pencil still stuck behind his ear but, to Flora's relief, the lit cigarette had gone. He frowned at her. 'You're a bit optimistic, aren't you?'

'Take a look.' She pointed across to his window where an expanse of blue sky was plain to see.

'Seems inviting, but everywhere will be soaked still, the terrace included.'

'I bet it's not. The sky is clear and the sun's bright. I'll meet you downstairs.' There was a challenge in her voice.

When he finally walked into the kitchen, Flora had the back door open and was arranging plates on the blue slatted garden table.

'See,' she said triumphantly, 'it's good.'

Jack stood on the threshold, blinking in the warm sun like a cat waking after a deep sleep. Stretching his arms high, he circled his shoulders.

'I'll make the tea,' he offered.

Flora liked that about him. He never begrudged her winning a tussle. The terrace proved what she'd initially guessed it would be – a veritable sun trap – and, after the inevitable sandwiches and pot of tea, they found themselves lulled into silence, in danger of dozing off in the warmth.

'So it's going well?' she enquired, trying to shake herself awake. 'The book?'

'It's going better,' he amended, 'but writing to order – even with some flexibility – is difficult. And this damn contract I've signed is for another two books.'

'They won't be set in Cornwall. Does that make a difference?'

'Not that I can see. I'll be facing the same problems.' He paused and kicked a small pebble to one side. 'Maybe it's just writing that's beginning to pall.'

Flora shot him a surprised look. 'That's quite a thought!'

'Don't you ever tire of selling books?'

She thought for a moment. 'At times, maybe. I enjoy advising customers and I like meeting new ones. And I *love* the smell of books... but the routine, yes, sometimes it can pall. Opening on time each day, cleaning the shelves, cashing up, paying invoices. The workaday jobs, I suppose. They can be wearying.'

There was silence for a moment until she asked, 'If you didn't write novels, would you go back to journalism?'

'I doubt it.' He sat for a while, his eyes half-closed, then turned to look at her. 'Perhaps we should both try something else.'

Flora laughed. 'Like what?'

He pulled a wry face. 'We could do a swap. I could run your bookshop and you could write my books. How about that? You'd probably be much better at it than me.'

'I hope that's a joke.'

'Kind of. I suppose what I'm saying is that there's no reason either of us should be stuck with the life we have. We've no responsibilities other than keeping a roof over our heads.'

It was true, Flora thought. Sadly. She'd owed responsibilities to Violet, and a year on from her aunt's death, she would have welcomed them back again even though, at the time, they'd felt onerous. The hurt of losing someone she'd loved so much was still raw.

Shaking off her gloom, she leaned forward. 'How about opening a detective agency together?' There was a wide smile on her face.

Jack leaned back in his chair and roared with laughter. 'Judging by our success in Treleggan, or lack of it, I don't think we'd have too many customers.'

'That's unfair. We've nobbled Lionel. The man is clearly the villain we're after – it's Mallory that's taking an age to see it.'

Lionel Gifford had motive and opportunity. Within a day of his brother dying, he'd been knocking on their door demanding Roger's papers. He was desperate for money to extricate himself from trouble and Roger was his only source. As for the mishaps they'd suffered, Lionel could easily have been behind the accident in Mullion and he was certainly the person who'd broken into their cottage and taken a kitchen knife with him.

There were a few things that didn't quite fit, Flora admitted to herself. The fall she'd had in Helston, for instance. There'd been no sign of Lionel in the town, but her tumble could have been down to a movement in the crowd rather than a deliberate act. And yesterday in Falmouth, when she'd felt threatened... the incident had taken on a haziness that bothered her. She'd begun to think she might have imagined a presence behind her. The gun embrasure had been narrow with only a low wall as protection from the sheer drop below. Realising how dangerous it could be might have triggered a reaction, her mind constructing a reality that wasn't there.

'I'll make another pot,' Jack said, interrupting her train of thought and picking up the tray. 'Maybe we can plan our next trip over a second cup. The weather has improved and I can just about spare the time now.'

'Apart from Land's End, where else do you want to visit?'

'I thought maybe further up the south coast, towards Mevagissey. After that, call it a day.'

'Does that mean you intend to finish the book in Abbeymead?' Jack had surprised her again.

'Treleggan hasn't turned out too well, has it? I won't be sorry to leave. Unless, of course, you want to stay on.' He smiled at her. 'I could always find more books for you to work on.'

'We'll go home,' she said decisively.

24

The next morning dawned bright, the sun shining from the
moment Flora woke, and the air fresh and crystal clear.
Selecting her prettiest summer dress from the wardrobe – a
navy polka dot with a wide skirt and a cinched waist – she felt
ready to explore. The Austin was still being patched up, but a
taxi to Land's End or some of the villages Jack had mentioned
seemed promising.

She was to be disappointed, though – Jack had changed his
plans. Woken in the night by an overactive mind, he'd discovered a flaw in his plotting. He had to put it right before he went
anywhere, he said, making a hurried retreat to his room once
breakfast was over.

Flora was unhappy. She'd been counting on leaving the
village today and, for the first time, the garden had lost its
appeal and the cottage felt cramped. Unable to settle, she
decided on a walk to the village, the sound of hammered keys
following her to the front door. She would make for the bakery
and buy those crumpets. Possibly doughnuts, too, for a mid-
morning snack. It seemed the time for indulgence.

Her stroll along the lane that fronted the cottage gave a lift to her spirits. Overnight, it seemed, the grass verges had filled to bursting with foxglove and dog-violet, wild rose and purple orchids. On the main road, hedges of white hawthorn had flooded into full bloom. And above her, the sun shone from a cloudless blue sky.

She had reached the greengrocer's, the first in the small cluster of shops, when she spied Jessie further down the street talking to a huddle of women, baskets in hand and their heads bent as though to hear better.

'Hello, Jessie,' she called out as she approached the group, but when the housekeeper turned, Flora was shocked to see her red-eyed and evidently tearful. One of the women began patting Jessie on the shoulder.

'Whatever's happened?' Flora was alarmed.

Jessie's mouth tightened as though she didn't want to let the words out.

'It's that Lionel.' A woman wearing a brightly coloured headscarf spoke first.

'Vandalised the house,' another said, clutching her wicker basket tight to her hip.

When Flora looked bemused, Jessie said with an effort, 'It's River House. I haven't been back since... since Mr Roger... but that Lionel has left the most awful mess.'

Flora felt relief. For a moment, she had thought that something truly terrible had happened. 'I'll help you clean it up,' she offered. 'Please don't upset yourself.'

'It's not just the mess,' the headscarfed woman said in a low voice. The group with one accord nodded their heads. 'It's the safe. Broken into!'

Flora's eyes widened though she felt little surprise. She had been certain that, if a safe existed in Roger's house, Lionel Gifford would have broken into it, and here was the proof.

'Have you told the police?' In the light of the sluggardly

murder investigation, Flora doubted it was worth the bother, but felt she should ask.

'I called on Will,' Jessie said, her voice unsteady, 'and he's writin' up a report.'

What good will that do? she was tempted to say, but didn't. Jessie needed comfort. 'Was very much taken?' she asked gently, expecting to hear that a large sum had gone missing. A sum large enough to buy a new Humber.

Instead, Jessie said, 'It can't have amounted to much.'

Flora frowned. 'Roger didn't keep money in the safe?' It seemed unlikely or what would be the purpose of having a safe?

'Jus' my wages. Mr Roger would go into Falmouth every month and draw the money.' Jessie had become more animated. 'Then every week, he'd open the safe and count out my pay. I'd already 'ad two weeks' wages when poor Mr Roger died, so there can't 'ave been much left.'

'Serve that Lionel right,' a voice from the back of the group put in. 'He 'spected to get rich, and all he got were two weeks' pay.'

The women laughed as one. The thought of Lionel expending huge effort to force open the safe, only to find nothing but Jessie's modest recompense, made a good joke.

'I suppose Roger didn't keep anything else in his safe?' Flora asked hopefully.

Jessie thought for a while. 'He 'ad a passport – it were a terrible photo of 'im. He used to go to France sometime, though why I never could see. And there may 'ave been a document or two,' she concluded.

Documents. A paper that Lionel had wanted badly and, whatever it was, he must have found. *I've the one piece of paper I need*, he'd said to her, the day Ralph Carrington had driven them back from Mullion. A piece of paper that in some way had provided him with the money to buy a new car. What was left of Jessie's wages would have bought little more than its wing mirror.

'You best go 'ome, Jessie love,' her patter-in-chief said. 'You can tackle River House tomorrow, when you've 'ad time to get over the shock.'

'And after the police 'ave been round to look, I 'ope,' the woman in the gaudy headscarf added severely.

'Tha's right,' another woman said. 'They need to get on, catch that rascal.'

'Scoundrel is what I'd call 'im.'

The conversation had dwindled into a general exchange of Lionel Gifford's iniquities when Flora saw a figure she knew at the end of the road.

'Will you excuse me?' she said, disentangling herself quickly. 'Jessie, please forget our supper tonight.'

'That I won't,' Jessie said indignantly.

Flora didn't waste time arguing but took to her heels, racing down the village street to catch the figure of Mercy Dearlove, as she disappeared into the copse of trees that ran parallel to the road.

'Mercy! Wait!' she called out.

The figure paused in its lengthy stride, and a tangle of long black hair swung around to reveal skin of brown leather and eyes of green, glittering in the shadow of the copse.

The eyes watched her gravely. 'Miss Flora Steele,' she said. 'You came then.'

'Came?' Flora was mystified.

'I called and you came.'

'I walked into the village and caught sight of you, that's all.'

'Ezackly. Arsk yerself, why did you walk this way this mornin'?'

'The sun was shining, I fancied a walk and a doughnut, so I walked. I didn't hear anyone call.'

'O'course you didn't, but I called nevertheless.'

Had that been the restlessness she'd felt? The inability to settle? 'You wanted to see me?' she asked, hoping a direct question would rescue her from this maze.

'No, it were *you* who wanted to see me,' the witch corrected.

Flora took a deep breath and tried to rein in her impatience. 'Now that I am here, can you tell me why you summoned me? Are you going to take me to the spot we talked about?'

'The sacred place,' the peller corrected her again.

Flora knew she needed Mercy's help as an intermediary, to make sense of the information Sally had given her. 'The sacred place,' she repeated obediently.

'Not today, my 'ansum. Tomorrow at noon. Polvarra Cove.'

'But—'

Flora was about to protest that she had no idea how to find this cove, nor did she have a broomstick to get there, but before she could say any of it, Mercy had gone.

There was a knock at the front door as Jack came down the stairs the next morning. Flora was already in the kitchen and he heard her call out, 'It's very early for someone to be knocking – be careful.'

Often these days she seemed jumpy, and Jack couldn't blame her – he'd not felt truly at ease himself since the moment they'd found Roger's body. But when he opened the front door, it was to find a young man in mechanics' overalls, who doffed his cap and smiled.

'I brought your car back,' he said.

Jack looked over the boy's head at his beloved red Austin, abandoned in Mullion days ago. Newly polished, it glinted in the early morning light.

'That's very good of you. I thought we'd have to find our way to Porthleven.'

'I were comin' this way, so I thought I'd save you the bother of collectin' it. My guv'nor sent the bill with me, but you can post a cheque later if you'd rather. The address is on the invoice.'

Jack opened the envelope and drew out a sheet of paper. 'A decent price,' he remarked. 'I'll write a cheque now and you can take it back with you – if you'll hang on for a minute.'

He passed Flora in the hall as she took his place at the front door.

'How will you get back to Porthleven?' she asked the boy, sounding worried. 'Could we ring for a taxi? I've enough cash in my purse, I think.'

'No need for a taxi.' The young man grinned at her. 'I'll not be goin' back right now. I can catch a bus to Helston from 'ere. Go and see my gran. Makes a decent heavy cake, does Gran, *and* I get time off.'

'If you're sure,' Flora said doubtfully as Jack returned, cheque in hand. He took the offered car keys and tipped several coins into the boy's palm.

'Thank you, mister. Tha's right proper.' The lad gave them a half salute and sauntered back along the path to the gate.

'No traipsing over to Porthleven after all. That's a bit of luck.' Jack followed her into the kitchen and began laying out the breakfast dishes. 'And no need to hire a taxi if we take that trip along the south coast.' The arrival of the car seemed providential.

'You managed to fill your plot hole then?'

'I did, and sorry about yesterday.'

Squirrelled away in his room for hours, he hadn't seen Flora properly since the previous morning and was feeling guilty. Today, he was determined to make up for it.

'How about exploring some of the places we talked about? There are some stunning villages further along the coast. The background I've sketched so far is Cornish, but a smidge too general for my liking. What I need is something more specific, small details that will bring the story alive. I need to talk to new people – hear *their* wartime experiences.'

'Sounds a good idea.' Flora reached for the marmalade.

'How about lunch in' – he unfolded the map he'd brought down from his room – 'in Looe? It would make a good base for the day.'

She finished spreading her slice of toast and he noticed her actions were slow and deliberate. 'I don't think so.'

Jack was surprised. After yesterday's disappointment, he'd thought she would have jumped at the chance of leaving Treleggan. 'We could go on to Polperro, on to Fowey – they're all lovely,' he tempted. 'We don't have to stop in Looe.'

'I think I'd rather stay home today.' Flora didn't look at him as she spoke and he couldn't stop a frown.

'Why would you want to, when you can spend hours in some of the most beautiful spots in Cornwall? I'll be back at my desk soon enough and the chance will be gone.'

'I've decided to go on with the garden, that's all. There's a lot that needs doing.' She still wasn't looking at him, her gaze fixed on the piece of toast she was eating.

Stubbornly, he refused to give up. 'The garden isn't your responsibility. We won't be here much longer and you've already spent days clearing the terrace. And look what's left.' He pointed at the kitchen window and the knee-high grass beyond, feeling his annoyance grow. 'What are you going to use to tidy that? A pair of nail scissors?'

'There are shears in the garden shed,' she said defensively.

'Possibly blunt. Almost certainly blunt. In any case, shears will be useless. You'd need a scythe to take the grass down to a level you can cut, and I can't see you wielding one of those even if you could find it.'

'I'd still like to try.'

She began collecting the breakfast dishes and that was the

end of the argument, Jack could see. He tried to shrug off his irritation, but there was also a hurt that he didn't want to acknowledge. She would rather play at cutting grass, it seemed, than spend the day with him in some of the most picturesque villages in the county. The garden was an excuse, that was clear enough. It was simply that she didn't want to be with him.

He was surprised she'd stayed around as long as she had and this breach between them – he felt keenly that it was a breach – was bound to happen. She was bored, needed time away from him. Their stay together in Cornwall had been a mistake, hastening the knell for a friendship that had always seemed unlikely. The few moments where he'd imagined that she liked him more than she was saying had been a mistake.

'I'll get off then,' he said, hearing his voice come thin and sharp.

'Have fun,' she responded. 'Tell me all about it when you get back.'

He shrugged again, and it wasn't until he was behind the wheel of the car that another thought struck. What if this was a ploy to get him out of the way? What was she planning that she didn't want him to know? He almost switched off the ignition and walked back into the cottage, but then decided he'd leave it be. She probably did prefer the garden to him.

25

Flora felt bad. She wished she could have told Jack of her plans for the day. Wished she could have had him alongside. She hated having secrets from him, and it was plain that refusing his offer of a day out hadn't just annoyed him but wounded him, too. It was a warning, if she needed one, that they'd grown too close for their own good, though it didn't make her feel any better. *And* she would have loved to have seen the glories of Polperro and Fowey. Loved to have eaten fish and chips at the harbour in Looe. But she had to find Polvarra Cove and get to her meeting with Mercy Dearlove.

She'd sneaked a look at the map when Jack had been upstairs collecting his wallet. The cove was a good three mile walk, perhaps more, but doable. She would wear her oldest pair of shoes to avoid blisters, and take money in case she saw a bus going anywhere near Treleggan on her return, though that seemed unlikely.

As soon as Jack and the car disappeared down the lane, she made ready to leave. Early mornings and evenings were still chilly, but if the sun shone as brightly as it had at times this week, it could feel like midsummer. Today, the clouds were huge puffs of white wool high in the sky, looking as though at any moment they could peel apart and allow the sun its full freedom. She would need only the lightest of jackets.

Walking along the lane, she followed the direction Jack had taken, but when she reached the main road, turned away from Treleggan. It was fortunate her route to Polvarra meant that no one was likely to see her leaving the village and ask where she was making for. Flora had no wish to tell more lies than was necessary. It was a brisk ten-minute walk along the main thoroughfare before she reached the signpost she was expecting, directing her along a smaller road that, three miles on, would lead her to the sea and the cove.

The three miles felt much longer than they should – country miles, she thought. After a while, the road began to seem endless, bend after bend, up one hill and down the next. Occasionally, it ran straight for a hundred yards or so, but another zigzag was never far off, and it made for weary walking. By the time she came across a carved wooden hand, the finger pointing out the path to Polvarra Cove, her legs had developed a dull ache and she still had the return journey to make. Turning into the sandy track that led down to the sea, she persuaded herself that no matter how long the walk, it would be worth it.

The path was mercifully short and a gap very soon appeared in the cliff, from where she was sure there would be a flight of wooden steps leading down to the beach. Before she could reach the stairway, though, she was brought to a halt. There was tape barring her way. As she drew near, she saw it was printed in large black letters with the word Police.

Confused, she stood staring blindly at it.

'There's a cordon, Miss Steele,' a voice said. It was Will Hoskins, having just climbed up from the shore. 'You can't go down. Best to find another beach. Plenty of 'em, though.' He gave her a friendly smile.

'But why? Why is the cove cordoned off?'

'I can't really say.'

'Can't or won't?'

Will gave a resigned puff. 'Well, I s'pose it'll be all round the village soon enough. It's Mr Gifford.'

The image of a short, stolid man with florid cheeks and a trimmed moustache filled her mind's eye. 'Mr Gifford?' she asked, puzzled. 'But he's dead.'

'Not Mr Roger,' Will spelt out painstakingly, 'Mr Lionel Gifford. He's dead, too.'

Flora had never believed it possible when a character in a book had their mouth fall open, but hers did now.

'He can't be,' she protested.

Will nodded gravely. 'A dog walker found 'im early this mornin'.'

'But what happened? Did he have an accident? Did he fall?'

'In a manner of speakin'.' Will moved closer and, bending his head, spoke into her ear. ''ad 'is throat cut like 'is brother.'

Flora's hand flew to her mouth. It was horrible, almost as horrible as finding Roger.

But how could Lionel be murdered, too, if he'd been the one to wield the knife in the orchard?

'What kind of knife...?' she trailed off. 'Was it the same as...'

'The one that did for poor Mr Roger?' Will nodded very slowly. 'I think tha's right. Leastways, this'un looks like somethin' you'd 'ave in your kitchen.'

A kitchen knife. A knife from Primrose Cottage. But if Lionel had taken the knife, and surely he had, how had he ended up murdered by it?

Dazed, she turned away, leaving Will to return to the beach. Lionel killed, and in the same fashion as his brother. The story she had so carefully constructed around his guilt fell to ruins. A kaleidoscope had been shaken and its pieces thrown into the air, landing – where exactly?

Stumbling back along the path, she thought about the

Gifford brothers. About Beatrice. Thought about the men who
had worked at the Mullion centre. What bound all these people
together – if anything? There were links between individuals,
but even these were tenuous. Lionel could be linked to the
signallers, possibly, through their days in the army. One of those
men might be connected with Roger, through the latter's
research, though Flora had nothing to prove it. And Lionel and
Beatrice had separately quarrelled with Roger over a will that
had or had not been changed. But there was nothing that tied all
of them into one large knot.

Was the timing of Lionel's murder significant? Had their
visit to Beatrice provoked the killing? If Roger hadn't, in fact,
changed his will and Beatrice had lied to them, pretending to
believe he had... if she'd killed her husband that morning in the
orchard, maybe she'd decided to finish the business completely,
to rid herself of the final obstacle to a comfortable life. It was
plain she was in deep trouble. The man for whom she'd left
Roger had rejected her, walked away to a better prospect, and
left her in financial peril – she had no home, no job, no money.
What had she said? Flora tried to remember the exact words. *I
may not benefit from Roger's money, but I'll do everything in my
power to ensure that little rat doesn't either.*

'That'un won't be much of a loss.'

Flora jumped at the voice coming from behind and spun
around. Mercy Dearlove stood to one side of the track, looking
out to sea. She might as well have risen from the earth since
Flora had heard nothing – not even the sigh of a single blade of
marram grass.

'I'm so glad to see you,' she said, a heady mix of relief and
excitement flooding through her.

It was more important than ever that Mercy used her
powers to see beyond this world. Flora had no idea how the
seeing might relate to Beatrice, to the Giffords, but she was
convinced that it mattered. The deeper Mercy delved and the

stronger vision she could conjure, the better chance there was of making sense of these murders.

'I'm so glad you're here,' Flora said again, her voice warm with welcome. 'I really need your help.'

Mercy had turned from the sea and was staring at her. Looking through her almost. 'There's no more, maidy,' she said.

Flora stared back at the witch. 'What do you mean?'

'No more help. Nothin' more I can tell you.'

'But you said for me to meet you here. Meet you at Polvarra Cove. The cove is sacred, you said, and you could call on your dead comrades to help you see more.'

Mercy shook her head. ''Tis true that pellers 'ave been buried in this cove for many a year. 'Tis a beautiful place – the grasses and the thrift and the stonecrop. Near to water, you see, and where the sprowl is strong.'

'So what—' Flora began.

'Violence, maidy. Violence came 'ere today and now the energy's gone.'

'Are you saying...' Flora stuttered, trying to make sense of a bewildering train of events. 'Are you saying the cove is no longer sacred? Because of Lionel's murder?'

Mercy nodded. 'Desecrated,' she said simply.

'But surely, you could try?' She was sounding desperate, she knew.

The witch shook her head. 'You got enough, maidy. You'll come good.'

'But how...' Flora began, but she was speaking to the air. Once again the peller had disappeared.

She could have wept with vexation, and for some time stood completely still, gazing unseeingly into the distance. Then, feeling an indescribable weariness, she resumed her trudge back to the road to finish the long walk to Treleggan. The day on which she had pinned so much had been a disaster. Far from discovering Roger's murderer, she was looking at a second killing, a killing that tore her assumption of Lionel's guilt to shreds. There couldn't be two murderers in such a small place. Whoever had killed Roger had killed Lionel, too. The dead men were brothers, tied together in all kinds of ways, and both had been killed in exactly the same fashion.

The murderer was still out there – waiting to kill for a third time? – and there seemed nothing she could do to prevent it. Other than Beatrice, there was no one else in the frame. For Roger's death, Flora could make a reasonable case against the woman, but instinct told her that, though Beatrice was embittered and desperate, she was unlikely to have arranged to meet her brother-in-law at a lonely cove. Unlikely to have wielded that knife this morning – and how, in any case, would she have got hold of it?

So where to look? How could she 'come good' as Mercy had said? All she had was the witch's brief vision of a body, not of Roger Gifford, but of a young man. Mountains of earth, Mercy had seen, a thicket of trees and petals that were blood red.

Suddenly, her feet refused to go further. Her mouth felt dry and her breathing became rapid. Mullion, she thought. It was Mullion. The wartime digging that had displaced mountains of earth, the plantation of trees that had come later and the rhododendrons – Ralph had slipped on the bloody mush of fallen blossoms.

A thought leapt hot and burning into Flora's head. What if the body Mercy had seen was that of a young soldier? What if Thomas Martin hadn't disappeared in shame? What if his body was buried on the cliffs above Mullion Cove?

26

Jack returned to Primrose Cottage in the early afternoon. He'd ruled out stopping for lunch as he'd originally planned; eating alone wasn't much fun, and he was keen to get back to Treleggan. There had been a shadowy misgiving in his mind all day, unsure of what Flora really intended. Still, the trip had been a good use of his time. The villages had been outstanding in their beauty and provided helpful context for the story he was building. In addition, he'd managed to strike up conversations with several of the villagers he'd met, and encouraged them to reminisce on their wartime experience.

A fisherman in Fowey had described how, as children, he and his mate had enjoyed cycling into the countryside, in the hope of finding the decoy sites they'd heard their parents talk about. Sites built to resemble towns or airfields at night, in an effort to fool the German bombers. It was one more example of how extensively war had touched the county, something of which Jack, despite his reading, had been only dimly aware. Realising how important Cornwall had been to the struggle made him determined to recount a story barely told before, as well as give his readers the crime they were looking for.

He was glad, though, to walk through the front door of the cottage, calling out to Flora as he squeezed himself into the hall, but was met by silence. Could she still be working in the garden? He walked to the kitchen and out of the back door onto the terrace. There was no sign of her. No sign either that any work had been done in the garden, the grass unsullied and as high as ever.

Looking at the neglected space, his heart received a nasty jolt. Where was Flora and what had she been doing? His misgivings seemed likely to be fulfilled. He'd gone back into the kitchen and lit the gas to make tea when he heard her key in the lock and, as soon as she walked into the room, her steps dragging, he knew for sure that she had been up to something. Her long hair was dishevelled and her hazel eyes tired as she slumped into a kitchen chair.

'Well?' he asked.

'Don't scold. Did you have a good day?'

'I did, but you... the garden must have proved really tough.' He made a play of looking out of the window. 'There's not a lot to show for all your hard work.'

Flora gave an irritated huff. 'You know very well I didn't do any gardening.'

'Now there's a surprise. What *did* you do?'

'I walked – to a cove called Polvarra. It was supposed to be three miles there and three miles back, but in reality it proved more like ten.'

'Tea?' he asked, subduing the questions frazzling his brain.

'Please. And a sandwich if you don't mind making it. I'm starving.'

Jack was starving, too, and took pleasure in cutting thick slices from the fresh loaf that Jessie had left them, and generously spreading the butter that had come with the milkman that morning.

Looking in the larder for something to fill the sandwich, he shook his head. 'There's only cheese. Is that OK?'

'Cheese is fine. I'm grateful for any food.'

'Now, Polvarra Cove,' he said severely. 'Why exhaust yourself getting there? And why,' he went on, bringing the sandwiches to the table, 'did you lie to me?'

'I'm sorry about that.' She looked sorry, he thought, and half forgave her before his fear of what she'd been doing made him bristle again.

'Lying was a horrid thing to do.' She took a large bite. 'But if I'd told you what I was planning, you'd have tried to stop me.'

'Which says loud and clear all I need to know. C'mon, Flora, spill the beans – tell me the worst.'

'It's not that bad, but you don't like Mercy Dearlove and I went to meet her.'

That was unexpected. What did Flora have to do with the witch and why traipse halfway round Cornwall to meet her? There was silence while they munched through their sandwiches, until Flora announced suddenly, 'Lionel Gifford is dead.'

'What?' Jack pushed his plate aside and stared at her.

'The police were at the cove when I got there. A dog walker had found his body earlier.'

That wasn't only unexpected, but inexplicable. 'I thought Gifford would have gone back to London by now. The solicitors must surely have asked him to vacate River House. What on earth was he doing in a cove miles from anywhere?'

Flora spread her hands. 'Your guess is as good as mine. It's possible, I suppose, that he was lured there in the same way Roger was lured to the orchard. It was a copycat murder, even down to the kind of knife that was used.'

'How do you know that? You spoke to the police?'

'Only Will Hoskins and he wasn't very communicative, but then I don't think he knew much. I didn't see Inspector Mallory or his team – they must have been on the beach. Will did tell me that Lionel's throat had been cut.'

Jack stirred the pot and poured them both a cup of tea. 'You must have been shocked to be greeted with that news.' He studied her for a moment. 'You don't seem too upset.'

'I'm not. Not really. For one thing, I wasn't forced to look at the body this time and, for another, Lionel was a thoroughly nasty man. I can't feel that sorry – except that by dying as he did, my journey lost its point. Today was the day I was going to find definite proof of his guilt.'

'I suppose Mercy Dearlove didn't put in an appearance?' She wouldn't, he thought cynically, not if she was implicated, and that seemed likely.

'Actually, she did. She came and went.'

'Did she, though?' he said quietly. Then decided to say what was in his mind, even though Flora wouldn't like it. 'Don't you think it's just a tad suspicious that Mercy was in the vicinity when both of these men were killed? I know you like her, but maybe you should think again.'

Flora looked mulish. 'Mercy had nothing to do with the killing. She didn't like Lionel – who did? – but she'd no reason to wish him dead. And if she had—'

'Yes, I know what I said. She would have hexed him rather than slicing him open with a knife. But the question remains as to why she was there. Why drag you all the way out to this place when she could have met you in Treleggan?'

It seemed to Jack too much of a coincidence that Lionel had visited the same cove on the very same day that Mercy Dearlove had arranged to meet Flora. He'd almost certainly been lured there, as Flora suggested – possibly by Mercy herself – though why the witch would have wanted Flora there as well, was decidedly odd.

'She asked me to meet her at Polvarra because the cove was

special.' Flora's voice faltered a little. 'You wouldn't understand. You're far too logical for it to make sense to you.'

'Try me.'

'A number of witches have been buried at Polvarra, apparently. It's near water and near sprowl. Don't ask,' she said, watching his face. 'Just accept that it's a special place. Sacred, Mercy called it. She hoped to tap into the energies that flow through the spot so that she could look back into the past. She was doing it for me.'

Jack was puzzled. He dismissed the talk of sacred places, hidden energies and whatever sprowl was – mumbo-jumbo, his father would have called it – but the mention of looking back into the past had him confused. He was used to Flora's sudden leaps into the dark, her jumping from idea to idea, from suspect to suspect. But this sudden lurch back into a hidden history was extreme even for her. Two days ago, it seemed, she had given up completely on Roger's wartime research. Accepted it was a distraction and plumped for his will as the one document that was significant, with Beatrice and Lionel as possible villains, both having killed for Roger's money.

He rested his elbows on the table and looked across at her. 'Let me get this straight,' he said, trying to sound measured. 'You're now back in the war? So what happened to Roger's will as the primary motive?'

Flora bit hard on her lips. 'I've come to think the will is a red herring. You'll scoff, I know, but everything is telling me that whatever happened all those years ago at Mullion has a connection with the present-day murders.'

'Everything? What is that, exactly?' He was no longer sounding so measured, he realised.

'Lionel isn't Roger's killer, even though we might want him to be – how likely is it that Lionel murdered his brother, only to be murdered himself? Added to which the two deaths are identical and whoever killed Lionel must have killed his brother. It means we need to look elsewhere for a motive.'

'Beatrice? You're dismissing her, too? She had a reason to kill them both. She could have murdered Lionel for any of the reasons we came up with, and today she could have been at that cove, slipping away without anyone knowing she'd ever been there.'

Flora stood up, holding tightly to the back of her chair. It was costing her to convince him, he could see.

'Beatrice could but she didn't. I had this moment of complete clarity, Jack, when I could see what I should have seen before. Mercy had told me of the body of a young man lying amid dense trees and piles of earth – I didn't tell you at the time because I knew what your reaction would be. The picture she painted has kept puzzling me, but then as I was coming away from Polvarra, I knew. I knew it was Mullion Cove that Mercy had seen and that the young man could be Thomas Martin.'

'Martin?' Now, he felt utterly bewildered. 'What has he to do with it? And how could you know any of this?'

'I don't *know*,' she admitted. 'But I can sense it – and it does add up. I've been thinking about it all the way home. What if Thomas wasn't guilty? Lord Edward always refused to believe it.'

'Lord Edward was hardly objective,' he countered. 'And others did believe, my father included.'

'Your father didn't know Thomas in the same way. Just suppose for a moment that the boy wasn't guilty. Isn't it possible that he knew who was? And, if he did, he'd have to be silenced.'

'Murdered?'

'That's what I'm thinking. Once he was dead, his disappearance would be taken as proof he was guilty.'

'Even if that were true, what relevance does it have now? If it happened at all – and your suspicions could be groundless – it was twelve years ago.'

'But don't you see? The murderer was never caught. He must still be at large and with a big secret to guard. He'd be desperate to ensure that no one else got close to it – and it will be a "he". One of the soldiers who worked alongside Thomas. Over the years, no one has come close to uncovering the crime. He must have relaxed, thinking that every year that passed kept him safer from discovery.'

She sat down again and leaned towards him, her voice urgent. 'But then Roger Gifford hits on the idea of researching wartime in Cornwall. He starts with searches about people's feelings about the war, how they coped with rationing, that sort of thing. Then he goes on to D-Day and the build-up of troops and tanks and ammunition in the county. In turn, that leads him on to how vital the signals centres were to the success of the invasion, and discovers to his delight a site that's highly secret and only a few miles from where he's living. Unfortunately for him, he was led into digging too deeply. His research brought to light whatever bad thing happened at Mullion, the secret our murderer has guarded for so long. Roger had to be silenced.'

'But the place was top secret,' he objected. 'How could Roger have uncovered something as damning as that?'

'To be honest, I don't have an answer, but I'm convinced he did.'

For a few minutes, Jack was too stunned to argue. Flora had thought it through step by step – she seemed utterly certain – and, despite his teasing, he respected the way her hunches so often turned out right. But could he accept such a crazy proposition? There *was* a major flaw, wasn't there? Apart from how Roger could have gained access to such information.

'How would the murderer know Roger had found the secret?' he asked quietly.

'He must have talked. From the short time we spent with our landlord, I put him down as a garrulous chap who loved speaking about his research. He was passionate about it, extremely proud of the progress he'd made, and could have boasted of it to anyone in the village, and beyond.'

'Surely, if he realised he'd uncovered a possible murder, he would have gone to the police rather than talk about it.'

'Perhaps he talked before he realised how crucial his finding was, then when the penny dropped, he might have hesitated, unsure what to do.'

Jack sat back in his chair, his brain full to bursting. For a short while, he'd been ready to dismiss this as one of Flora's hare-brained forays, but he had to admit that as she'd talked he'd found himself becoming more convinced. 'What about Lionel?' he asked, keen to keep testing her theory. 'His death doesn't fit.'

'That has me in a bind,' she confessed. 'Unless he knew the secret, too. I'm sure that Roger wouldn't have told him, but Lionel has been boasting about a paper he found – according to him, the only one that mattered. And I learned from Jessie that the safe at River House has been broken into.'

Jack gave a low whistle. 'You think Roger might have hidden the secret in his safe?'

'It's possible, isn't it, while he decided what to do? He could have been working himself up to going to the police with what he'd found.'

'Why would he need to work himself up? He was a stalwart of the community – he'd know the police would give him a hearing.'

'They would, but Roger wouldn't want to appear foolish. If all he had was suspicions based on the research he'd done, he could have been reluctant to share what he knew.'

'And we're left with much the same dilemma, aren't we? In fact, worse – we don't even have the research Roger dug up. There's absolutely no evidence. Somehow, I don't think a peller's vision is going to interest Mallory.'

'That's the problem,' she said gloomily, walking over to the sink and running water into the washing-up bowl. 'We have no evidence and, until we do, going to the police is pointless. The inspector will laugh at us.'

It was more than likely. In silent agreement, he picked up a tea towel to dry the dishes. But what evidence could they supply? What on earth could they say to convince Mallory? He hadn't come across as the most imaginative of men.

Flora's thoughts had been following his. 'Mallory hasn't been too impressive, has he? Don't you think you could—'

'No,' he said decisively. 'I am not ringing Alan Ridley. He's a useful contact and I want to keep him. Asking him to intervene in a case that's not his would risk him never answering my calls again.'

She leant back against the kitchen counter, her arms folded, while he watched her closely. Different options were passing through her mind, he'd bet on it. What fate, he wondered, was facing him?

'*We'll* have to find the evidence that Thomas was murdered,' she said firmly. 'There's no other way. Once we have it, we can pass details on to Mallory and even he won't be able to ignore where it leads.'

'By evidence, I take it you mean ...'

'Thomas Martin's body? Yes.'

'What if there isn't a body? What if Mr Martin is currently enjoying the Riviera?' It was a desperate last throw.

'He isn't. The poor boy is dead,' she said with finality. 'Don't forget, if we find Thomas, we can ensure he's returned to his parents for a proper burial at St Saviour's. Let's think how best to do this.'

Jack waited, half-amused and half-fearful. How she proposed to find a body supposedly buried years ago on a wild headland of the Lizard would make interesting, if terrifying, listening.

'There's a decent spade in the shed.'

'Flora!' he exploded.

'What? If we want to find a body, we need to dig. It's a pity we can't be more certain of where exactly we should start. That copse of trees stretches a long way. If Mercy had managed to see more, it would have been helpful.'

'Very helpful,' he said drily. 'Perhaps we can ask her to conjure up a little more energy, when the mood takes her. Until then, I think I'll pass.'

'Witches don't work like that,' she chided, 'and you won't dip out. Roger needs justice and we're going to give it to him. And don't forget that finding the murderer will keep us safe as well.'

Storing their china back in the cupboard, she stopped midway, a plate still in her hand.

'Just a thought,' she said slowly, 'but why don't we go back to the place your father had his fall? Remember, he slipped on a pool of red blossoms that had become mashed by the winter rain? He was tripped up by some kind of ridge. At the time, I thought it was strange, a raised mound in what was otherwise flat terrain. But now I'm suspicious. In fact... now I'm thinking that mound was grave-shaped.'

'*Now* you're thinking it! You're fitting the facts to suit your theory.'

'Jack' – she put out her hands to him – 'can we go back to that place? Please. We can take the spade and dig. If I'm wrong, there's no harm done.'

'No harm to you. I'll be the one digging. And I'm not sure you're right. There'll be people around. Logan and his mate, for one thing, walkers out with their dogs, visitors to the cove – there are tourists at this time of year. I don't fancy explaining to them that we're digging for a body.'

'Then we'll go at night.'

'You have to be joking.'

Really, Flora was more impossible with every day. It might be her theory had something going for it, but realistically there was little they could do. Except, perhaps, try talking to Mallory. If they presented Flora's reasoning in the right way, it was possible they could interest the inspector and get his men to do the digging. Searching for bodies themselves in the dead of night felt decidedly ghoulish.

'We'll never find the place in darkness,' he said flatly.

'We have a torch.'

'A small torch, almost useless on that terrain.'

'There might be something better in the cottage. There are no street lamps in the village and Roger would need a good light to get home if he ever stayed late here. Why don't you look in the bedrooms and I'll search downstairs?'

Jack gave up the argument and thumped up the stairs to begin searching. The sheer madness of what she was suggesting – *The Boy's Own Paper* nature of the exploit – had decided him. He'd do it. He'd always loved that comic. And there was no resisting Flora.

27

Flora was surprised that he'd agreed so easily. Not exactly agreed, but gone along with her plan without too much fuss. She was convinced she was on the right track, but Jack was a doubter who liked things clear and precise and, unless they were, he would dismiss them as irrelevant. Her theory made sense, she told herself, more sense than suspecting Beatrice Gifford of telling lies about the will, of killing her husband and then Lionel. It wasn't easy to overcome a grown man and Beatrice hadn't looked particularly strong. She'd also looked a defeated woman and to set out deliberately to kill someone must require huge wells of energy and self-belief – that you were doing the right thing, that the person you were despatching didn't deserve to live.

Making a swift search of the sitting room – only a single cabinet and a few shelves to look through – Flora began on the kitchen cupboards, her mind all the time busy with that moment on the road from Polvarra. If Thomas Martin were dead, buried where Flora suspected, it would explain all the years in which he'd never once attempted to get in touch with his parents. A loving son who had allowed his mother and father to suffer the shame of rumour, and the pain of never knowing the fate of their only child. The disjunction had jarred on Flora the moment she'd heard the Martins' story.

If she were proved right, his parents would at last learn the truth, terrible though it might be. It was indisputable there had been a spy in Thomas's small unit, and if it hadn't been Thomas, it had to have been one of the other three. A spy with a reason to kill. She skimmed through the names Ralph Carrington had mentioned. Ronnie Brooks – had he killed Thomas before being felled himself by a random bomb? No, that didn't work. A dead man couldn't have killed Roger or Lionel, unless he'd never really died. But Ralph had written to his parents to tell them of their son's death and that seemed pretty final.

Could it have been the colourfully named Randy Paradis? After the war, he'd returned to Canada apparently, but that didn't mean he couldn't travel. What was to stop him from taking a flight to London and making his way back to Cornwall? Why would he, though, unless he'd realised that his secret was about to be exposed?

It was possible that Roger had managed somehow to track him down, maybe written to him asking about the man's time in Mullion. The letter need not have made any direct accusation for alarm bells to start ringing. The mere enquiry would have alerted Randy to the fact that someone was digging into a past he wanted kept closed. Roger would need to be stopped. And Lionel? If Lionel had discovered the Canadian's secret after Roger's death and threatened him with it, he would be signing his own death warrant.

Finally, there was Lofty Price, the teacher from London, and the sad boy remembered by Sally's former colleague. He wasn't dead, as far as Jack's father knew, and he wasn't in

Canada. Yet he wasn't apparently in Cornwall either. But, like Randy, he could have been tracked down by a prodigious researcher such as Gifford. It was all supposition, though. A conundrum. On the surface, none of these three could be guilty, yet Flora was adamant in her mind that one of them was.

Her search for a stronger torch had been unsuccessful but she could hear Jack still looking. Drawers being opened, a wardrobe door banging. Then the tramp of feet on the stairs.

'I've found something,' he said, coming into the sitting room, an old army flashlight in his hand. 'Tucked away in a mouldy haversack under my bed. A relic of the Home Guard, I should think. I'm not sure it will be strong enough. It's likely to be pitch black on the cliffs.'

'Then we'll take your torch as well. It's bound to help.' She smiled at him, trying to get a smile in return. 'It makes a nice symmetry, doesn't it?' she said, pointing at the flashlight. 'Roger provides the light that's destined to uncover his murderer. Eventually.'

'If you say so. I suppose I better hack my way to the shed and hope the magic spade has an edge to it.'

'Why are you so grumpy, all of a sudden?'

'Because while I was searching, I started using my brain and realised how impossible this trip is. Think, Flora, how did we get to that site when we went with Dad? Along the coastal path from the village, then up a narrow track, and from there we wandered – left, right, I don't remember – amongst a host of trees to the place you've identified. The spot where Dad slipped. We'll have to do that again, in the dark with just two torches to light us, both a bit rubbish, and a heavy shovel to carry.'

'We know the place we're looking for, more or less. It's possible there might be a track that's accessible by car, one that would take us reasonably close. When we walked down to the harbour from the village, we took the footpath, didn't we? But there was also a lane that we could have driven down. If there was a track branching off that... before it reached the cove...'

'If? You're suggesting we start looking for it in the dark?'

'I might be able to go one better.' She tried to sound patient. 'I'll take another look at the leaflets that Roger left for his guests. I did flick through them the other day and I'm sure there was one that showed tracks you could drive along.'

'You find it then,' he muttered, and stomped out of the kitchen door.

She watched him through the window, scything his way through the long grass, and smiled to herself. Jack might mutter and grumble, but he was enjoying this, she was sure. There was a part of him that was still a boy in search of adventure. It was the part that had done nothing more dangerous since the war than write crime novels – until he met her, she thought. But she refused to feel guilty.

Pulling out the sheaf of leaflets from their resting place beneath the coffee table, she shuffled through them. The one she remembered was near the top, a leaflet devoted entirely to the Lizard, and more detailed than she'd expected. With her forefinger, she traced the track they'd seen signposted from the village to Mullion Cove, and found halfway along a faint line, suggesting the existence of a narrower track that swung off to the right. It looked as if it might take them to the right place, or as near as possible. Certainly easier than lugging a spade and flashlight up and down dale and along pathways that could prove treacherous at night. The worst that could happen was the car would get stuck and they'd have to rely on Logan and his friends to pull them out the next morning.

'I'm going for a walk,' Jack announced, heaving the spade into the kitchen.

'Would you like company?'

'No,' he said, definitely. 'I need to clear my head.'

Flora looked through the car window and up at the sky. There was hardly a cloud visible, a hint only of something darker hovering in the distance. A moon, nearly full, flooded the silent village square, the Mullion church clock striking midnight as they glided past its ghostly outline. Steering the car along the vehicle track they'd previously ignored on their way to the cove, Jack had half an eye on the road ahead and half searching for the turning Flora had found on the leaflet.

'I hope you're right,' he said, 'and it wasn't just someone's sticky paw that made that line.'

'Don't be silly.' She craned forward. 'It should be some-where around here.'

He slowed the car even further, creeping forward yard by yard. The landscape was lit as though it were a stage set and if there was a track to follow, they couldn't help but see it.

'There!' she cried out, making Jack stop so suddenly that the ignition failed.

Cursing, he started the engine again and negotiated the turn, inch by inch, into a track that ran between two high hedges, with barely room for even a small car to travel between them.

'If we ever find this place, there could be a problem,' he said, smiling for the first time since they'd left Treleggan. 'Or one more problem. How do we get out of the car when we're wedged in so tightly? Oh, and how do I get back to the village?'

'Reverse?'

'Thanks. That should be fun.'

They continued to travel at a snail's pace when, half a mile further on, the narrow ribbon of lane suddenly disappeared, swallowed, it seemed, by the encroaching landscape. The track had come to an end but delivered them to an enclave of spiky grass, surrounded by a host of trees.

'That's the copse,' she said excitedly, pointing ahead at the dense thicket of branches, silver in the moonlit stillness. 'And look, those are rhododendron bushes scattered between the trees. The track doesn't go any further than this.'

Jack looked around. 'Why stop here? It's not exactly a destination.'

'Maybe it is,' she said thoughtfully. 'When we came to Mullion with your father, we walked along the coastal path, then turned into the track that climbed uphill. From that point, we walked eastwards as though we were going back to the village. Which means—'

'That the signals site can't be far into those trees, and this was where their vehicles parked up.'

She gave a vigorous nod. 'We've done well, Jack. *And* there's room here for you to turn the car when we leave.'

'It gets better all the time.' He switched off the engine and sat staring through the windscreen. 'Why did I let you talk me into this, Flora?'

'I didn't. You wanted to come.'

He said nothing, but swung himself out of the car and walked round to the boot. 'The moonlight's bright enough for us not to need the extra torch. The less we have to carry, the better.' He lifted the spade out of the boot and handed her the flashlight. 'OK, Livingstone, I'm in your hands.'

Flora's sense of direction was generally good, but the moonlight filtering through the crowded thicket of trees was patchy, and finding her way in near darkness wasn't easy. The sounds of night were all around and, for a moment, she had a frightening premonition that they were not alone, but shook it off – it was the crackle of leaves beneath their feet, the whisper of small animals in the undergrowth.

Venturing deeper into the coppice, she began to relax. The

place felt right. It wasn't just the abundance of blossoms on the ground, their fiery red eerie beneath the flashlight, but the way that the trees ahead were beginning to thin and the ground to become smoother. She'd noticed that before, and assumed the original builders had levelled the ground once the site was finished.

They had reached a clearing, a fairly large open space, when her foot stumbled against a bank of turf. She looked down, trying to focus in the wavering light. 'Here,' she said. 'This is the ridge, I'm sure, the ridge your father tripped over.' She swung the flashlight back and forth. 'It's overgrown with grass, but it's a definite mound.'

'And grave-shaped,' Jack said, joining her. 'You were right, but don't get too excited. We may have found the place, but there's an awful lot of digging to do, and nothing to say there'll be anything at the end of it.' He took off the waterproof jacket he was wearing and dropped it on the ground. 'One thing's for sure, I'm going to get very hot.'

'I'll help. Tell me when you want a rest and I'll take over.'

But as soon as Jack began digging, she knew the task would be beyond her. Over the years, the earth had become heavily impacted and, after an hour's strenuous labour, a sweating Jack was only two feet down.

'Six feet, isn't it supposed to be?' he said, passing a hand over his forehead.

'It would have been a hasty burial, so perhaps not quite so deep,' she said hopefully, trying to keep the flashlight trained on the widening trench.

It must have been a hasty burial, since only half an hour later and another foot deeper, there was a loud crack that echoed and re-echoed in the silent air.

Flora held her breath.

'Bring the light closer,' Jack said. 'This cloud is a darn nuisance. We could have done without it.' Over the last hour, the previously clear sky had begun to fill, first with a light mistiness, but now a more solid darkness was pressing down on them.

Flora held the flashlight high above the trench and peered into its depths. Something glinted beneath its light, something white. Bone white.

'It's him,' she gasped. They had found Thomas, she was sure.

28

'It's a body and it could well be Martin's,' Jack said grimly. 'Can you find your way back to the car and bring the extra torch? There might be an identity tag buried alongside, or something else that would confirm it. I need more light so I can scrape away the soil. I can't go on digging – I don't want to hurt him.'

It sounded odd, but Flora knew exactly what he meant.

'I'll have to take the flashlight. Is that OK?'

'Don't mind me. I'm in a good place, in the middle of nowhere, darkness all around and a dead body to keep me company.'

'He's only a skeleton,' she said. 'Poor Thomas.'

Grabbing the flashlight, she weaved a path through the belt of trees as quickly as she could, reaching the car in record time. The torch was where she'd left it on the passenger seat and, stuffing it into her pocket, she closed the car door quietly behind her, and hurried back the way she'd come.

As she approached the site, her ears picked up a sound. A sound that was foreign to this night-time world. Not the crackling of leaves, the snap of twigs, the snuffling of small animals, but a voice. It couldn't be a voice. She must have taken a wrong turning, arrived in the wrong place, but then who would be out on this headland past midnight, apart from them? As a precaution, she switched off the flashlight and moved cautiously forward. The clouds were on the move and the glade was once more bathed in moonlight. Peering through the trees, she saw a figure. And it wasn't Jack's. A man was standing over the hole that Jack had dug, talking to someone. And he held a gun.

'Poor Thomas!' the voice exclaimed. 'I heard what that stupid girl said. But what about me? The years of terror *I've* endured. The hangman's noose always dangling in my face, never truly safe, no matter how much I made of my life.'

Flora stayed rooted to the spot, swallowing her breath in an effort to remain unheard. For a moment her ability to think clearly deserted her, her mind battling to make sense of what she was seeing. Who was the speaker? Why was he here? Most painful of all, where was Jack?

The figure crouched down, talking, it seemed, to the dead boy. 'I did make something of my life, believe me. Seeking promotion, pretending an interest. It wasn't the life I wanted, mind you, the one back in Fulham among friends and colleagues. For my sins, I was forced to stay in Cornwall. I dared not move away, had always to be on the alert. A life spent in a backwater. Only occasionally did anything interesting come along. Roger's research – that turned out to be very interesting.'

Flora crept a few yards forward. Roger's research – she'd always known it would come back to those papers. But where was Jack? Hiding in the shadows while this man talked to a skeleton? Once more the light had become opaque and she could see no further than the hunched figure. Her stomach hardened as she realised how trapped they were.

'I helped Gifford a lot,' the voice went on. 'Translated the German documents he found. That was fun, a rare indulgence. I never admit to anyone I can speak the language. It's French

I'm fluent in, that's my pretence. Living a lie, always living a lie. I thought I could trust Roger not to delve too deeply. He was a pretty hopeless researcher, that was my opinion. But the man was like a terrier, he wouldn't stop, no matter how many obstacles I put in his way. Loading him with useless books as a distraction, regaling him with anecdotes to put him off the scent. Nothing worked. Gifford had to keep poking until he knew, or thought he knew. And when he did, he found it difficult to believe. I could see that. He never spoke to me about it, but I could feel it. Feel him eyeing me differently, assessing whether the chief librarian of a Cornish town could really be guilty of treachery.'

Saul Penrose! The man from Helston library. The man at Pendennis Castle. She hadn't been wrong to feel threatened. It had been Penrose who'd trapped her in that embrasure, who'd somehow managed to disappear before Jack saw him, then emerged afresh from behind the keep wall.

But what connection did Penrose have with this ruined site? It took seconds for Flora's brain finally to jerk into action. Of course! SP, the initials she'd seen carved on the entrance wall to the signals centre, no more than a hundred yards away from where she stood. The initials of the corporal in charge of Thomas Martin's unit. SP was Stephen Price, and now, it appeared, Saul Penrose, too.

'I took a Cornish name,' Penrose went on, 'though it grieved me to do it. Goodbye Stephen, hello Saul. I rather liked Saul. It had the touch of the biblical about it. Rather like this scene – an eye for an eye, that kind of thing. I'm sorry, old chap, as your idiot father would have said, but you brought this on yourself. I did warn you to keep away, but you couldn't. And when you got here, you couldn't just sit and write a story – you had to be an actor in one. An actor in *my* story. Regretfully, yours is about to end and with no one to write it for you. Or for that annoying little busybody you brought along – when I find her. Which I will.'

The penny had at last dropped. He was talking to Jack! Jack was in that gaping hole, not sheltering in shadow, but lying side by side with Thomas. While she'd been gone, Saul Penrose must have thrust him at gunpoint into the trench. Flora was thinking quickly now. She had to distract Penrose, give Jack the chance to climb free. She cast wildly around for a means. The car, that was it. Or rather the car's hooter. She would run back to the Austin and sound the horn. Hopefully, it might wake some of the villagers, but in any case it should confuse Penrose.

It was as she prepared to creep away that she realised the man had put down his rifle and picked up the shovel that Jack had brought from the garden shed. He thrust it into the pile of soil Jack had displaced and began to shovel the earth back into the trench.

He was burying Jack alive! Flora's stomach turned to water. There was no time to get back to the car. She had to do something now. But why didn't Jack scramble from the trench and take the man on? There was no longer a gun pointing at his head. Could it be... could it be that he was he dead already?

She stifled a sob and tried to steady herself for the battle she must fight. *Now, Flora!* she told herself. Clutching the flashlight in one hand and the torch in the other, she crept forward until she was within a yard of Penrose. He turned to take another shovel of earth and, in that instant, caught sight of her. She swung the heavy metal object at his head, forcefully enough to knock him off balance. The flashlight landed with a thud a few yards from the trench.

Staggering upright, Penrose bent to grab the rifle but, dazed, fumbled with the weapon and in that split second, she hit him again, this time with the torch, landing a blow squarely on his temple. He crumpled at the knees and, as he fell, engaged the gun's trigger. The sound of a bullet sliced through the stagnant air.

The firing of the gun brought transformation. A previously monochrome world became full of colour and, from nowhere, there were lights, noise, feet. Men in uniform swarming across the clearing.

'Are you all right, miss?' It was Inspector Mallory.

Flora staggered to her feet, unsure that what she was seeing was real. Shocked that it might be – how was it possible the police were here?

'Yes,' she managed to say through choking breath. 'But Jack.' She pointed to the trench.

'We'll have him out in a tick, don't you worry.'

Mallory bent over the fallen Penrose, then turned to one of the uniformed men behind him. 'Get back to the car and radio for an ambulance,' he instructed. 'He's alive, but his shoulder's a mess – the bullet seems to have ripped right through. Looks like he's lost a lot of blood.'

'Should we go to the hospital, boss?'

'Two of you go with him. If he survives, get him to talk. If not, it will be one less for the hangman. And you other two, help me with... Mr Carrington, isn't it?'

A uniformed policeman stood either side of the trench and, leaning down, gripped hold of Jack's arms, heaving his body up and out of the grave. Very carefully, they laid him flat on the grass, Mallory shrugging off his overcoat and using it to cover Jack's unconscious form.

'Looks as though he's got concussion, sir,' one of the policemen said. 'Seems to have had a rifle butt cracked over his head.'

Flora remained motionless, riveted to the small square of earth she stood on. Only very slowly did she emerge from the paralysis that gripped her. Retrieving the flashlight – amazingly, it still worked – she walked towards Jack and, pinched with anxiety, held the torch high above his prone body. At the sight of the blood streaming from one side of his head, she forced herself to swallow her nausea.

Mallory bent down to his overcoat and fumbled in the pocket, bringing out a bottle of golden brown liquid. Kneeling beside the unconscious man, he forced a few drops between Jack's lips. 'Brandy should do it,' he said cheerfully.

Jack's eyes half opened, blinking rapidly. Then, as though a curtain had suddenly been pulled back and the play set in motion, he tried to stagger to his feet. 'Flora,' he croaked.

'I'm here,' she said. 'Right here.'

Mallory helped him up and, barely able to stand, Jack turned to her, catching her roughly in his arms and holding her tight. For several minutes they stood, locked together, until the inspector took her gently by the arm and indicated she should follow his colleague to the waiting police car.

29

A gentle knock on the door had Flora stir. For an instant, as she swam into consciousness, she heard herself whimper, grabbing hold of the counterpane and thrusting it away, her body pressed rigidly into the bed, as though braced against suffocation. Then her gaze took in the sun streaming through blue striped curtains and the homely shape of a painted dressing table, and she relaxed. On the floor a heap of clothes lay bedraggled where she'd dropped them last night. More like this morning, she thought. It had been nearly dawn before Jack had been seen by a doctor, they'd answered some rudimentary questions, and Inspector Mallory had driven them back to the cottage.

'How are you, my luvver?' Jessie's anxious face appeared around the door.

'I'm fine, Jessie. Come in. But Jack?'

'Mr Carrington's OK,' Jessie said, availing herself of the invitation, 'though he looks a bit battered, I 'ave to say. I made him a good Cornish breakfast and tha'll set 'im up for the day. The inspector, too. They're both down there.'

'Inspector Mallory is here?' Flora pulled herself upright.

'Been 'ere this last hour.' Jessie walked across to perch on the bed. 'My word, what a kerfuffle you've caused. I've never seen anythin' like it. Nor Treleggan neither.'

'I take it the village knows.'

Jessie gave a cackle of laughter. 'All of Helford knows, more like. That Logan came over from Mullion – he brought your car back, by the way. He were full of it. How there were a body buried at the old signals site, how Mr Carrington had been hurt – nearly died, he said – and how that man, Penrose – he were the one who murdered Mr Roger.'

'And Lionel, too,' Flora reminded her.

'Oh, 'im. But you can't believe it, can you? Penrose! To think, I borrowed a book from 'im. I must 'ave touched a murderer's hand!'

'So did a lot of people, I imagine.'

'A terrible thing.' She sat, staring at the worn pattern of the bedside rug, sunk in thought. 'Still' – she brightened – 'I'll tell you what. It'll give Treleggan somethin' to talk about fer a good few months. Mebbe, a good few years.'

It would give Abbeymead the same, Flora thought, if they ever got to know. Villages were notorious for absorbing and recycling gossip, and it would take something very big to dislodge the Penrose saga from being the main topic of conversation in any village, whether in Cornwall or Sussex.

'What time is it?' She shuffled across the bed to peer blearily at the small travelling alarm she'd brought with her, but the clock looked hazy and its hands seemed to dance in a very odd manner.

'Midday, my luvver,' Jessie answered for her. 'And if it 'ad been up to me, I'd 'ave let you sleep, but that inspector... he wants to talk to you.'

'Then I'd better get up.' Flora swung her legs out of bed, her eyes attempting to focus more clearly.

'Shall I bring you a cuppa? It'll 'elp you put yourself together.'

'No thanks. I'll feel brighter when I've washed and dressed.'

'Bacon with scrambled egg?' Jessie asked hopefully. 'You need feedin' up.'

Flora's stomach lurched uncomfortably. 'Toast might be better, if that's OK.'

Within twenty minutes, she was walking into the sitting room where Jack and Inspector Mallory were enjoying a late breakfast cup of tea. The inspector rose from his chair as she walked in, but Flora's attention was on Jack. His lanky frame seemed relaxed in the chair, but he looked pale and there was a slight stain on the white pad the doctor had fixed earlier that morning.

'The inspector has some news,' he said, by way of greeting.

She sank down on the knobbly sofa. 'I'm keen to hear it, but first can I ask a question, Inspector? Something that's bothering me. How was it that you appeared so opportunely last night?'

The inspector looked across at Jack and Jack looked guilty. 'I rang Alan Ridley before we left Treleggan,' he confessed.

'You were adamant you wouldn't!' Flora didn't know whether to feel angry or relieved. If it hadn't been for Mallory's men arriving, she couldn't imagine how that scene would have played out.

'I didn't do what you spoke of.' Jack was being deliberately hazy, she could see, not wanting Mallory to suspect they'd ever considered going behind his back. 'But I thought I should tell somebody what we planned. At first, going back to Mullion seemed harmless enough, in fact I didn't really think that in the dark we'd find the site again. But then I started getting a bad feeling about the expedition and I wanted someone in authority to know what we were doing. If I hadn't rung him by this morning, I asked Alan to contact Inspector Mallory. That way, we'd at least be found – dead or alive.'

'It's why you took yourself off on that walk yesterday. You went to the phone box,' she accused him.

Jack ignored the accusation. 'We were lucky that Ridley didn't wait until this morning. He telephoned the inspector straight away, seriously concerned we were out of our depth. I'd told him as best I could where exactly we were headed and, fortunately for us, Inspector Mallory recognised the location.'

'My son and his mates used to cycle down that track from Mullion, when the centre was still working,' the inspector confessed. 'No one was supposed to go near the place, but you know what kids are.'

It was clear Jack hadn't wanted her to know about the phone call, either because he hoped to hide how concerned he was or because he didn't want her demanding again that he should get Alan Ridley to intervene. Well, he had intervened, and in a good way. He'd rescued them and without putting anyone's nose out of joint.

'Satisfied?' Jack asked her, a challenge in eyes that this morning were silver grey.

'You could have told me,' she said mildly.

Inspector Mallory cleared his throat. 'I thought you might like to know what we've learned from Saul Penrose, or Stephen Price, as I suppose we should call him.'

'He's alive then?'

The inspector nodded. 'Very much so. The bullet went through his shoulder but the medics managed to stop the bleeding pretty quickly.'

'I suppose we'll have to return to Cornwall,' Flora said heavily, 'to give evidence in court.'

Mallory shook his head. 'I had a long chat with Price in the hospital. He's under police guard there, but as soon as the doctors say he's OK to leave, we'll make sure he has a nice comfortable cell. He intends to plead guilty. In those cases, there's no trial. Just a record of his plea, and a second hearing for sentencing.'

'He's going to plead guilty?' Jack repeated. The information was obviously new to him. 'He does understand the penalty?'

'He knows all right. Seems almost to welcome the idea. A bit of a loner, our Mr Price. No family, no friends, as far as I can make out. We offered him a call to someone but he declined. Won't even call a solicitor.'

'And he's made a confession?' Jack pursued.

'Couldn't stop him talking. Written down and signed as I left him. A confession to all three murders – Thomas Martin, Roger Gifford and his brother, Lionel. And to the theft of Mr Gifford's watch, not that it matters too much now.'

'Not a random mugger then?' Flora couldn't resist asking.

The inspector looked sheepish. 'The watch smashed when poor Mr Gifford fell and Price didn't want to leave a possible clue to the time of the murder. It was carefully planned, all very clinical. He doesn't seem to have felt any personal enmity against any of the men.' The inspector paused. 'Well, that's not strictly true. He hated Lionel Gifford, but that's understand-able. The man tried to blackmail him. Apparently, he found papers incriminating Price in his brother's safe at River House.'

'A safe Lionel broke into,' Flora interrupted.

Mallory nodded. 'We haven't gone through all the docu-ments yet, but it seems they're copies from an archive belonging to the French resistance. A unit based at Dieppe.'

That would explain why Roger had made those trips to France, Flora thought. 'The documents are in French?'

'The originals that Mr Gifford had copied, yes, but several of the sheets are English translations. As far as we can make out, they're a record of messages sent to a German source and inter-cepted by the resistance in Dieppe. They'd come from the Mullion signals centre and gave the Germans information on airfields, troop movements, armoury, in the run-up to D Day.'

'And the sender?' Flora already knew the answer.

'He called himself Hoch, which I believe is German for tall.'

'Lofty,' Flora said. 'Lofty Price.'

Mallory nodded. 'Pretty damning.'

'Penrose, or rather Price, told me that he'd translated documents for Roger,' Jack said. 'But presumably not these messages?'

'No. The stuff he looked at for Mr Gifford was written in German and was pretty innocuous. Gifford must have gone elsewhere with these papers, maybe because they were in French or perhaps he'd begun to have suspicions of Penrose. There was a question scribbled in one of the margins against the sender's code name – *Saul Penrose?* – so he was on to our villain.'

'And that question would have alerted Lionel Gifford to the fact that he had something highly incriminating in his hands,' Jack put in. 'Something worth trying a spot of blackmail for.'

'If Lionel's new car was anything to go by, he succeeded.' Flora hated what Price had done but, if it was possible, hated Lionel's grubby opportunism even more.

'He managed to extort a payment out of Price,' Mallory agreed. 'A large payment, in fact most of the man's savings. But when Lionel came back for more – they always do – Price had little to give and, he must have reckoned, little to lose. Despatching Lionel Gifford was his only way out.'

'If Lionel knew too much, so did we – and Price tried to kill *us*,' she said.

'Well, yes—' the inspector began.

'I mean before last night. He must have followed us for days. Miss Hodges, his assistant, mentioned he was often away from the library. I believe he targeted our car when we first went to Mullion – it had to have been him – and,' she added, 'he tried to harm me. At Pendennis Castle. You remember, Jack?'

He nodded. 'You were right that day,' he said slowly. 'You *were* being threatened, and no doubt I was next on the list. Presumably it was Price, too, who sent the anonymous letter before we'd even left Abbeymead, hoping to keep us away.'

'He said as much when he was bending over the trench, pointing a gun at you. You were unconscious and didn't hear him, but I did.'

'The fate of being a crime writer, Inspector!' There was a glimmer of a smile on Jack's pallid features.

'I don't think it was just that.' Flora tilted her head to one side. 'Though it probably helped. It was also the fact that you were renting Roger's cottage and Roger had become the enemy. Price must already have been planning to kill him and didn't want anyone in the way.'

'You would think he'd have changed his mind,' Jack said. 'Found somewhere else to murder Roger, when he knew we hadn't been deterred by the letter and had actually moved in here.'

'He strikes me as a man who has, what you might call, tunnel vision,' Mallory said. 'Once he's decided on a course, nothing sways him.'

'Tunnel vision would certainly have been useful, holed up for years in that signals centre!'

The inspector didn't respond to the joke, but was following his own train of thought. 'He was clever, I'll give him that. He still had hold of his old army issue knife, we found it in his house, but he chose not to use it in case it was traceable. Instead, he killed Roger Gifford with a knife from his own kitchen.'

'How did he get hold of it?' Flora asked. The knife had always been a puzzle.

'Gifford had it on him, Price told me. For protection probably. Price had asked to meet him quietly, telling Roger he had important information on the war that was too secret to divulge in public. The riverbank early in the morning was where he named.'

'And Roger met him, even though he was suspicious?'

'Mr Gifford had the same tunnel vision, I reckon,' the inspector said. 'He was desperate to know what Price had to say – perhaps he hoped he was wrong about the chap – but armed himself with a knife, just in case, which was probably his undoing.'

'Price turned the knife on him?' Jack asked.

'Exactly. Did the same thing to Lionel, too. In both cases, he intended to kill with his bare hands – neither of the Giffords were particularly young or particularly fit – but in the event, Price was gifted a knife each time. And both from this kitchen.'

Jack pushed the flop of hair back from his forehead. 'It was definitely Lionel who broke in here?'

His question sounded tired as though putting even a few words together was becoming too much of an effort. Flora looked across at him and saw his pallor had, if anything, increased. It was time for the inspector to go.

But Mallory was now in full flow. 'Your break-in was definitely down to Lionel. A last throw, I think, to find the papers he was after – until he discovered them in his brother's safe. That was hidden away behind the study's wood panelling, and it took him some time to find it. He broke into Primrose Cottage all right, but went away with a knife rather than papers. Lionel might be greedy but he wasn't stupid. It seems from police records that he'd lost his own knife at some mêlée at the local pub and probably figured he'd need protection in the future. After he'd plundered the safe and found something more immediately lucrative than the will, the knife came in handy. Or would have done, if it hadn't been used against him.'

Jack frowned. 'I guess Lionel was pretty easy to overpower.'

'No problem for Price to turn the knife on him,' Mallory confirmed. 'He'd suggested Polvarra as a meeting place – nice and quiet, no one around – promising Lionel he'd hand over the next tranche of money. Except there was no money and, when Lionel appeared, no doubt knife in hand, it was wrested from him and his throat cut. They'd both been soldiers but Price was by the far the fittest.'

'Did he speak of his army days?'

'Strangely enough, he seems to have enjoyed being a soldier. Like I say, he doesn't appear to have disliked Thomas Martin personally. Only that the lad found him out – you'll know about the spying, of course – and Price couldn't let him tell tales.'

'Instead, he told his own tale,' Jack murmured. 'According to my father, he convinced the powers that be that Thomas had disappeared to save his skin. That he was the spy they were hunting.'

Mallory nodded. 'Price got a lot of enjoyment recounting that story. He seems to have delighted in hoodwinking the authorities. Called Mr Ralph Carrington a turnip, I'm afraid.'

Jack gave a faint grin. 'Not wholly lacking in discernment then.'

A lull in the conversation was broken by Jessie bustling through the door, plate in hand. 'Toast,' she announced, standing over Flora. 'Make sure you eat it!'

'Thank you, you're a dear.' She sank her teeth into thick marmalade and, satisfied, Jessie turned back to the kitchen.

'If his days in the army were reasonably happy, why turn spy?' Flora demanded through a mouthful of toast. 'It makes no sense.'

'He liked the camaraderie. Least, that's the impression I got. He liked being part of a group, of belonging. That's what made him happy.'

'Sally Jenner – she's a friend from Sussex – had a colleague who'd worked with Price's father. This woman mentioned to Sally what a sad child the son was, taken away, quite brutally it seemed, from his friends and a school he loved.'

'The chap touched on that. Said he'd never been truly happy since he left Berlin. He seems to have loved his father and thought him a wonderful man. Maintains the bloke was persecuted for what Price says was a simple mistake with the books. After he saw his father wither and die, it made him determined to pay Britain back for what it had done, by going over to the enemy. His spying for the Germans had nothing to do with politics, nothing to do with money. It was wholly personal.'

'Some vendetta,' Jack remarked. 'One that threatened the safety of an entire nation.'

'He admired Hitler, so what can you say? Saw him as a strong man when our leaders were weak and divided. He'd do what he could to help by passing on information. In particular, he wanted to damage the D-Day invasion by alerting the Germans to what was happening along the coast here.'

'How did he kill Thomas?' Flora asked. The boy's fate seemed even more poignant now she knew for sure that he'd died doing his best for his country. 'The signals centre must have been a crowded workplace, and the men a close-knit group. How could Price murder a fellow soldier without anyone having a clue?'

'He says it was easy enough. He knew the boy was on to him – apparently Martin had been watching him closely, writing notes which unfortunately Price found and read. The boy sealed his fate with those notes. Price invited him outside for a chat, to clear the air, he said – and the boy went willingly enough. I imagine he was hoping that maybe he'd been mistaken in his corporal. Then Price offered him a cigarette and, when his attention was diverted, he killed him. The lad wouldn't have seen the blow coming. Price had already fed the authorities with his own story – that he was growing increasingly uncomfortable with his subordinate, that Martin just might be the spy they were looking for. When Thomas disappeared suddenly and without explanation, it wasn't difficult to persuade those in charge that his story was authentic.'

'Easy enough to convince the turnip,' Jack put in.

'He wasn't much more polite about Edward Templeton. According to Price, Thomas Martin was Lord Edward's pet, part of his feudal family, which for Price summed up all that was wrong with Britain. Not that it matters now. The end result was that Price got away with the killing and lived free for another twelve years.'

Flora toyed with a second slice of toast. 'But twelve years with a noose dangling in his face.'

'That might be some consolation for the boy's family, I suppose, but not much. Altogether, a pretty sad story.' The inspector turned to Jack. 'I believe you write stories, Mr Carrington?'

'Used to.'

Flora was stunned. Surely, Jack wasn't thinking of covering his typewriter for good? Her head buzzed with questions, but she bit them back until the inspector had left. Obligingly, Mallory rose from his chair at that moment, placing his empty cup on the tea tray.

'I'd best be off. Price might be pleading guilty, but that doesn't lessen the paperwork. One of my men will come by in the next day or so to take your statements.'

'Then we'll be free to leave?' Jack asked.

'Or free to explore more of Cornwall – without the shovel this time, sir!'

After seeing the inspector to the door, Jessie returned for the tray. 'You're never thinkin' of givin' up the writin', are you?' she asked Jack, before Flora had time to speak. The housekeeper must have been listening attentively from the kitchen.

'I need a few weeks to think things over,' Jack said to them both. 'Then we'll see.'

Three days later, Jack loaded his typewriter into the back of the car and turned to say an affectionate goodbye to the woman who had made their stay more comfortable than they deserved.

'Make sure you use that,' she said, nodding towards the boot of the car. 'I want to read this Cornish story.'

'All in good time,' he said gently.

Jack was keenly aware that he'd need space when they got back to Abbeymead. Since the attack, he'd been plagued by headaches and the stitches in his wound were tightening by the day, or so it felt.

He looked up to see Flora coming out of the cottage, bag in hand and her jacket slung across her shoulders. 'Jessie has packed us a picnic for the road,' he called out.

'Wonderful!' She gave a wide smile and began walking down the path towards them. Then stopped for a moment and looked along the lane.

When Jack followed her gaze, he saw a tall lean figure standing yards away. Mercy Dearlove, he presumed.

'I need to say goodbye,' Flora said, her voice flustered. Jessie stared at the woman in outrage.

'Wha's the girl want to go and talk to 'er for?'

'Flora quite likes her,' he said apologetically, watching his friend hurry towards the woman and greet her with a warm handshake.

Jessie was clearly fuming still when Flora returned, but apparently had forgiven her sufficiently to land a big kiss on her cheek.

'You look after yourselves in that village of yours,' she said. 'No more adventurin'.'

Flora hugged her back. 'We will, but why don't you visit us, Jessie?'

'Travel all that way? I couldn't do that.'

'Yes, you could. I'll introduce you to Alice. She's a wonderful cook, too. You'd have fun swapping recipes.'

'I'll think about it,' Jessie extemporised. 'You 'ave a good journey now.'

'You were lucky to escape with a frown,' he said, as Flora closed the car door behind her. 'Jessie is not best pleased with you, consorting with a witch.'

'I had to say goodbye.'

'And?'

'That's all, though Mercy did have some interesting ideas on my future.' He saw the mischievous smile appear.

'More bloody visions, I suppose.'

'Tut-tut, Mr Carrington. Such language in front of a lady. And no, don't answer that.'

They were pulling away from the verge when Jessie came bounding back through the front gate and ran after them, tapping at the rear window.

Concerned, Jack pulled to a halt, while Flora wound down her window.

'I forgot to tell you the latest. Roger's will. He did change it and guess what?'

They shook their heads in unison.

''Cept for a nice little sum to me, he's only gone and left River House and this 'ere cottage and all 'is money in the bank to...'

They waited.

'The local dogs' 'ome. And he never even owned one!'

30

Flora and Jack had been back in Abbeymead for several days when Alice decided on a welcome-home tea at Overlay House. Jack had seen nothing of Flora since he'd dropped her at home after their long journey from Cornwall, but he knew she'd been busy shopping and cleaning and tidying the garden. What she hadn't been doing was call at the bookshop. *I've said to Sally I won't be in till next week,* she'd told him. *I don't want her to feel pushed out.*

Charlie Teague was the first to arrive that afternoon. He'd come straight from school, crashing his bicycle outside Jack's front door and haring round to the back garden to help him find whatever furniture they could. Jack had never had cause before to explore the crumbling shed that stood at the very end of his garden – he kept his own tools in a much newer construction nearer the house – and they were forced to fight their way through a mountain of abandoned hardware, cupboards and chests, to find anything that looked a possibility, eventually dragging a foldaway table into the daylight. The table had certainly seen better days, but they set it up on the grass square at the rear of the house and made several more journeys back to the shed to uncover a motley collection of ancient wicker and faded deckchairs.

Jack left his young helper to arrange the seating while he returned to the kitchen, emerging a few minutes later carrying a tray of sandwiches in each hand.

'Is this OK, Mr Carrington?' the boy asked, having wrestled the final deckchair into position.

'Perfect, Charlie. You've almost earned your tea. Last task – just whip back to the house for some plates and cutlery. Miss Steele is bringing the scones and jam, I think, and Mrs Jenner the cakes.'

On cue, Flora emerged through the French doors with Alice a step behind, pink-faced from manhandling Jack's unreliable oven. The smell of fresh baking followed in her wake.

'Sally's shuttin' the shop early today, so she can come by and welcome you home,' Alice said, bringing to the table two large white plates filled with cakes. 'Katie might pop along later as well, but if she can't get away, she'll see you at the Nook, mebbe tomorrow. But don't let's wait. We should tuck in.' She took hold of one of the slatted chairs and plumped herself down. 'This feels a bit rickety, Jack. Am I goin' to end up in the bushes?'

'If you do, there are plenty of flowers to cushion your fall,' he said laughingly. 'The garden is ablaze with them. Charlie has excelled himself while we've been away – nothing has been allowed to die.'

'Where is Charlie?' Flora looked round for the boy, just as he was crossing the lawn, staggering slightly, his hands full of patterned china.

'Bless you, lad, let's have those before you drop the lot.' Alice heaved herself out of the chair and fussed around the table.

'How is Katie? I haven't had time to call on her yet.' Flora reached for a sandwich, narrowly beating Charlie to the potted meat. 'And how's the Nook?'

'Katie's well, I'd say. In some ways, I think she's relieved she don't have the worries that husband brought down on her, but in others, well the lass is lonely. But the café's doin' well. Better than it was.'

Jack gave a small grimace, stretching his long legs beneath the table. 'Better since you started working there?'

His head wound had healed nicely – Flora could see only a small scar beneath the flop of hair that would never quite stay flat – and his headaches had gone, he'd told her. It was a relief.

'Don't you believe it,' Alice said vigorously. 'Nothin' to do with me. It was all that stuff she had to cope with when Bernie Mitchell was alive. Katie's got more time for the café now, though I daresay my cakes have helped a little.'

'I daresay they have,' Flora said, amused. Not that Kate herself wasn't a dab hand at baking, but she'd had too much to do running the café single-handed.

A swirl of wind sent the ends of the linen tablecloth flapping across the food and Alice jumped up to rescue the small meringues she'd baked that morning.

'This weather don't want to settle,' she muttered.

'At least the rain has held off.' Flora offered round the tray of sandwiches, then helped herself to a second. 'I thought we might be picnicking in the sitting room, but the garden looks brilliant, Jack.'

In the last few months, Overlay House had seen a transformation. A wild expanse of ragged grass and weeds had been turned into something that approached a lawn, enclosed on two sides by flower beds filled with scented roses, pink and mauve phlox and the deep blue of iris. Colourful pyramids of sweet peas, Flora's favourite, flourished at each corner.

On the terrace that lined the rear of the house, pots of geraniums were ready to flower and, on the fourth side of the garden, neat rows of vegetables were making themselves at home. Even the cedars had received a trimming, their branches bending in the breeze but no longer a hazard to those sitting beneath.

'This wind's getting up,' a voice called from the house.

Sally walked through the French doors, laughing as she rescued the scarf half blown off her head. 'How are you both?' She sank down onto the faded stripes of a deckchair. 'It's good to have you back – *and* safe and sound.'

Alice, teapot in hand, nodded knowingly. 'And here you should stay. Didn't I warn you that Cornwall was a dangerous place?'

'You were right,' Flora said, wiping crumbs from her chin, 'though we brought some of it on ourselves. Or I did. But I hope we did some good, too.'

'That's for sure. The Martins will never be able to thank you enough. Lily is heartbroken, naturally, now she knows for sure her boy is dead. But she's glad, too, if you know what I mean. They've got certainty at last, and their son is back where he belongs, and with his reputation restored. The funeral is next week and they're hopin' you'll both come.'

Flora felt Jack glance at her and knew what he was thinking. Since their first meeting, they'd attended a good many funerals together – Cyril Knight, Kate's father, her husband Bernie, then poor Polly Dakers. Now there was Thomas to add to the list.

'We'll be there,' Jack said. Flora heard the reluctance in his voice and hoped she was the only one to notice.

'Have you heard what's happenin' to that wicked man back in Cornwall?' For Alice, the county would be lucky if it ever emerged from the Dark Ages.

'Saul Penrose, Stephen Price, whatever his name, is in prison awaiting sentencing,' Flora said. 'But he's confessed and there can only be one result.'

'The judge putting on the black cap,' Sally said ghoulishly.

There was silence as the finality of Penrose's fate became real.

'Leastways, him pleadin' guilty means you don't have to go back there again.'

'It's a beautiful spot, Alice, really beautiful,' Flora told her. Her friend gave a loud sniff. 'And Jessie Bolitho. You'd like her a lot. She's a great cook and looked after us very well.'

'This Jessie can come and see me then,' Alice said decidedly, 'I'm not stirrin' my stumps. Anyways, I'll be too busy soon to do any travellin'.'

Flora was surprised. 'Don't say you're taking over the Nook from Katie?'

'I'm not takin' anythin' over, thank the Lord. I'll keep cookin' for Kate, but probably a bit less than I do now. No, it's Sally who's doin' the takin' over. The Priory!' Alice announced proudly.

Jack frowned. 'You're going to manage the hotel, Sally?'

'Not only manage. I'm buying it.' Sally jumped up from her chair and did a jiggle around the deckchair.

'What!' Flora couldn't help the exclamation. It seemed an extraordinary development.

'Exciting news, isn't it? While you've been away, I made a big decision – to spend the money Dad left me on what I know will be a brilliant project. I'm sure he'd be pleased.'

There was an uncomfortable silence, Jack appearing as stunned as she was.

'The Priory is going cheap,' Sally hurried on, 'and I've found a partner to buy with. I've always liked the idea of running a hotel. The bank manager likes it, too, thank goodness.'

'But liking the idea...' Flora's voice trailed away.

'It must sound mad, I know, but we're getting it for a song and at least Vernon Elliot's creditors will get paid.'

'Who is "we", Sally?' Jack asked quietly.

'Would you believe, a relative of Lord Edward Templeton's?'

Flora was perplexed. 'I didn't think he had any relatives, other than the one in Australia who sold the house to Elliot.'

'He's a second cousin of a second cousin, something pretty obscure, but a complete sweetie.'

Alice frowned. 'You're buyin' the place to put it back on its feet, young lady, not for any other reason.'

'I'm going to, Auntie, but it's good to get on with your business partner, isn't it?'

'Do you have a name for him?' Flora felt fearful even asking.

'Dominic,' Sally pronounced. 'Dominic Lister. We sign the contract next week. Dominic is putting in the money he raised from selling a chain of bars he ran in London – and he was terrific at persuading the bank to lend us the rest! He'll be in charge of the financial stuff and I'll do the day-to-day managing. There'll be a lot to learn, I realise. I've worked in shops and I did have a chambermaid's job for several months before I joined the Foreign Office, but I've never managed a large staff before. Still, I'll have Auntie with me to advise. She'll be our number one cook.'

'It will be an awful lot of work for you, Alice.' Flora felt concerned for her friend. 'If you continue to help Kate as well.'

'I'll be gettin' help, too. The Priory kitchen is going to have an under-chef.'

'Sous-chef, Auntie.'

'Whatever fancy name you like. It means another pair of hands. Skilled hands this time. More useful than that dozy Ivy that Elliot hired. Now eat up, I don't want all this cake goin' spare. And I'm not just talkin' to you, Master Teague.'

On their walk back to Flora's cottage, Jack seemed preoccupied. Eventually, he said, 'What do you think about this Priory business?'

'I don't know what to think. I suppose it's all right. Sally seems pleased, Alice, too. You're not so sure?'

'She seems to have rushed into it rather. The hotel might be going for a song, as she says, but it's a money pit. Vernon Elliot found that. It's why he's banged up in gaol for the next ten years. And she's leaving all the financial stuff to this man Lister, whom we didn't know existed until a few minutes ago.'

'There's no point in either of us saying any of this. Sally isn't the kind of girl who will be easily dissuaded. I've a feeling that Alice may have tried already and failed.'

They walked on for a while in companionable silence until Jack asked, 'How do you feel about losing your manageress?'

Flora turned a bright face to him. She knew exactly how she felt. 'I'm looking forward to getting back to the All's Well. Running the shop myself, in my own way. I'm grateful for all Sally has done – it's clear she's got the place buzzing – but it's my baby and it was Aunt Violet's baby before me.' She paused. 'Actually, Jack, would you mind if we did a detour?'

'To the bookshop?'

She nodded. 'We came back from Cornwall sooner than I expected and I haven't liked to interfere while Sally was in charge. But I can't wait to walk through the door again.'

'No more dreams of travelling then?'

'Maybe for holidays, but nothing too lengthy. Abbeymead is my home and I love it. Perhaps I didn't realise how much until I went away. But how about you? I know this contract is still hanging in the air. Have you heard from Arthur yet?'

'A letter arrived yesterday, as it happens, and it was the best piece of news I've had all year. Somehow my wonderful agent has wriggled out of the contract. The last two novels have been scrubbed.'

'And the Cornish book?'

'That's in abeyance at the moment – still to be decided. In future, though, I won't be writing to order. I got the impression he considered it safer after what happened in Cornwall. I don't think he trusts me to keep out of trouble.'

'At least, not when you're with me.'

'And I would be, wouldn't I?'

'I think it's inevitable,' she said, smiling up at him.

They walked on, saying little, but thinking a lot more, until they reached the high street. Passing the bakery and Mr House-man's shop, a few more steps had them standing outside the All's Well.

'Do you need to check on Betty first?' he asked.

'I can't imagine Sally ever rode her, but perhaps we should say hello. She can be grumpy if she doesn't get the attention she thinks she should. Then I get a difficult ride!'

Turning into the cobbled yard behind the bookshop, they found the bicycle beneath her shelter, exactly where Flora had left her several weeks ago.

'It doesn't look as though Sally ever braved a journey,' Jack said.

Flora smoothed Betty's handlebars and adjusted her wicker tray. 'Probably just as well. Betty looks fine, doesn't she? I'll walk to the shop tomorrow and ride her home at the end of the day.'

'I think she heard that.'

'Of course she did. Now she won't sulk.' Flora fumbled in her handbag for her spare set of keys. 'C'mon, I'm longing to check on my brilliant books.'

Inside the shop, Jack stood back, allowing her to breathe in the atmosphere he knew she loved. Smoky, earthy, with the faintest hint of vanilla.

'Happy?' he asked.

She beamed. 'I couldn't be happier. I'm back where I belong and it looks as though Sally hasn't changed a thing, bless her.'

'Have a saunter around. I'll wait.'

She did as Jack suggested, wandering slowly in and out of the angled bookshelves, her eyes feasting on the volumes she loved, but widening at the sight of so many new titles.

'I'd better start reading this very evening,' she joked, strolling back towards him. 'So many books have arrived while we've been away. Customers are bound to ask me about them.'

'Before you bury yourself in their pages, why don't we spend the evening together? For old times' sake?' He sounded diffident.

'A last supper,' she teased.

The glimmer of a smile lit Jack's face. 'Let's hope not.'

Flora looked up into a pair of warm grey eyes. 'It was fun, wasn't it? Cornwall?'

'When we weren't finding dead bodies, you mean?'

'It wasn't all dead bodies.'

'No, you're right. It was more than that.' His hand reached out to stroke her hair, the unruly waves slipping through his fingers.

Flora caught hold of his hand and held it tightly. 'Let's walk back to the cottage,' she said. 'I've a bottle of Mrs Teague's elderberry wine in the cupboard – we can eat in style!'

A LETTER FROM MERRYN

Dear reader,

I want to say a huge thank you for choosing to read *Murder at Primrose Cottage*. If you enjoyed the book and want to keep up to date with all my latest releases, just sign up at the following link. Your email address will never be shared and you can unsubscribe at any time.

www.bookouture.com/merryn-allingham

The 1950s is a fascinating period to write about, outwardly conformist but beneath the surface there's rebellion brewing, even in the very south of England! It's a beautiful part of the world and I hope Flora's and Jack's adventures there entertained you. If so, you can discover their adventures before they even get to Cornwall in *The Bookshop Murder* and *Murder on the Pier*.

If you enjoyed *Murder at Primrose Cottage*, I would love a short review. Getting feedback from readers is amazing and it helps new readers to discover one of my books for the first time. And do get in touch on my Facebook page, through Twitter, Goodreads or my website – it will make this author's day!

Thank you for reading,
Merryn

KEEP IN TOUCH WITH MERRYN

www.merrynallingham.com

 facebook.com/MerrynWrites
twitter.com/merrynwrites

Milton Keynes UK
Ingram Content Group UK Ltd.
UKHW010732131223
434284UK00006B/120